PRAISE FOR CATHERINE BYBEE

WIFE BY WEDNESDAY

"A fun and sizzling romance, great characters that trade verbal spars like fist punches, and the dream of your own royal wedding!"

—Sizzling Hot Book Reviews, 5 Stars

"A good holiday, fireside or bedtime story."

—Manic Reviews, 4½ Stars

"A great story that I hope is the start of a new series."

—The Romance Studio, 4½ Hearts

MARRIED BY MONDAY

"If I hadn't already added Ms. Catherine Bybee to my list of favorite authors, after reading this book I would have been compelled to. This is a book *nobody* should miss, because the magic it contains is awesome."

—Booked Up Reviews, 5 Stars

"Ms. Bybee writes authentic situations and expresses the good and the bad in such an equal way . . . Keeps the reader on the edge of her seat."

—Reading Between the Wines, 5 Stars

"*Married by Monday* was a refreshing read and one I couldn't possibly put down."

—The Romance Studio, 4½ Hearts

FIANCÉ BY FRIDAY

"Bybee knows exactly how to keep readers happy . . . A thrilling pursuit and enough passion to stuff in your back pocket to last for the next few lifetimes . . . The hero and heroine come to life with each flip of the page and will linger long after readers cross the finish line."

—*RT Book Reviews*, 4½ Stars, Top Pick (Hot)

"A tale full of danger and sexual tension . . . the intriguing characters add emotional depth, ensuring readers will race to the perfectly fitting finish."

—*Publishers Weekly*

"Suspense, survival, and chemistry mix in this scintillating read."

—*Booklist*

"Hot romance, a mystery assassin, British royalty, and an alpha Marine . . . this story has it all!"

—Harlequin Junkie

SINGLE BY SATURDAY

"Captures readers' hearts and keeps them glued to the pages until the fascinating finish . . . romance lovers will feel the sparks fly . . . almost instantaneously."

—*RT Book Reviews*, 4½ Stars, Top Pick

"[A] wonderfully exciting plot, lots of desire, and some sassy attitude thrown in for good measure!"

—Harlequin Junkie

Taken by Tuesday

"[Bybee] knows exactly how to get bookworms sucked into the perfect storyline; then she casts her spell upon them so they don't escape until they reach the 'Holy Cow!' ending."

—*RT Book Reviews,* 4½ Stars, Top Pick

Seduced by Sunday

"You simply can't miss [this novel]. It contains everything a romance reader loves—clever dialogue, three-dimensional characters, and just the right amount of steam to go with that heartwarming love story."

—Brenda Novak, *New York Times* bestselling author

"Bybee hits the mark . . . providing readers with a smart, sophisticated romance between a spirited heroine and a prim hero . . . Passionate and intelligent characters [are] at the heart of this entertaining read."

—*Publishers Weekly*

Treasured by Thursday

"The Weekday Brides never disappoint and this final installment is by far Bybee's best work to date."

—*RT Book Reviews,* 4½ Stars, Top Pick

"An exquisitely written and complex story brimming with pride, passion, and pulse-pounding danger . . . Readers will gladly make time to savor this winning finale to a wonderful series."

—*Publishers Weekly,* Starred Review

"Bybee concludes her popular Weekday Brides series in a gratifying way with a passionate, troubled couple who may find a happy future if they can just survive and then learn to trust each other. A compelling and entertaining mix of sexy, complicated romance and menacing suspense."

—*Kirkus Reviews*

NOT QUITE DATING

"It's refreshing to read about a man who isn't afraid to fall in love . . . [Jack and Jessie] fit together as a couple and as a family."

—*RT Book Reviews,* 3 Stars (Hot)

"*Not Quite Dating* offers a sweet and satisfying Cinderella fantasy that will keep you smiling long after you've finished reading."

—Kathy Altman, *USA Today,* "Happy Ever After"

"The perfect rags to riches romance . . . The dialogue is inventive and witty, the characters are well drawn out. The storyline is superb and really shines . . . I highly recommend this stand out romance! Catherine Bybee is an automatic buy for me."

—Harlequin Junkie, 4½ Hearts

NOT QUITE ENOUGH

"Bybee's gift for creating unforgettable romances cannot be ignored. The third book in the Not Quite series will sweep readers away to a paradise, and they will be intrigued by the thrilling story that accompanies their literary vacation."

—*RT Book Reviews,* 4½ Stars, Top Pick

NOT QUITE FOREVER

"Full of classic Bybee humor, steamy romance, and enough plot twists and turns to keep readers entertained all the way to the very last page."
—Tracy Brogan, bestselling author of the Bell Harbor series

"Magnetic . . . The love scenes are sizzling and the multi-dimensional characters make this a page-turner. Readers will look for earlier installments and eagerly anticipate new ones."
—*Publishers Weekly*

NOT QUITE PERFECT

"This novel flows extremely well and readers will find themselves consuming the witty dialogue and strong imagery in one sitting."
—*RT Book Reviews*

"Don't let the title fool you. *Not Quite Perfect* was actually the perfect story to sweep you away and take you on a pleasant adventure. So sit back, relax, maybe pour a glass of wine, and let Catherine Bybee entertain you with Glen and Mary's playful East Coast–West Coast romance. You won't regret it for a moment."
—Harlequin Junkie, 4½ Stars

NOT QUITE CRAZY

"This fast-paced story features credible characters whose appealing relationship is built upon friendship, mutual respect, and sizzling chemistry."
—*Publishers Weekly*

"The plot is filled with twists and turns, but instead of feeling like a never-ending roller coaster, the story maintains a quiet flow. The slow buildup of a romance allows readers to get to know the main characters as individuals and makes the romantic element more organic."

—*RT Book Reviews*

Doing It Over

"The romance between fiercely independent Melanie and charming Wyatt heats up even as outsiders threaten to derail their newfound happiness. This novel will hook readers with its warm, inviting characters and the promise for similar future installments."

—*Publishers Weekly*

"This brand-new trilogy, Most Likely To, based on yearbook superlatives, kicks off with a novel that will encourage you to root for the incredibly likable Melanie. Her friends are hilarious and readers will swoon over Wyatt, who is charming and strong. Even Melanie's daughter, Hope, is a hoot! This romance is jam-packed with animated characters, and Bybee displays her creative writing talent wonderfully."

—*RT Book Reviews*, 4 Stars

"With a dialogue full of energy and depth, and a twisting storyline that captured my attention, I would say that *Doing It Over* was a great way to start off a new series. (And look at that gorgeous book cover!) I can't wait to visit River Bend again and see who else gets to find their HEA."

—Harlequin Junkie, 4½ Stars

STAYING FOR GOOD

"Bybee's skillfully crafted second Most Likely To contemporary (after *Doing It Over*) brings together former sweethearts who have not forgotten each other in the eleven years since high school. A cast of multidimensional characters brings the story to life and promises enticing future installments."

—*Publishers Weekly*

"Romance fans will be sure to cheer on former high school sweethearts Zoe and Luke right away in *Staying For Good*. Just wait until you see what passion, laughter, reconciliations, and mischief (can you say Vegas?) awaits readers this time around. Highly recommended."

—Harlequin Junkie, 4½ Stars

MAKING IT RIGHT

"Intense suspense heightens the scorching romance at the heart of Bybee's outstanding third Most Likely To contemporary (after *Staying For Good*). Sizzling sensual scenes are coupled with scary suspense in this winning novel."

—*Publishers Weekly*, Starred Review

FOOL ME ONCE

"A marvelous portrait of friendship among women who have been bonded by fire."

—*Library Journal*, Best of the Year 2017

"Bybee still delivers a story that her die-hard readers will enjoy."

—*Publishers Weekly*

HALF EMPTY

"Wade and Trina here in *Half Empty* just might be one of my favorite couples Catherine Bybee has gifted us fans with so far. Captivating, engaging, lively and dreamy, I simply could not get enough of this book."

—Harlequin Junkie, 5 stars

"Part rock star romance, part romantic thriller, I really enjoyed this book."

—Romance Reader

FAKING FOREVER

"A charming contemporary with surprising depth . . . Bybee perfectly portrays a woman trying to hold out for Mr. Right despite the pressures of time. A pitch-perfect plot and a cast of sympathetic and lovable supporting characters make this book one to add to the keeper shelf."

—*Publishers Weekly*

"Catherine Bybee can do no wrong as far as I'm concerned . . . Passionate, sultry, and filled with genuine emotions that ran the gamut, *Faking Forever* was a journey of self-discovery and of a love that was truly meant to be. Highly recommended."

—Harlequin Junkie

SAY IT AGAIN

"Steamy, fast-paced, and consistently surprising, with a large cast of feisty supporting characters, this suspenseful roller-coaster ride will keep both series fans and new readers on the edge of their seats."

—*Publishers Weekly*

My Way to You

"A fascinating novel that aptly balances disastrous circumstances."
—*Kirkus Reviews*

"*My Way to You* is an unforgettable book fueled by Catherine Bybee's own life, along with the dynamic cast she created that will capture your heart."

—Harlequin Junkie

Home to Me

"Bybee skillfully avoids both melodrama and melancholy by grounding her characters in genuine emotion . . . This is Bybee in top form."
—*Publishers Weekly* (starred review)

Everything Changes

"This sweet, sexy book is just the escapism many people are looking for right now."

—*Kirkus Reviews*

A Thin
Disguise

Faking Forever
Say It Again

Creek Canyon Series

My Way to You
Home to Me
Everything Changes

Richter Series

Changing the Rules

Paranormal Romance

MacCoinnich Time Travels

Binding Vows
Silent Vows
Redeeming Vows
Highland Shifter
Highland Protector

The Ritter Werewolves Series

Before the Moon Rises
Embracing the Wolf

Novellas

Soul Mate
Possessive

Erotica

Kilt Worthy
Kilt-A-Licious

A Thin Disguise

Book Two
of the
Richter Series

CATHERINE BYBEE

Published by Montlake, Seattle

www.apub.com

Amazon, the Amazon logo, and Montlake are trademarks of Amazon.com, Inc., or its affiliates.

ISBN-13: 9781542009959
ISBN-10: 1542009952

Cover design by Caroline Teagle Johnson

Cover photography by Regina Wamba of MaeIDesign.com

Printed in the United States of America

Ethan and Eloise
Enjoy every day of your Happily Ever After

CHAPTER ONE

Inside the eye of a scope, there is a spot where two lines come together. If that scope is mounted on top of a high-powered rifle and is in the hands of someone who understands the mathematical calculation of how much the projectile will descend before it reaches its target, that spot becomes deadly.

Olivia noted three snipers positioned south, east, and west of the entrance to the courthouse. SWAT . . . all of them. While she had no doubt they'd do their job well if put to the task, the fact that none of them had noticed her pissed her off.

She positioned a camera behind her scope and snapped photos of the uniformed men.

Once she was satisfied with what she had, she wrapped up her location and moved to the next. It took ten minutes to change her appearance, and ten more to get in position.

The familiar thump of her heart pounded blood up to her brain. The first time she'd ever squeezed the trigger, she'd pictured a video of red blood cells pushing through veins. With each beat, her blood pushed forward and stopped as valves closed off behind them only to be pushed forward again with another beat of her heart.

After pulling the trigger . . . the imaginary blood in her mind manifested into real puddles on the pavement.

The images she'd put in her head were nothing next to the real thing.

Nothing had prepared her for what followed.

Not one of the classes she'd been forced to take at Richter equipped her for what she needed to survive.

And yet here she was.

Heart still beating.

Soul still bleeding.

She refocused on her position and searched.

"Don't disappoint me," she muttered as her scope scanned the places she would have used.

Her lens narrowed in and found one solo player.

From the outside, it appeared as if the back door to the courthouse would not be in use, although Olivia's sources said it would. So instead of moving to the front of the building, she flattened herself on her hidden perch and waited.

A buzz on her watch told her the time had come.

Her body tensed and her eyes kept in constant motion.

The door opened and several men and women in black suits emerged. Although Olivia knew the target, the team did a damn good job of blending her in.

They moved in a herd, alert but swift as they climbed into two SUVs. Once the doors shut and the cars were in motion, Olivia scanned the area again.

The lone sniper still had aim and didn't move until the cars were out of sight. Once he did, Olivia snapped a photograph of the man to add to the others.

She waited until he left before disassembling her tools and packing them away.

An hour passed, her appearance changed once again, and Olivia vacated her position. Once on the ground floor, she blended into the overrun streets of the Vegas Strip. The hot September sun hadn't even considered letting up as the temperatures hovered in the triple digits.

The heat under Olivia's wig was enough to give her a stroke, but she moved along, dodging the Nevada visitors that had no need for sobriety even on a Tuesday. Young women with long hair and short shorts laughed and stumbled around while young men urged them to have one more drink.

Innocent fun . . . until it wasn't.

Like Marie Nickerson. The girl hidden in a black suit sliding into the back of an SUV. Marie had a bounty on her head that would disappear only with her death. But once the hearing was over, and the protection program did its job, she'd never be seen again.

Even though Marie had no idea who Olivia was, she'd been Marie's shadow for nearly a year. Much as Olivia would have loved to say, even to herself, that she had no interest in the girl, that would be a lie.

Olivia knew Marie's crimes, and more importantly, the atrocities that had been committed against her. The girl had been forced into childhood prostitution, sold like chattel to the highest bidder, and nearly lost her life when she'd tried to break free. Olivia understood all too well what it meant to belong to someone who only wanted to use you for their personal gain. While Marie didn't have the skills or access to shoot the man responsible, the girl did have testimony that was in the process of putting that man deep inside a federal penitentiary.

Olivia's job was to keep Marie alive so she could do just that.

She knew where the girl was right then, knew the federal marshals who were guarding her. Marie deserved to live the rest of her life in some kind of peace. She was young enough to put this behind her, so long as the system could keep her alive.

Olivia wandered off the Strip on foot until she was far enough away from the courthouse and anyone who'd seen her in her current disguise. Inside a smoke-filled casino, one that didn't depend on the glitz of the Strip but the desire of old-school gamblers for its income, she found a public bathroom and eased into the appearance that had rented a room a few blocks away.

She hoisted her bag over her shoulder and checked the feeds to the surveillance system on her phone. Once she knew it was safe, she left the smoky casino.

Inside her room, Olivia deadbolted the door, did a sweep, and then finally sat down.

Her right hand reached for her head and pulled the third wig of the day off. With it gone, she removed the cap that held her natural hair out of the way and shook it loose.

She sniffed . . . twice.

Her hair stunk.

She flopped back on the mattress, arms wide, and closed her eyes.

Thirty minutes elapsed, giving her brain enough time to tune out and her body a chance to soak in the cool air of the air-conditioned room.

A few more days and she could disappear . . .

Again.

Maybe this time she'd leave and stay that way. Find that beach, that mountaintop . . . that sanctuary that allowed her to forget.

Olivia pushed herself into a sitting position and placed both hands on her thighs.

Once the trial was over and Marie was in the hands of the good guys, Olivia could walk away. The promised money would go far so long as she relocated outside of North America.

Dismissing the thoughts of her future—any future—she pushed off the bed and took a few steps to the bathroom.

The water out of the shower was hot, even on its coldest setting.

Adjusting the water temperature was a simple thing when considering life's pleasures. But cheap hotels in Nevada as summertime winded down didn't always have the ability to do such a minimal task.

Hard, hot water washed the grime of the day and refreshed her enough for round two.

She dried her hair completely before putting it back in the cap and donning a wig. This time dishwater blonde and halfway down her back. Blue contact lenses, a beauty mark on her cheek . . . a pair of short shorts and a sparkly tank with a jacket that covered her enough to suggest she wasn't looking for a paid date. Although she'd play that card if she needed to.

Once she was far enough away from her hotel, she grabbed a taxi and made her way to the Wynn. Upscale, cosmopolitan without the themes that many of the other resorts on the Vegas Strip used.

Inside, the hotel bells and whistles of the casino floor were slightly muted in comparison to the other resorts on the Strip. It was early and very few chairs in front of the slot machines were occupied. A handful of tables were open, and most had lone dealers standing behind them with their hands folded waiting for someone to sit down and open their wallet.

Olivia knew how to play all the games, but never saw the point. She only dipped her hand in when it suited her assignment.

She circled around the casino, making mental notes as she went. Where the secluded rooms that high rollers congregated in for private gambling were located, where employees slipped behind walls and into kitchens or bars, the exits that dumped deeper into the casino, or close to an actual exit. She landed in the cocktail lounge with a view of the casino floor.

After ordering a club soda and lime, Olivia pulled her cell phone out of her pocket.

A security screen masked her activity from anyone sitting close by, and certainly from any cameras above. She logged in to a secure space and pulled open a handful of pictures.

Players. All of them from the same family.

That's what the mafia called those close to them.

Family.

And in the case of Mykonos Sobol, the man standing trial, he was both blood and chosen. Some of his extended family had flown in to support him. By *support*, that meant take over his connections and operations until his name was cleared. Olivia knew from experience that the same family was busy trying to bribe witnesses and make those that wouldn't cooperate disappear.

The case against Mykonos was as solid as it could get so long as Marie was alive to testify.

Mykonos had bought the girl when she was sixteen.

For three and a half years, he sold her out as he saw fit. When she stepped out of line, or tried to escape his clutches, he made her pay. The last attempt at his idea of discipline nearly killed her.

At that point, Olivia stepped in. She'd been asked to return a favor. Be Marie's shadow while the right people gathered their case and the girl could recover from her physical injuries. As her shadow, Marie never knew Olivia existed. She'd been by Marie's side while she convalesced in the hospital and again when she was in the rehabilitation center. Her protective custody was taken care of by the federal marshals, but that didn't mean Olivia wasn't watching and following. And now, when tensions were high and the gavel was about to drop on the accused, moves would be made.

Navi, Mykonos's "cousin," had a presidential suite at the hotel. If he was a good little criminal, and Olivia already knew he was, the man and his entourage would be visible tonight. After all, they were all upstanding men with nothing to hide. And staying tucked away, out of sight, would bring suspicion to their activities. Navi knew he was being watched. Any "family" had a team assigned to them.

Since Navi was the biggest fish, Olivia was tracking him.

And the teams knew nothing about her.

Olivia scrolled through pictures and names and profiles, most of them Russian. Not Russian American, not born there and raised here . . . but born, lived, and killed Russian. Filthy rich, dirty money, mafia that lived and breathed by their own code.

With a tap on the screen, the images she'd been studying disappeared and a video game replaced them.

She lifted herself off her perch and left the lounge. The casino was picking up.

Families skirted the perimeter of the gaming sections with children in hand. Parents were not allowed to stop and toss even a quarter in a machine while their children stood by and watched. Nevada gaming did have its laws, loose as they were about everything other than gambling.

Olivia moved closer to the elevator tower that accessed the highest-price suites and waited. For nearly an hour, she moved her location to avoid suspicion. If she'd had even a little notice as to what hotel Navi was going to use, she would have set up something in the man's room to alert her to his actions. But that hadn't been possible, so now she was doing this the hard way.

Eventually, the hard way paid off.

Navi's arrival on the ground floor of the hotel was hard to miss. Two men the size of small school buses flanked him, and one long-legged brunette hung on his arm like he'd paid for her.

If there was something Olivia prided herself on, it was her ability to gauge people and her surroundings. Navi's men both had weapons, an easy deduction since they were obviously bodyguards. Their eyes were on the move and assessing the situation as they walked beside their boss. Navi wore a wedding ring, but his female companion did not. Men like Navi married for the social expectation and to bring legitimacy to their children's names. Not to stay faithful to their wives.

Olivia stayed well beyond the eyes and ears of Navi's party and watched as they walked into a steak house. She waited a few minutes before meandering by the entrance of the restaurant. When she did, she noticed the bodyguards taking a seat in the waiting area while Navi and the girl disappeared inside.

By her estimate, she had at least an hour and a half before Navi would emerge. She'd do a quick check inside the restaurant to ensure

Navi and the girl were dining alone or make note of anyone they may have joined, and then retreat to watch him later.

She waited for a larger party to enter the restaurant and walked in quietly behind them. With her face diverted from the bodyguards, Olivia did a quick redirect and headed toward the restroom. She found a stall, waited a full minute, flushed, and emerged to wash her hands. When she left, she moved into the restaurant and looked around. It wasn't long before an employee approached her.

"Can I help you find your table?"

Olivia smiled and glanced left and right. "I thought my party was already here, but I don't see them."

The waiter tilted his head. "The hostess would know if your party arrived."

"Yeah, she was busy, so I thought I'd just duck in." Over the waiter's shoulder, she zeroed in on Navi and his date. A table for two with wine and candlelight.

How cozy.

The waiter leaned in and whispered. "We have a dress code in here. The manager isn't fond of shorts."

Olivia let her jaw drop. "Oh, shit. I should probably run up to my room and change."

He smiled. "No one will force you to leave, but you might get a few dirty looks."

She lowered her voice. "Thanks for the tip."

The waiter looked her up and down. "Anytime."

Turning on her heel, she made her way back to the front of the restaurant. She noted the bodyguards once again when someone's shoulder nudged hers as they walked by.

"Excuse me."

"It's okay," she said, looking up.

Her eyes caught his, and her smile froze on her face.

What the hell was Leo Grant doing there?

CHAPTER TWO

Leo diverted his attention from the couple that had walked into the restaurant and toward the woman he'd just bumped into. Dishwater blonde with mysterious eyes and full pink lips. Beautiful.

The back of his throat itched as if he should know the woman staring at him. Only he didn't. He would have remembered.

"Do I know you?" he asked.

Her lips instantly closed, and she stood taller. "No."

She turned to leave, and for some reason his hand found her arm and halted her.

"Are you sure?"

"I'm quite positive." She glanced over his shoulder, eyes wide, and walked swiftly away.

Is that an accent?

Yeah, he would have remembered her.

He watched her leave before shaking off thoughts of the confusion on her face and turned back toward the restaurant. Then, because he felt someone's stare, he looked to his left.

Brutis A and Brutis B stared, recognition on their faces.

Fuck.

He shifted from one foot to the other, weighed his options.

Brutis A stood.

Leo squared his shoulders. "He in there?" The question was rhetorical.

Brutis B met his friend on his feet.

It was then that Leo pushed his jacket back enough to display his badge and the butt of his gun holstered at his side.

They didn't flinch, and they didn't sit down.

They knew who he was.

"I'll just look," Leo said as he moved into the restaurant.

Navi Sobol's bodyguards right at his back, he marched in.

Sobol spotted him, put his drink down.

With every step, Leo knew his boss wasn't going to be happy with him. But he moved forward anyway. He had no choice.

Leo arrived at the table with a smile. "I see you're making yourself right at home."

Navi folded his hands and placed them in his lap.

"Is there something I can do for you?"

Leo moved his gaze around the room.

Plenty of people were watching them. Hard not to when three men, two admittedly a little larger than him, stood in the center of a posh restaurant talking.

"No, no . . . I'm good." Leo turned his stare to Navi's female companion—young . . . but not Marie Nickerson young—then looked back. "How's the food?"

Navi opened one palm to the empty table. "I couldn't tell you."

Leo grinned. "Well, let me know. I'll put this place on my list."

Navi tilted his head, looked Leo dead in the eye.

"You kids enjoy yourselves," Leo said. He'd gotten what he wanted by seeing the man in the restaurant with only the woman.

He turned and found Navi's bodyguards push in just enough to stop him from walking past without bumping into one of them.

There was no way Leo was going to brush shoulders with them. As much as the men were trying to intimidate him, Leo knew their kind.

Hired men who held no value for life other than their own and the man they were paid to protect.

An accidental touch of a shoulder could be considered battery in front of the right judge.

Leo put his hands up, his playful smile still in place. "If you'll excuse me."

A noise behind him suggested Navi had called his dogs off.

Brutis A and B separated, allowing Leo a path.

Leo made eye contact with at least two people in the restaurant as he slipped past the paid help.

He felt both bodyguards at his back as he left.

A few yards into the noisy casino, Leo muttered, "Well, fuck."

~

Olivia broke her own code and called in. "Get him out of here."

"Who?"

"The teacher. He's fucking up."

"Grant?"

"I don't care who he works for, he's fucking up! I can't do my job if he's lurking."

"Consider it done."

The person on the end of the line disconnected the call.

Leo walked out of the restaurant with an audience.

As he headed toward the door, the bodyguards peeled off. Leo lifted a cell phone to his ear and paused.

Olivia was too far away to hear the conversation, but she imagined what was being said. Leo looked around the massive room as if searching for someone he recognized. Olivia knew that wouldn't be her. Outside of walking past him in the restaurant, they'd never met.

He turned a full circle, gestured with his hand, and walked out of sight.

She released a breath of relief.

If Navi Sobol had planned on meeting with anyone after dinner, that plan was likely to change.

She should probably call it a night, but instead she walked over to a penny slot machine, put a hundred bucks in, and sat down.

In the time it took Navi to have his dinner, the cocktail waitress had stopped by several times and filled up a sparkling water with lime, and Olivia had managed to keep the machine eating pennies a few at a time. She'd pulled out a cigarette only to realize she was in a nonsmoking section of the casino. Just as well, but it would have added to her leisure status, as she'd sat at one machine for well over an hour.

She saw the bodyguards first. But once Navi and the woman stepped out of the restaurant, the guards took position from behind, following like the puppy dogs they were.

Waiting until the entourage had passed, Olivia cashed out of her machine and held her winning ticket in her hand as she followed from a safe distance.

The casino had filled with people, and with them the noise level increased. But even with all that, it was easier to duck into a bank of slots when one of Navi's dogs turned around.

Olivia played shadow while Navi stopped at a craps table and pulled out several hundred-dollar bills. This was where she would have approached, but since Leo had stopped her in the restaurant, she knew better than to make her face seen twice by the bodyguards. They looked as if they were all muscle and no brain, but she wasn't going to risk it. Instead, she kept her distance and watched to see who, if anyone, approached the man.

An hour passed, he won some, lost more, but the only conversation was with the woman and a thirtysomething man wearing a plaid shirt and jeans. His accent said Deep South, and the only reason she knew that from a distance was the loud nature of the man. No one Navi would be in contact with on purpose.

Eventually Mr. South moved on, and Navi collected his chips and did the same.

After a brief stop at a roulette table, the couple headed back to the elevators.

It wasn't even ten o'clock and the man was turning in.

For the second time that night, Olivia wished she'd bugged the man's room.

She waited until his group entered the elevator, then stepped closer to watch the numbers. Sure enough, the elevator stopped on the top floor.

She considered hanging around longer, see if the man was dropping off the woman only to reemerge, then decided against it. If she'd stashed another disguise in the hotel and could change her appearance, she would have. But as it stood, the longer she hung around, the better the chances of being seen.

Outside the resort, the hot desert night had cooled down enough to be tolerable. The dryness of the air gave the atmosphere a spark of electricity. Or maybe that was the buzz of people that swarmed like bees to honey.

Olivia walked past the valet and the line of high-end cars all parked in a way to be noticed. As tourists snapped pictures of the Ferrari that sat next to a Bentley, she rolled her head and loosened the tight muscles in her neck as she strolled by.

She was hungry, and tired.

Deeply tired.

She made her way onto the Strip and slowed her pace. If Marie's testimony wrapped up the next day as expected, this would be Olivia's last night in Vegas. Maybe even the States. That forgotten island somewhere sounded better and better.

Groups of people passed her in both directions. Several homeless limped along in no hurry while a few single locals, high on God only knew what, zipped around talking to themselves.

The closer she was to the trendier hotels, the bigger the crowd.

Street drinking was encouraged, and nearly everyone took part.

She found an understated convenience store and stepped in under the blinding fluorescent lights. The air-conditioning grew colder as she moved deeper inside the building. In the back she found what she was looking for. She favored a turkey and cheese over tuna and discovered an apple that didn't look half bad. And since the water coming out of the tap at her hotel tasted like dirt, she grabbed a big bottle of water.

"Someone as beautiful as you shouldn't be eating that piss-poor excuse for dinner."

The words registered, and Olivia turned to find a pair of blue eyes staring her way. The guy was twenty-five, tops. The sunburn on his face and the way he wasn't completely steady on his feet suggested he'd been out day drinking and continued the party into the night. His eyelids closed halfway and had a hard time opening back up.

The man wasn't interesting enough to even respond to.

Olivia turned away from the refrigerator and toward the checkout.

"Wow, not even a hello?"

She kept her eyes forward and didn't look back.

He was still behind her when she set her stuff on the counter.

Her neck tingled, and she looked toward the open doors.

"Is this all?" the clerk asked her.

She offered a tired smile and one quick nod. From her back pocket she removed a twenty-dollar bill and handed it over. All the while the hair on her arms stood up. Much as she wanted to look behind her, she didn't.

She accepted the plastic bag and her change and started toward the door.

The man who'd been watching let out a low whistle.

Let it go, Olivia.

She made it a block outside the store when the chill on her neck made her stop and turn around.

Her spidey sense ratcheted up another ten notches when she didn't see the object that was watching her.

The streets were loud, with people everywhere and cars cruising the Strip, music blaring into the southwestern air.

Her intention was to zigzag back to her hotel so long as the neck tingling went away.

With a twist of her heel, she turned around and stopped dead in her tracks.

Leo stood two feet away, eyes glued to her.

"We meet again," he said, his voice calm and even.

She paused . . . shocked to see him. "Are you following me?"

He shifted his weight from one foot to the other, and then he opened his mouth and lied. "No." The corners of his mouth lifted, and a smile that could only be described as flirtatious manifested on his face.

This was not happening. "Don't you have somewhere to be?" she asked him, knowing damn well he did.

Her question pulled some of the tension out of his shoulders. "As a matter of fact, I do."

She looked him dead in the eye. "So, go there."

He paused, let that flirty smile expand. "What's your name?"

A car horn sounded from the street.

"You've got to be kidding me." The man was trying to pick her up.

He cocked his head to the side. "You're beautiful, you're not wearing a ring . . ." He shrugged. "What's your name?"

For a moment she stood in shock. In her line of work, she didn't believe in coincidences. So what were the chances of Grant not knowing whom he was talking to?

Considering she'd sniffed out his earlier lie, and the one he just delivered by saying he hadn't been following her . . . no, Leo Grant wasn't that great of an actor, even if she knew he was capable of taking on the persona of someone he wasn't. Undercover federal agents had a knack for things like that.

In an attempt to deliver the same message to him as she did to the guy in the convenience store, she shook her head and walked past him.

He followed. "Wait."

She stopped, did a quick pivot, causing him to step into her personal space. "Go away!"

"You don't mean that. I see something in your eyes . . ."

"You see me being . . ."

Car horns blared.

Olivia shifted her gaze from Leo to the street.

In an instant, she saw the barrel of a gun pointing out of a car, the face behind it.

"Get down!" she yelled.

Everything happened all at once.

Surprise on Leo's face as she dropped her bag and lunged for him.

Her knees buckling as she attempted to become a smaller target.

And a flash of light from the tip of a gun that fired without a sound.

CHAPTER THREE

One minute she was growling at him, the next she was grabbing his arm, and they were both down on the dirty sidewalk of the Las Vegas Strip.

He heard a horn blaring and tires screeching.

Leo rolled over to see the taillights of a car speeding off and around the corner.

"What the hell?"

Then someone screamed, pulling Leo's attention to the woman at his side.

She was still.

Too still.

The small jacket she was wearing had moved enough for him to see blood coming from the left side of her chest.

Adrenaline surged and he pushed himself up to hover over her.

"Hey," he said, gently touching to see if she would open her eyes.

Nothing.

He leaned down, put his ear to her lips.

The air on his face said she was alive.

Leo reached for his phone and dialed 911 as the crowd surrounded them.

He took the liberty of lifting her jacket to see if there were any other holes in her and then did a scan of her body with his eyes and fingertips as the phone rang and rang.

"Come on, damn it. Answer the phone."

Not finding more, he moved to her shoulder. He wanted to turn her over, see if there was an exit wound, but she was out cold, and moving her wasn't an option.

"911, what's your emergency?"

"Special Agent Leo Grant. I need an ambulance. Single gunshot wound to the chest, female, approximately thirty years old." He looked up. "We're in front of the Venetian on the sidewalk."

"Is the victim breathing?"

"Yes, but unconscious. Hurry."

His breath came in short, fast pants. What the hell had happened? A drive-by, of course, but who? She must have seen the gun and reacted. If she hadn't, he'd likely be the one on the ground and not her.

Security guards from the Venetian showed up first. Then a local black-and-white.

Between them, the crowd was pushed back to keep Leo and the woman from being stepped on.

Leo disconnected from the 911 operator and stared down at the woman who'd taken a bullet aimed at him. All because he found her attractive and intriguing and wanted to know who she was.

He'd hung around the Wynn for more than two hours, watching those coming and going in an attempt to find who it was that had generated the call from Claire.

"You're following Navi at the hotel," she'd told him once he'd picked up the phone the second he left the restaurant.

"Do you have a bug on me?"

"No. We have one on him. And you're messing up our intel."

"You know that's not your job here."

Claire worked for a security detail that had been essential in flushing out Mykonos and all the sordid details of Marie Nickerson's case. And while they weren't the ones protecting the woman at the moment, he knew Claire's team was just as invested in seeing Mykonos locked away. So having Claire call him wasn't as much of a surprise as it would have been in any other case.

"I'm a private investigator, licensed in the state of Nevada," she reminded him. "Navi knows who you are, but not who we have on him. So get out of there."

"I liked it better when you were the student and I was the teacher telling you what to do." When he met Claire, he was undercover as a high school teacher and she was in his class.

"Ha! Even as my teacher you didn't stand a chance of telling me what to do. Now leave the casino."

Even though he knew she was right, he grumbled and bitched before hanging up.

He left the inside of the hotel, but that didn't mean Leo was gone.

And when the blonde in shorts walked out and headed toward the Strip, Leo abandoned his post and followed her.

Yeah, maybe it was creepy, but something told him to keep his pace.

It was the first time a woman turned his head this much since . . . well, in a long time.

And now his flirting had resulted in her unconscious with a gunshot wound.

Her breathing was steady and fast, and although there wasn't an excessive amount of blood on the pavement, it didn't mean she wasn't bleeding on the inside.

When the paramedics arrived, Leo finally stood back.

It took only a few minutes for the team to expose her chest and find the hole the bullet had put in her.

The older medic on the team found a small wallet in her pocket and a cell phone.

Once they put a collar on her neck and had her on a gurney, they were rushing toward the ambulance.

Leo followed and climbed inside after them.

"Has she been drinking? Drugs?"

"I don't know. I don't think so."

He needed to call this in. Let his boss know what was going on. The person who did this was likely long gone by now. Or waiting for another shot.

The medic spread his fingers and pushed around on her head.

That's when they noticed a wig.

Leo looked closer as they attempted to remove the blonde and reveal the brunette. Because some of the blonde strands were trapped inside the cervical collar, the medic found a pair of scissors and started cutting at the thing.

He pulled bits of the wig away, and with it, a significant amount of blood flowed.

A moment of panic struck Leo. "Was she shot in the head?"

The medic looked closer as the driver wove through traffic.

"I don't think so. I don't see a hole. Probably happened when she went down."

Minutes later they backed into an ambulance bay at the hospital.

Leo jumped out first, and the medics rushed past him to the waiting staff members, who hurried the woman out of sight.

He walked in and stopped at the trauma bay doors while the emergency room staff did their jobs.

"Damn it!" He pulled out his phone to call his boss.

Blood stained the tips of his fingers.

~

Gunshot victims always generated a lot of activity in emergency rooms. But bullets put into people while in the presence of the police or, in Leo's case, a federal agent generated a small army.

Las Vegas police had a good showing of force, and a few agents from Leo's team joined him. Leo's boss was en route to an airport along with that small army.

"Who's the girl?" Kelsey Fitzpatrick, or Fitz, as everyone called her, had partnered up with him as soon as he finished his undercover assignment six months ago. They both lived in Southern California and were in Vegas for the trial.

Fitz was eight years older than him and had celebrated her fortieth birthday a few years back by divorcing her husband of ten years.

They were both in transition, and so far, the partnering was working out.

But the way Fitz was looking at him, with her sharp eyes and hair pulled back to the nape of her neck, Leo felt as if her words were more of an accusation than a question.

"Just a girl."

Fitz looked down the length of her nose with a practiced stare.

"I swear."

"She come to you, or you go to her?"

Leo sat back in the waiting room chair. The staff had designated a small space for the officers and agents to come and go. Isolated and out of the way.

The woman they were talking about had been rushed from the ER to the OR where they were working on her.

"I approached her."

"Why?"

He'd be asking the same questions if it were Fitz who'd nearly gotten shot.

"She's attractive."

21

Those eyes that were focused on the tip of her nose closed, and Fitz shook her head. "You were picking her up?"

"No." That wasn't exactly the truth. "I was looking for a name . . . maybe a phone number."

Fitz wasn't amused. "Trying to hook up."

"For later. After the case."

"Tell me again how she went down."

Leo sighed, told the story again. "We were talking. She was facing the oncoming traffic. Suddenly she looked behind me and shouted. She must have seen the shooter. She grabbed me, and the next thing I knew we were both on the pavement."

"How many shots were fired?"

"Couldn't tell you. I didn't hear the shot. They obviously used a silencer. The people around us didn't react until the car sped away." If he concentrated hard enough, he could remember the dull thud of a gunshot through a silencer, but the commotion of being pulled to the ground and tires . . . yeah, he wouldn't swear to what he heard.

Fitz started to pace. A habit when she was thinking. "Did she push you away, or pull you toward her?"

"She didn't push. She grabbed my arm." He looked at his forearm as if seeing her fingers gripping him.

"Let's hope she wakes up so we can question what she saw."

Leo ran a hand through his hair. "Let's just hope she wakes up. We both know that gun was pointed at me. If she hadn't yelled, and I hadn't moved . . ."

"I don't know what the hell you were thinking going in there after Navi."

"I was watching. Seeing who he talked to . . . met with. It's called investigating."

"Doesn't do any good if you're seen."

Leo knew Fitz's words were going to be repeated once their boss arrived.

"Can't imagine Navi is dumb enough to try this after talking with me face-to-face." Mob bosses might be complete scumbags, but they weren't stupid.

"Unless the alibi for him and his men is rock solid."

"I'm sure it is."

"Which means you almost got popped for nothing. Did you at least get her name?"

"I was working on it." The hospital had her listed as a Jane Doe. The wallet in her pocket had some cash and a casino voucher for two hundred and change. No ID. They weren't able to get into her cell phone without facial recognition, and no one thought to try and unlock it until after she'd been wheeled off to the OR.

That had been two hours ago and no word on her condition.

"I need a cigarette," he said aloud.

"You don't smoke."

He'd quit two years prior, but that didn't stop his desire to smoke.

Leo pushed out of the chair and rolled his head around in an effort to clear the kinks.

It didn't work.

The door to the waiting room opened, and the surgeon walked in, still wearing blue surgical scrubs complete with a hat. "She's going to make it," he said.

Leo released a long breath and sat back down.

"The bullet made a bit of a mess before exiting her body. A centimeter more and she would have likely bled out on the street before getting here. She's lucky."

"When will we be able to talk to her?" Fitz asked.

The doctor shook his head. "I'm keeping her sedated and on a ventilator for at least the next twelve hours."

"Any idea why she was unconscious?" Leo asked.

"She hit the pavement pretty hard, decent laceration on the back of her head, but there wasn't anything on the CT to indicate any long-term issue. A repeat CT will confirm that. When we take her off the vent, she should wake up."

Leo and Fitz exchanged glances.

"Do you have her identity yet?"

"No," Fitz answered.

The doctor shook his head. "We get a lot of Jane and John Does in Vegas. Eventually someone comes looking for them, often the police."

"I'm sure that's true." Vegas didn't earn the name Sin City for nothing.

When the surgeon turned to leave, Leo stood and put out his hand. "Thank you."

"Of course."

With a nod, he left the room.

Leo looked at his watch. "We have about four hours until Brackett arrives. You might as well go back to the hotel and get some rest."

"What about you?"

He shook his head. "Better I stay here, get as much information from the locals so I have something to tell our boss when he gets here."

Fitz looked as if she wanted to say something, but instead turned toward the door. She stopped. "If you do come back to the hotel . . ."

"I'll take a police escort. No need to give the shooter a second chance."

Fitz glanced over her shoulder. "For what it's worth, I'm glad it's her in the ICU and not you."

Leo couldn't say the same.

He lifted his tired ass out of the chair in search of fresh coffee.

It was going to be a very long night.

~

"You look like shit."

Leo had managed an hour of chair sleeping in the waiting room before Brackett arrived and delivered a crap sandwich.

Now, in the early hours of the following day, Leo stood outside the courtroom doors with Neil MacBain passing judgment.

"Rough night."

Neil was the head of the investigative team that had taken Mykonos down.

The man was big, the kind of big that you saw walking toward you in a dark alley and you hopped barbwire fences to avoid. Retired military, with a team filled with highly skilled special ops individuals that the feds would love to get their hands on. But those talents were happy in the private sector.

"I heard. How's the girl?"

"Still in the ICU. Hoping she's awake by the time I get back."

"Any idea who did it?"

"Who squeezed the trigger and who asked for it to be squeezed are two different things." Leo nodded toward the closed door of the courtroom. "Your guess is as solid as mine."

Neil shifted his gaze without moving a muscle in his body. "I've sent Claire and Cooper back to LA. They were visible, you were visible."

Yeah, Claire had pretended to be a high school student and Cooper a substitute teacher and coach in the sting to flush out Mykonos. It would be easy to assume Neil's team could be a target as well. "Smart. Although I doubt they liked that."

"I'm the boss."

"When I spoke with Claire last night, she said you had eyes on Navi."

"We do."

"Wanna elaborate?"

Neil looked at him dead-on, then away without answering.

"Okay. If you have anything solid, you'll share?"

Neil gave a quick nod, and then focused on the open space in the foyer. "Claire and Cooper's replacements are here." Without saying anything else, Neil stepped away.

Behind him, Fitz walked up with two cups of coffee, handed one to him. "You look like—"

"Shit! I know." Leo accepted the coffee and added the new caffeine to the old. "Thanks," he muttered, putting the cup to his lips.

Leo was halfway through his coffee when the lawyers arrived.

Mykonos had three high-profile, high-dollar, and high-attitude attorneys wearing suits that cost more than Leo made in a month.

It was nauseating.

Whoever said crime didn't pay had their head up their ass. As that thought drifted through Leo's mind, he followed the district attorneys into the courtroom and took a seat. One look at the victim . . . the twenty-year-old girl who'd lost her dignity, her innocence, and any value she had for her own life reinstated Leo's desire for cheap suits and the path for right versus wrong.

Marie Nickerson had been sold into the sex trade at the age of sixteen.

Human trafficking took the form of a boyfriend who convinced her to join him in Vegas with a fake ID and the promise of a good time. Next thing the girl knew, she belonged to Mykonos.

And when she tried to escape Mykonos and the life he'd forced upon her, she was rewarded with attempted murder and dismemberment.

Her physical wounds had healed. The bruises gone, her hair grown back. But if you looked close enough, you saw a thinning at the base of her skull where the burn was too deep and the hair wouldn't regrow.

Then there was the look in her eyes.

Empty.

Soulless.

Her eyes tracked Mykonos with palpable fear.

Every second of the trial was one second closer to her throwing in the towel and backtracking on her testimony.

Fear stopped victims from righting wrongs every second of every day.

The way Mykonos stared at Marie would make most people shrivel into a ball of dust as if Medusa herself had narrowed her gaze on them.

Every once in a while, Mykonos splayed his lies for the jury to hear, his easy smile and charming personality weaving a tale just as fanciful as Cinderella's. Only he used broad strokes to describe his role as fairy godmother giving a young woman a home and security even though she was unfaithful to him. The defense's case was based on a relationship where Marie was in the wrong, addicted to sex and drugs, and Mykonos was the hero.

But today was about cross-examination and closing arguments. His story wouldn't hold up.

Or so Leo hoped.

The district attorneys wanted Mykonos and all of his kind exiled from Las Vegas as soon as humanly possible. He, and those like him, soiled the already slippery landscape that encompassed the Vegas life-style. Gamble, drink, have sex with strangers . . . but leave the kids out of the equation. Nothing infuriated the powers that be more than sexual predators targeting children.

No matter how much Mykonos tried to convince the jury that Marie was an adult, one look at her said something different. Yes, she was twenty now . . . but the photographs of her at sixteen running for her high school cross-country team painted a different picture.

All of those visuals were courtesy of Neil and his team.

The evidence against Mykonos trumped everything his fancy-suit-wearing attorneys could come up with.

The only way the jury would deliver anything but a guilty verdict would be with someone fucking with them. Which was where Navi stepped in.

The jury, however, had been sequestered for the duration.

And hopefully that safeguard hadn't been compromised.

The courtroom filled, the doors closed, and the judge made his way to the bench.

CHAPTER FOUR

Life exploded in her brain like brief psychedelic, drug-induced, painful flashes on a movie screen.

Bright lights hovered over her face. Voices echoed, and machines made unfamiliar noises.

And when she tried to take a breath, the pain blurred her vision until she fell back into the darkness she'd crawled out of.

The next time the movie aired, it was darker. Quieter.

Something obstructed her ability to breathe. When she reached for the thorn in her side, her hands were too heavy to move. Even opening her eyes wasn't a possibility. Tiny slits of light passed before her as if she were inside a dark closet looking at the draft space at the bottom of the door.

A voice spoke in soft tones before a feeling of warmth flushed through her body and the worry of the thorn and heaviness no longer mattered.

Each time she tried to wake up was different. But every time she fell back into the abyss, the dream was the same.

She was alone, walking barefoot across wet grass. At first the grass felt refreshing and soft, but soon the earth started to harden, and the prickly edges of each green blade turned brown and filled with thorns. With each step she asked herself, Where are my shoes?

There had to be shoes somewhere.

Soon the grass was gone altogether, and the earth was covered in jagged rocks brought up from the depths of hell.

With each step she burned and bled, and still she walked. The compelling need to move forward was as important as taking her next breath.

But like her breathing, each step was as painful as the last.

"Just stop," she heard a voice say.

But staying in place would give the rocks the opportunity to carve out bigger sections of her skin . . . and maybe the next step would be better.

Her gaze moved around the content of the dream, searching for something to look forward to. A place where the rocks were gone and the earth was soft and healing . . . but all she could see in the vastness of her dream was hell's landscape of pain.

~

"This is going to hang on another day." Fitz voiced what Leo had already figured out.

It was lunchtime, and the court was in recess for the next hour and a half.

"I know," Leo said.

The expensive lawyers were dragging it out. Which would likely leave closing arguments for the next day.

They stood just inside the courthouse while most of the occupants walked past them in search of something to eat.

Leo looked out the windows to the tops of the adjacent buildings. He knew his people had extra coverage on watch. Unlike the night before, the chances of someone shooting at him here were slim. That didn't stop his heart from beating a little too fast at the prospect of doing a simple task like ordering a greasy burger from a local fast food joint.

That thought brought him around to the woman in the hospital.

He needed an update.

Fitz reached for the door to push her way outside.

Leo hesitated.

Fitz stopped, looked at him.

"I need to make a couple calls."

"Right. Sure. I'll grab you something." She saw through his excuse.

Leo reached for his wallet, handed her a twenty.

"No onions."

She waved the bill in her hand and walked out.

Behind him, a voice demanded his attention. "You have a second?"

Neil stood over him.

"Yeah. What's up?"

Neil nodded to a quiet corner of the building.

"Are your people any closer to finding who took a shot at you yesterday?"

"Couldn't tell ya. No one has contacted me if they are." His phone had been put on silent in the courtroom, and it hadn't buzzed once during the proceedings. "Why?"

Neil looked away. "My eyes on him haven't checked in today. It's not unlike them, but considering your activity last night . . ."

"You think Navi's men took your guy out?"

Neil kept his lips pushed together. His silence was his answer.

"Damn," Leo said for him.

"I'm not jumping to conclusions. My contact is smoke and shadows. You never know they're there."

Leo couldn't help but feel there was more that needed to be said. "Why are you telling me this?"

"Because if my contact was compromised, you need to go underground."

"Why?"

Neil looked him dead in the eye. "If they're gone, then you don't stand a chance."

That didn't sound promising.

"Your guy is that good, huh?"

For a second, it looked as if Neil was going to laugh.

All Leo got was a half of a smile. "Yes. *She* is."

~

Chandler Brackett was the man Leo reported to. The man was fifty-five and two years away from being forced out of the bureau. Why the federal government wanted to retire their agents at such an early age was beyond Leo. The man would likely find a new, high-paying job once he retired that would make him question why he stayed with the FBI as long as he did.

From the courthouse, Leo and Fitz returned to the hotel and met Brackett in his room.

Unlike Leo's accommodations, which were equipped with a bed and a bathroom, Brackett's had a living space with a conference room–type table and enough seating for eight.

"Have a seat," Brackett told them the second they walked through the door.

At the table, an agent by the name of Hector Lopez sat in front of a laptop computer and a portable printer.

"What do you have?"

Lopez handed Leo a stack of images. "With the help of Vegas's surveillance cameras, we were able to narrow down the type of car the shooter was in. A black Cadillac Escalade, newer model."

Leo looked at the dark images of the car Lopez described as it drove down the Vegas Strip.

"From what we can tell, they circled the block twice before making their move. I have headquarters combing through audio feeds from the Venetian to see if we can hear the actual shots."

"How many casings did they find?" Fitz asked.

"Two. One traveled through the girl, the other was lodged in a pillar on the street," Brackett informed them.

"Have we located the car?"

Lopez sneered. "Do you know how many black Cadillac SUVs are in this town?"

"A lot?" Fitz asked.

"All the limousine services use them, most of the hotels, and then there's the private sector. And since the license plate had been removed, we can't trace that."

"Why can't people do drive-bys in Ferraris?" Fitz teased.

"Don't think that would narrow much down," Lopez countered.

"What about Navi . . . Any movement on him or his boys after I left last night?"

"The hotel footage showed him enter his room, one of the bodyguards went in with him, the other moved across the hall. Sometime after two in the morning, the men switched."

"Couldn't be that easy."

Leo glanced at Fitz. "Just means Navi made a phone call."

"Do we have a list of calls yet?" Fitz asked.

"That's a little bit harder. The only calls on his landline at the hotel were to room service."

"Any word from the hospital?" Leo asked.

Brackett shook his head. "I'll leave that one to you. Considering your attempt to pick her up got her shot, you're going to have to talk her into not hiring lawyers of her own."

Leo hesitated.

Shit, he hadn't given that a thought.

"I should probably go, then."

Brackett took a deep breath. "Not alone."

Fitz let out a deep sigh and started to stand. "I'll change my clothes."

"Fifteen minutes?" Leo asked her.

She nodded through a tired smile.

~

"You're okay. Don't struggle."

Pain flickered and came into red-hot focus.

Breathing was an effort, and her head was thick with fog.

"You're in the hospital," a male voice told her.

Her throat was on fire.

"Can you open your eyes?"

She tested her eyelids and found the bright lights invasive to her brain.

There were two men and one woman at her bedside. All three of them stared down at her, watching. The antiseptic smell of a hospital assaulted her senses. And the sound of her own breathing was accompanied by a strange sensation in her chest. She looked toward the window and felt the movement just as painful as her breath.

"W-what happ—" She didn't get the question out before a cough tore at her lungs.

The woman she assumed was a nurse pressed a button on the bed, lifting her head, while one of the men brought a small cup with a straw to her lips. "Just a sip," he told her.

The tiny taste of water felt as if it were going through sandpaper that was once her throat.

"Better?" he asked.

"Yes." She swallowed again and tried to shake the curtain in her brain. "What happened?"

The Asian man removed a pen light from his pocket and flashed it in her eyes. "I'm Dr. Lee. You're at the University Medical Center in Las Vegas. You were shot last night."

"I was what?" She attempted to look down at herself. Saw the rise and fall of her chest through a hospital gown and wires that were attached to her chest.

"Do you remember anything?"

No. She didn't. "No." But getting shot didn't sound right.

"It's okay. That's not uncommon. The bullet went through your lung. You have a chest tube that's helping you breathe. That's the pain in your side . . ." Dr. Lee went on to talk about a surgery she didn't remember and terms she didn't know. Then, as she was watching him talk, she had a hard time concentrating on his words.

Who was he again?

"What's your name?" the nurse asked.

"It's, uhm . . ." *My name.* She closed her eyes, searching for it. "It's . . ." This was not a hard question. "My name is . . ." The harder she concentrated, the more pain filled her head.

She attempted to sit up taller, as if doing so would bring the answer to her lips.

The doctor and the nurse looked at each other in silence.

"My name is . . ." She took a deep breath to answer. But it didn't come.

"Do you know where you are?" the doctor asked.

"A hospital." That was an easy question.

"What city?" he asked.

Didn't he just tell her that? "Atlantic City."

The doctor flashed the light in her eyes. "You're in Las Vegas."

"Why am I in Vegas?"

He smiled at her, didn't answer. "I want you to remember three things for me. Can you do that?"

"Yes."

"Elephant, moon, and peanut butter. Can you repeat that for me?"

"Elephant, moon, and peanut butter."

"Good. Just remember that for me."

She could do that.

"Do you know today's date?" he asked.

"It's May."

The look on the doctor's face told her she was wrong. She looked around the room, searching for clues. There was a whiteboard on the wall across the room. On it was a date. "September."

The doctor glanced over his shoulder. "That's cheating," he said, teasing. "What's the last thing you remember?"

She closed her eyes . . . searched. "My feet hurt."

"Your feet?"

The doctor walked to the end of the bed and moved the blanket off her feet. He touched each one. "Does this hurt?"

"No."

He pressed and poked before returning the blankets. "Okay, sweet-heart . . . what were those three things I asked you to remember?"

"Uhm . . ." It was there. Close. Something big. As she pushed her brain to remember, she forgot his question altogether. Her stomach started to churn, and her body felt cold. "I'm going to be sick."

Her words put the strangers at her bed in motion.

CHAPTER FIVE

Leo and Fitz were buzzed back into the ICU and were instructed to check with the nurse before going into Jane Doe's room. Once there, they showed the nurse their identification.

"How is she doing?" Leo asked.

"Physically? Better. We took her off the vent a couple of hours ago. She's breathing on her own."

A weight lifted from Leo's chest.

"You said 'physically,'" Fitz pointed out.

"Her memory is taking some time to come back."

"What do you mean?" Fitz asked.

"Transient amnesia. She doesn't remember what happened that brought her here or even her own name," Maureen, the nurse, reported.

"Transient? It won't last?" Leo asked.

The nurse shrugged. "Most of these things resolve on their own. Could be a few hours or a couple of days. Dr. Lee ordered more tests for the morning to make sure there isn't something else causing it."

"This is from the head injury?"

"Appears that way."

"This is normal?"

"I wouldn't say normal, but it happens. You were with her when the shooting happened, right?" Maureen asked.

"Yeah."

"Maybe seeing you will spark a memory."

Somehow Leo doubted that. "Worth a try."

Leo and Fitz followed Maureen into the room.

Once the curtain was pulled back, Leo took in the stranger. Her head was slightly elevated, eyes closed. Long brown hair splayed on the pillow, and a canula was fitted in her nose, delivering oxygen. The vibrant color of her skin the night before, before a bullet penetrated her body, was gone. Here she was drawn, pale. Evidence she'd lost enough blood to make a difference. Or maybe it was the stress of everything on her body.

"Hey, hon." Maureen coaxed her awake. "You have visitors."

Janie, which was how Leo had been referring to her in his head instead of Jane Doe, opened her eyes. Green eyes . . . not the blue he remembered. The sharpness of those eyes had lost some of the focus from the night before. But the beauty of them was still there.

"How is your pain?" Maureen asked.

"I'm okay." Janie looked past Maureen toward Leo and Fitz, her stare blank.

"Do you remember my name?" Maureen asked.

Without words, she shook her head. "You're a nurse."

"I am." She pointed to the wall opposite the bed. "My name is written up there."

"Maureen."

"Right. Do you know where you are?"

Janie tried to smile. "A hospital."

"What city?"

"Atlantic City," Janie said a little too quickly.

Leo heard Fitz sigh.

"Vegas. But I would guess they're a lot alike." Maureen looked at the two of them. "She keeps saying Atlantic City."

"Is that where you live?" Fitz asked.

"I don't think so." Janie started blinking as if forcing away tears.

Maureen reached for the water at the bedside and helped her drink. "Do I know you?"

Leo stepped closer, took a seat in the only chair in the room. "We met last night. My name is Leo. This is my partner, Kelsey. We're federal agents."

Janie's eyes grew wide. "Agents?"

"Yes."

She started breathing a little heavier. "I was shot?" It was a question.

"That's right," Maureen told her.

"Am I . . . did I do something?" Her hands fisted in her lap.

Leo placed a hand on her bed. "No, no . . . you didn't do anything. That's not why we're here."

Janie's eyes tracked his and stayed there. "You're sure."

Leo found a smile, tried to calm her down. "I'm sure. I was there. We were talking. It just happened. Wrong place, wrong time."

Maureen reached for the monitor that showed Janie's pulse elevating. The blood pressure cuff on her arm started to inflate.

"Were you there?" Janie asked Fitz.

"Ah, no." Leo knew she wanted to say more.

"What were we talking about?" Janie asked him.

Fitz started to laugh behind him.

Leo turned to stare her into silence.

She motioned out the door. "I'm going to call in, give Brackett an update."

Leo nodded his agreement.

Another nurse popped her head into the room. "Maureen, your patient in five needs you."

"Be right there." She turned back to Leo. "She might ask you the same questions over and over and likely not remember what you said, so don't press her for answers, it only frustrates her and causes her blood pressure to go up. We don't need that."

Leo smiled. "I won't."

When he turned back to Janie, she was smiling at him. "You're a cop?"

"Federal agent."

That smile faded. "I was shot."

Leo nodded and started to see the repetition and surprise in her eyes with everything she said.

"You hit your head pretty hard."

"What did I do?"

Leo patted the hand lying at her side. "Nothing."

He looked around the room at a loss. There was no use in asking questions when she didn't even know her own name.

His gaze landed on a white plastic bag that said "Patient Belongings" on the front.

Leo stood and walked to the bag, opened it up.

He expected to see the clothes she was wearing the night before. All he found was a wallet and a cell phone.

The phone he couldn't get to work.

"Have you tried to open this?" he asked.

"I don't know. I don't think so."

He pressed the power button. It still had enough juice to turn on.

"Maybe we can find someone who knows who you are."

She shrugged. "Okay."

Leo moved closer, swiped at the screen, and held the camera close enough to her face to pick up the features that would open it.

It took three times for it to work.

"Okay . . . good. Do you mind?" he asked before he started prying.

"No."

Good. He sat down and clicked into contacts.

Only it came up blank.

Not one contact. How was that possible? "Interesting." Leo glanced at the patient, saw her eyes drifting shut. He noticed the collection bag hanging from the side of the bed. Inside showed a small amount of blood he assumed was from the chest tube inside her lung.

He pushed her condition out of his head and moved around the contents of her phone.

Pictures . . .

Empty.

Internet searches?

No history. Though he knew those could be erased.

None of this made sense. Why would a cell phone be completely void of anything?

He fished around to see what apps were on the phone.

Every one he clicked into acted as if it were being opened for the first time.

He moved back to the phone calls. One number showed up in recent calls.

He pressed the number and put the phone to his ear.

Leo looked over, saw Janie fast asleep. Her pulse on the monitor a slow, steady beat.

The telling sound of a call being connected shot Leo's hopes high.

"What the hell, Olivia. Where are you?"

Olivia. Her name was Olivia. He liked it.

"Olivia?" The voice was male, deep . . . and pissed.

And familiar.

Leo cleared his throat. "I'm sorry . . . I'm calling—"

"Who is this?" The question was slow and measured.

The hair on Leo's neck stood on end.

"Who is this?" Leo asked back.

Silence suggested the person on the other end might not answer.

"You hurt one hair on her head and I'll—"

The voice triggered in Leo's head and he turned stone cold. "Neil?"

A pause.

"Grant?"

Their earlier conversation came back to him.

"If my contact was compromised, you need to go underground."

"Why?"

"If they're gone, then you don't stand a chance."

"Your guy is that good, huh?"

"Yes. She is."

Leo stared at the woman in the bed.

"Ah, fuck."

"What the hell are you doing with Olivia's phone?"

Voices outside the door brought Leo's attention behind him.

"I'll call you back." Without anything else, Leo disconnected the call and slipped the phone into his pocket.

Fitz walked in, and Leo placed a finger over his pursed lips before pointing to the sleeping patient.

~

"There isn't a reason for us to stay," Fitz told him a few minutes after Leo discovered the name of the patient.

For reasons he couldn't identify, Leo kept the new information to himself. His people knew Neil and his team were watching the trial and doing what they could to keep the victim safe from any foul play. But so far, Neil was the only visible member of the team. Everyone else was in the shadows. And from the sound of it, Olivia was deep undercover.

Leo knew a thing or two about being invisible to those around him. Hell, he'd spent nearly a year of his life acting as a high school teacher in an effort to flush out a bad cop responsible for girls like Marie Nickerson.

All things considered, Leo made a decision to hold off on the truth until talking with Neil.

"What are the chances of Navi being the one behind this?" Leo indicated Olivia, who was asleep. The two of them stood at the far end of the room talking in hushed tones.

"Him or someone associated with the case."

"Right. These are professional dirtbags. They missed the shot because she saw the gun and grabbed me. It wouldn't be a stretch to assume the people responsible for this might conclude that and come around and eliminate an eyewitness."

"She doesn't remember anything," Fitz said.

"They don't know that."

Fitz looked around the room, took a peek beyond the curtain. "You're right."

"And considering she doesn't know who she is, anyone could come in here pretending to be family and . . ."

Fitz blew out a breath and made a grand gesture, while she pulled out her cell phone and walked out of the room.

The second she left, Leo removed his phone and called Neil.

He picked up on the first ring. "What room is she in?"

"ICU bed four."

"We're parking now. Don't leave her side."

"Wasn't planning on it."

Olivia moaned, taking Leo's attention away from his phone.

Her eyes fluttered open, and her hand reached for her side.

For a moment Leo thought she was going to pull at the tube sticking out of her lung.

"Hey," he said, distracting her.

Their eyes met and held. She smiled, at first, and then those green eyes clouded and her smile fell. "Do I know you?" she asked.

"We met earlier," he informed her.

"Why don't I remember?"

"The doctors say it's temporary." And maybe when Neil walked in the room something would click into place.

Fitz returned, offered a nod to Olivia, then turned to Leo. "Brackett is calling the locals for around-the-clock protection."

"Good."

Fitz addressed Olivia. "How are you feeling?"

"I can't seem to stay awake."

Leo looked around the sterile space. "It's not like there's a lot of excitement going on in here."

For the first time since he'd run into her, she offered a true smile. Amused.

"Excuse me." Maureen poked her head in the room. "There's a Neil MacBain asking to come back."

"What's he doing here?" Fitz asked.

Leo shrugged and got to his feet. "Maybe he came to the same conclusion we did."

Leo followed the path to the locked door of the ICU and opened it. Neil stood on the other side, a stony mirror of the man that had been in the courtroom only hours before. Instead of escorting him directly back, Leo stepped outside to talk first.

"My partner is in there."

Neil seemed to accept the need to delay his trip to the bedside. "How is she?"

Leo smiled. "Recovering. Off the ventilator, awake . . . only she doesn't remember anything."

Neil looked away as if not believing Leo's words.

"Anything. Even her name," Leo reiterated.

"Olivia would never tell you her name," Neil informed him, reaching for the door.

Leo stopped him. "She has to be reminded that she's in Vegas. She has some type of amnesia." Leo removed her cell phone from his pocket and handed it to Neil. "When I asked if I could use her phone to try and find someone who knows her, the only number on it was yours."

Neil took it and stared. "She wouldn't do that."

"Right . . . well, she did. I didn't tell Fitz that you know her." He sighed. "I'm not sure that was the right call."

"No one in your department needs to know who she is."

"Not sure that's possible," Leo told him. "If her memory comes back and she can ID the people holding the gun . . ."

"She won't do that."

"Someone nearly killed her," Leo reminded him.

Neil fixed him with a cold stare.

Leo felt the chill down to his toes.

Neil tucked her phone in his pocket. "Keep this silent. I'll explain more later."

Leo hoped he could.

Neil followed him through the doors, past the nurses' station, and into Olivia's room.

Leo kept his eyes on the woman in the bed when Neil came into view.

She looked at him and then past him as if he might be there to empty the trash.

The only visible change in Neil was a muscle twitching in his jaw.

Fitz stood and put out her hand for Neil to shake. "What brings you here?"

"I know Leo didn't get a lot of sleep last night, and I thought my team and I could help with backup." Neil shook her hand, and then moved his eyes back to Olivia.

"That's thoughtful, but we should have help here within the hour," Fitz said.

Neil didn't comment and walked to the edge of the bed. "How are you feeling?"

Olivia narrowed her eyes. "I was shot."

Leo smiled. "That's an improvement. An hour ago, she needed to be told that over and over again."

"Do I know you?" she asked Neil.

"I'm hard to forget."

Leo heard Fitz laugh under her breath.

Leo asked the same questions the nurse had. "Do you know where you are?"

Olivia squeezed her eyes shut. "Atlantic City."

He looked at Neil as if to say, *See . . . she doesn't remember a thing.* "Wait."

Leo turned back to her.

Olivia's features twisted in pain. "That's not right. Not Atlantic City." She brought a hand to her face and pressed her fingers to her temples. "Why is this so hard?"

The monitor over the bed started to ping.

"It's going to be okay." Leo dropped into the chair beside the bed, placed a hand over hers.

Her eyes welled with tears. "I don't know you."

"No, you don't. And you didn't before either."

The nurse walked back in, took one look at Olivia, and glared her disapproval. "My patient needs her rest, not this overstimulation. You're not getting your answers tonight. You might as well come back in the morning."

"We've scheduled continual security," Fitz told her.

Maureen wasn't amused. "In here, I'm the boss. If one of you needs to stay, I'll put a chair outside the door of her room."

"Completely fair," Neil spoke up. "A chair would be appreciated."

The three of them filed out while Maureen spoke in soft tones to Olivia.

"I've got this," Neil told them both.

"We're bringing in local PD," Fitz said.

"Police officers who haven't been vetted? Rookies who wouldn't know to stop a housekeeper from walking in the room." Neil shook his head. "I got this. I have resources. Save the taxpayers their money."

Neil's argument was solid.

"Why?" Fitz questioned him.

Neil didn't miss a beat. "A bad cop kidnapped one of mine trying to bury what Mykonos and his family were doing. Now there's a woman in the ICU without a memory. I take that personally. If she remembers the shooter, she's going to need more than a local anything to keep her safe."

Leo placed a hand on Fitz's arm. "I think Brackett will agree."

Fitz put both hands in the air. "It's your aching back," she said.

Leo shook Neil's hand. "I'll be in touch."

CHAPTER SIX

Neil stood outside the doorway of Olivia's room. His eyes fixed on her sleeping features. She was softer here. The sharp edges of her personality had been chipped away with one bullet.

Two years before, she'd reached out to him.

The gesture caught him off guard, but he knew what it was.

A cry for help.

The woman walked the world completely alone. More than once she'd pointed out that there was no other way for her.

Part of him believed she might be right. But that didn't stop him from trying to hook her into his team. A team composed of retired military, recovered thieves, private investigators, orphans, and the latest acquisitions from a military school in Germany.

Richter wasn't like anything else out there. Many students like Olivia left the school employed by less-than-honorable entities. They exploited the talents Richter taught them. Skilled in weapons and hand-to-hand combat, versed in a handful of languages, masters of disguise, students like Olivia were shaped into spies . . . or worse.

Olivia was one of the *worse*.

Neil had finally convinced her to help him out. A favor, he phrased it. No, she didn't need to be in contact with anyone but him.

Keep an eye on Marie Nickerson while she was in the hospital and wherever the protection program took her until the trial. Once the trial was over, so long as the jury delivered the verdict deserved, the job would be over, and Neil would pay Olivia for her time. If the man went free, the assignment would go on.

He didn't think for a minute Olivia needed his money. The woman would be able to con, steal, or maybe even earn money the old-fashioned way by simply working . . . but she'd taken the assignment.

And now she was lying in a hospital bed, vulnerable. With no idea who she was or what was dormant inside of her.

Leo Grant thought the bullet she'd taken was for him.

But Neil knew it was highly probable that wasn't the case.

Which meant, memory or not, Neil needed to get Olivia out of Las Vegas as soon as she was safe to transfer.

And he needed to do it without clueing Leo in to exactly who she was.

~

The world fell into focus much faster than it had the day before. It helped that the sun shining through the window was the catalyst for disturbing her sleep and not pain.

Her eyes fluttered open. Familiar beeping and the squeezing of her arm inside a blood pressure cuff offered a swift explanation as to where she was.

She vaguely remembered falling asleep and the mantra she had chanted to herself as darkness engulfed her.

Remember where you are.

Remember what happened.

Remember.

"Las Vegas," she whispered to the empty room. "I was shot."

Why?

Deep inside she knew why . . . or so the churning of her gut told her. But the answer wasn't found when she closed her eyes and tried to remember.

What's my name?

Her throat constricted as she searched for the answer.

"Good morning."

She opened her eyes, saw a young man enter the room wearing blue scrubs and a stethoscope around his neck. *Nurse,* she thought. *Not a doctor.*

"Good morning," she tested her voice.

"Do you remember me?" he asked.

She noticed a face peeking from behind the curtain, but the woman stayed outside.

"You're a nurse," she said. Across the room she found the whiteboard with his name. "Ben."

He smiled, removed his stethoscope, and put it in his ears. "I wouldn't expect you to remember my name. I came in last night to give you pain medication. Every other time you were asleep. But I'm glad to see you knew where to look for the information."

He pressed the scope to her chest and asked her to breathe for him.

He poked around a little, pulled out a computer that was attached to a wall across the room, and started to type. "Dr. Lee will be in shortly."

"The surgeon."

"Yes. That's right. What else do you remember?"

She tried to sit taller, prompting Ben to help her.

"I'm in Vegas."

"Right." He smiled.

"I had surgery for a gunshot wound. Collapsed lung. I hit my head."

"I'm impressed."

Her smile was short lived. "I don't remember my name."

Ben kept his expression neutral. "One day at a time. Do you remember getting shot?"

"No. Just that everyone keeps telling me that's what happened."

"That's a hundred times better than yesterday." While Ben praised her efforts, he plugged in an IV bag, told her it was an antibiotic, and explained that a new nurse would be in shortly to take over for the day shift.

When Dr. Lee walked in the room, his face looked familiar, and with that simple observation, she was comforted by the fact she could grasp the memory of him talking to her before. Though she couldn't remember what he talked to her about. Likely her condition, but she was speculating.

He took his time examining her, asking questions. Many she couldn't answer, but like Ben, he seemed impressed with her progress.

"When will I remember who I am?" she asked him.

"There is no timeline for these things. Statistically, you could remember everything at any moment, or it might take a couple of days. Or . . ."

"Or?"

"There are cases of people taking longer to recover their memory. The brain is protective, and often the mechanism of injury is too painful to remember. At least temporarily. I asked for a neurology consult, maybe Dr. Everett can shed more light on what you can expect."

"I've been in the hospital for two nights," she told him.

"That's right."

"You thought I'd remember by now or you would have asked for a neurologist earlier." As she said the words, she knew them as fact. How she knew them as fact, she couldn't name.

"Your brain scans don't show any reason to believe the amnesia is anything but temporary."

"I should remember more by now."

"Let's get Dr. Everett's advice."

Passing the buck. The man didn't have the answers. "Okay."

As the doctor left the room, the curtain exposed the woman standing outside.

"Are you hungry?" Ben asked, distracting her.

Just the mention of food had her stomach growling. "Yes."

"A good sign. Don't get too excited, the food here sucks."

She tried to find his humor and failed.

Before he walked away, she stopped him. "Ben . . . do you have a mirror?"

He regarded her for a moment. "I'll find one."

Ten minutes later she sat staring at a stranger.

Green eyes she couldn't remember. Full lips and shaped eyebrows. Did she pluck them or have them waxed? And how was it possible that she knew that women plucked and waxed but couldn't remember what she preferred?

Her eyes started to water, and even that felt unfamiliar.

People cried. Emotions, pain . . . or both. So why did tears slipping down her cheeks feel like they were doing so for the first time?

"Take it," she said, pushing the mirror into Ben's hands.

"It will come back."

She looked away and ignored his look of sympathy as he exited the room.

A few minutes passed, and the curtain moved.

"I know you're out there," she said to the woman lurking outside.

Finally, the woman exposed herself by walking around the curtain.

Tall, rail thin, rich dark hair pulled back into a single ponytail. Dark eyes, olive skin. She wore black from head to toe. She neither smiled nor frowned.

What she did do was stare.

"Do I know you?"

The woman didn't answer the direct question. "My name is Sasha."

"We find the defendant, Mykonos Sobol, guilty of . . ."

Leo blew out a long breath as the foreperson rattled off a dozen charges.

His fists clenched at his sides, and the smile in his heart punched his gut with relief. He glanced at the back of Marie Nickerson's head. A head with a pixie cut courtesy of her assailants.

Her shoulders slumped, and her female attorney placed an arm over her shoulders while the male whispered in Marie's ear.

Leo pulled his cell phone out of his pocket and immediately texted Claire. He knew Neil would inform her of the outcome, but he'd likely wait, and if it were him, Leo would want to know, real time, if he wasn't there.

Guilty.

She texted back almost instantly.

Thank God.

Leo tucked his phone away and listened while the judge thanked the jury for their time and quick deliberation.

Mykonos sat huddled with his attorneys, eyes glaring across the room toward Marie.

Sitting behind him, Navi and his henchmen kept their eyes forward.

The courtroom itself was humming with activity as reporters undoubtedly texted their bosses in an attempt to get a jump on the headlines.

The judge closed the session by telling the defendant when sentencing would take place, then dismissed the jury and adjourned the trial.

Reporters rushed out.

The bailiff approached Mykonos to take him back into custody.

"Watch, the judge will go easy on him," Fitz whispered at Leo's side.

They'd seen it before. The jury did the right thing. The bad guy received a guilty verdict. And then the judge slaps him with a prickly rose and not a sledgehammer. Though there were too many charges for him to get off without doing real time in jail, there were no guarantees the judge would do the right thing.

Marie's attorneys hugged the girl and offered their congratulations.

While she did have a slight smile on her lips, her expression was blank.

Numb.

One of the attorneys turned to Leo and Fitz. "Thank you. All of you."

"I'll pass that on to everyone."

Marie looked in Leo's eyes. "Thank Claire for me."

"I'll do that." Leo smiled . . . wanted to give her some kind of assurance. Once she left the room, he'd likely never see her again. "Go grab that life you deserve."

She lifted her chin ever so slightly. "I'll try."

A noise on the other side of the courtroom caught their attention.

Everyone turned to see Mykonos offer a confident smile to Marie.

Her attorney stood in front of her as Mykonos was escorted from the courtroom.

"Don't let him rattle you, not now," Leo told Marie. "We have the area secured. Once you're settled, that man will have no way of knowing where you are."

She looked blankly at a wall. "That won't stop me from looking over my shoulder for the rest of my life."

No, he didn't imagine it would.

Navi made his way to the end of the aisle and stopped only a few feet from where Leo and Fitz stood.

"We meet again," Navi said to him.

Leo squared his shoulders, put himself between Marie and Navi.

"Get her out of here," Fitz told Marie's personal detail.

Out of the corner of his eye, Leo saw Marie being escorted away from the activity. Once she was out of view, he turned back to Navi.

"I hear you had an unfortunate accident the other night," Navi said.

"And where did you hear that?"

"Shootings in Vegas are commonplace, but they still make the paper."

Leo narrowed his eyes.

"Glad to see you're in one piece," Navi said, his charming smile firmly in place.

"I somehow doubt that," Leo said. His jaw tightened.

The man laughed. "Oh, of course. You probably think I had something to do with it. I assure you, I didn't. Though it does make me wonder who your enemies are."

Leo matched the man's energy and confidence. "I'm one of the good guys."

That made Navi laugh. "Right." He looked above Leo's head. "I missed the halo. But I see it now."

"Is there a point to this conversation?" Fitz asked.

Navi looked down at her, didn't comment, then back to Leo.

The dismissal rippled through both of them.

"Be careful out there," Navi advised as he turned to walk away. But before making it two feet he looked back. "How's the woman doing?"

"The woman?" Leo played dumb while the hair on the back of his neck stood on end.

"The woman who was shot? The paper didn't disclose her name. I imagine with the good guy standing right there, she fared well."

"She's fine."

He nodded. "Good. I hate to see innocent people getting hurt."

Navi started to turn away.

"Plan on staying in town for long?" Leo asked.

"This is a filthy city. Never did see what my cousin saw in it. Can't trust the women." He motioned toward the door Marie had disappeared behind. "Can't walk the streets. Can't have a quiet meal without someone harassing you."

Leo didn't comment. Once Navi broke eye contact, Leo watched him walk out of the room flanked by his goons.

"That guy's a prick," Fitz muttered.

"Any of that sound like a threat to you?" He stood a little taller, felt some of the tension ease from his shoulders.

She shook her head. "Nor a confession."

"That doesn't mean it wasn't both."

Fitz stretched her neck from one side to the other. "Let's get out of here."

CHAPTER SEVEN

The drop ceiling tiles of the hallway were broken up by long fluorescent lights in various stages of function.

Olivia had a vague memory of being wheeled down this path before. A hospital staff member pushed the gurney while Rick, a bodyguard, walked alongside them.

She felt like an observer. One with limited space in her brain to carry any information she'd been given.

"So you get paid to sit in a chair?" the staff member asked Rick as they waited for an elevator to open.

"You could say that."

The door dinged, and once again Olivia was in motion.

Each bump shot pain up her side and had her closing her eyes to try and manage the discomfort. She'd started saying no to the pain medications in an effort to recognize herself in the mirror.

When someone wanted to join them on the short ride down to radiology, Rick lifted his hand. "Mind taking the next one?" he asked.

Without question, the person waiting backed up as the doors closed.

"Do people always listen to you?" Olivia asked.

"Not my wife," he said with a smile.

"Good to know."

The lower levels of the hospital were a series of catacombs and relatively deserted.

The hospital employee parked the gurney outside a closed radiology door and disappeared inside, leaving Rick and Olivia alone.

Rick stood taller as a man walked toward them.

"By any chance do you know which way I need to go to find the cafeteria?" the stranger asked Rick and glanced around him to Olivia.

She blinked a few times.

Rick positioned himself in front of her and pointed in the direction they'd just come. "There is a map by the elevators just around the corner," he told him.

The tall stranger looked at Rick briefly, then at her again. "Thanks."

Olivia tried to smile, despite the pounding in her head.

As the man walked away, Rick moved to keep himself between her and the stranger.

"He didn't look like he wanted to hurt me," she offered.

"The more innocent they look, the more dangerous they are," Rick said.

Olivia started to comment, but the hospital employee opened the door to the CAT scan room and moved her inside.

～

"What do we have?" Neil sat in his hotel room, Sasha at his side. Isaac and Lars were on point monitoring Marie Nickerson's transfer. Once the woman was in the air, her whereabouts were between her and the federal marshals involved in hiding her in plain sight. Neil had to trust the witness protection program, even if it cut at him to do so.

Rick and AJ, two other members of his team, were assigned to Olivia.

Cooper, Claire, and Jax were back in LA doing the legwork.

Or hacking, as it stood.

The hotel suite had duffel bags tossed on the floor and three computers set up on a conference table.

Sasha sat at one, Neil at another.

Claire was on speaker so they could both hear.

"Olivia knows how to cover her tracks," Claire stated. "She spoofed someone's phone in North Dakota, making it almost impossible to locate where she was making her calls from. I spent some time digging and found a ping from her phone to the cell tower at the Wynn when she called you the night of the shooting. The next ping was when she called you again, this time the call bounced around. But we have a general area when you triangulate where she was walking when she was shot and the most likely places she would feel safe to stay—"

"All I want is an address." Neil liked Claire's skills, but didn't need a detailed dossier of how she managed to obtain it.

"I have a block. There are three small hotels, not the kind that have cameras in every corner. My guess is the management doesn't want to know what goes on there."

"What about city cameras?" Sasha asked.

Jax's voice carried over the line. "I'm working on it. Going back from when the trial began. The problem is I don't know what I'm looking for. Was she wearing a wig, a costume? Dressed as a man? I'm going with the description from the night at the Wynn and the blonde wig."

Neil looked over his computer screen at Sasha.

They needed to narrow this down, find out where Olivia had been staying, and empty it out before her bill came due and someone went into the room and found Olivia's belongings. Sasha insisted the woman wouldn't leave anything incriminating where others would find it, but that didn't mean her fake IDs wouldn't be found and eventually handed over to the feds.

That wouldn't bode well for anyone.

"Give me the address you have," Sasha told them. She jotted it down and stood.

"Don't go in alone," Neil instructed her.

The look on her face said she'd do what she damn well pleased if it suited her.

She grabbed her bag and walked out of the room.

Neil wanted to growl. "Where do we stand with medical and location?" he asked the team instead.

"Found a place in Colorado just outside of Durango. Remote enough to go unnoticed, but close to a hospital if the need arrives. We have a nurse, retired army. Spent some time living in tents in the Middle East in the nineties. Looking forward to combat pay."

Sounded right up Neil's alley for the team.

"Soon as Lars and Isaac are free of their assignment, I'll dispatch them to Colorado. Claire, keep digging in that phone."

"Will do. But, Neil?"

"Yeah?"

"What are the chances of Olivia remembering who she is and just bailing?"

"She'll bolt the second she remembers. But if we can get her someplace safe, maybe she'll give herself some time to heal and regroup."

"And if she doesn't recover her memory?" Cooper asked.

"That's unlikely." Neil just hoped it was later rather than sooner.

~

"Look who's sitting up and eating."

Leo had shown his ID to Neil's man sitting in the chair outside Olivia's room before walking in.

Her face had color, and someone had brushed her hair into a sweeping ponytail that trailed down one shoulder.

She put her fork down and lifted a napkin to her lips while she finished chewing. "I'm sure I've had better. I think."

Leo had already gotten the report that her memory had yet to resurface. So he took her words as the joke they were meant to be.

"May I?" he asked, pointing to the chair beside her bed.

When the woman smiled, a small amount of light he hadn't seen before reached her eyes. "Thank you for asking. Yes, please."

He supposed her experience in the hospital was a steady stream of people doing without asking day in and day out. "You look better."

"Hurts like a horse kicked me across an arena. But clearing my head from the narcotics is helping."

"How is saying no to painkillers helping?"

She tapped her head with an index finger. "Less fog."

"And the pain?"

She shrugged. "It's just pain."

He peered at the side of the bed, saw the same drainage bag that had been there since she returned from surgery. Same IVs, probes, and things that squeezed her legs since she was lying in bed. Her saying *It's just pain* was unexpected.

"Don't let me keep you from eating."

She smiled and pushed the overhead table away. "I was done anyway."

Now he felt bad. It didn't appear as if she'd eaten a third of what was on her plate.

"Your name is Leo, right?"

It was his turn to smile. "Yes."

"You're a federal agent." Her face twisted as she said those words.

"I am."

"Have you found the person who shot me?"

"We're working on it."

"I suppose that's all I can ask. For all I know I deserved to get—"

"Whoa, back up. No. You were standing there minding your own business. You didn't deserve any of this." He waved a hand at the room.

She lowered her eyes to her lap.

"I'm sorry," he said.

She brought her gaze to his. "Did you shoot me?"

"No," he choked out.

"Then why are you sorry?"

Because it should be me in that bed.

"I'm sorry it happened. That you were hurt."

She frowned. "That's a waste of an apology."

He laughed. "I thought women liked apologies."

"Not me, apparently." She gifted him another smile. "Did you tell me what we were talking about when this happened?"

He cleared his throat and sat up a little taller. "It was a warm night . . ."

"We spoke of the weather?"

He licked his lips . . . stalled. "I was trying to get your name."

Her eyes narrowed as she looked down her pert nose. "You were flirting with me?"

Leo repositioned himself in the chair. "Ah . . . yes."

Now her smile was forced back, as if she were trying not to grin. "And was I flirting back?"

"Well . . ." What the hell was he supposed to say to that? *No, you were trying to walk away.* In this case, honesty was likely not the best route. "You weren't running away," he told her. Which wasn't a complete lie.

"I was busy getting shot." This time she chuckled.

"You're laughing about it."

"I'm not happy I took a bullet . . . or at least I think I wouldn't be happy about something like that. Who would want that?"

He didn't have time to answer before she kept talking.

"I'm much more upset that I look in the mirror and don't recognize myself. That's quite a bitch, isn't it?"

"I can't imagine."

She moved her shoulders and started to cough. Short bouts of breathing between each eruption.

"Should I get the nurse?" He moved closer to the bed.

Olivia reached for her side and attempted to take a deep breath and started to struggle.

Leo jumped up and stopped at the door. "I need a nurse."

The man in the chair brushed past him and looked into the room.

Both of them stepped back when a nurse rushed in. Calm and collected, the nurse soothed the anxiety swimming in Olivia's eyes. When she lifted the bedsheets to look at Olivia's side, she pivoted and closed the curtain between them.

Only when Leo heard Olivia's cough start to subside did he step completely out of the room and start to pace.

"Hey?" Neil's man stood a little taller than Leo and spent more hours at the gym. But his smile was easy, and his eyes were kind. "You okay?"

"She shouldn't be in there."

"And the Dodgers should have won the World Series . . . and?"

Leo stared. "What's your name?"

"Rick. Neil and I were in the service together."

That made sense. The men were cut from the same physical cloth.

Leo stepped closer, lowered his voice. "Do you know her?"

Rick shook his head. "I overheard the doctors. They want to transfer her out of the ICU. I encouraged them to wait until tomorrow. It's harder to get in here than the main floors."

Leo didn't like the sound of that.

"If all goes well, the chest tube comes out tomorrow, and within a day or so she'll be ready to leave."

Leo's heart started to pound. "And go where? She doesn't know her name."

Rick's voice was a whisper. "We have it covered."

Of course they would.

Except she was a witness . . . or could be at any moment. "We'll bring her into the protection program," Leo told him, knowing that would be the next step. "My superiors will insist on it. At least until she regains her memory."

Rick paused.

Leo looked at him.

"Do you want to keep her safe?"

"I'm the reason she's in here. I fucked up. Approached Navi, pissed the man off . . ." He ran a hand through his hair.

"Then you'll do, tell, lie, or whatever you need to in order to get your superiors to go along with our plan. She is not safe in a protection program, or more to the point, those protecting her are not safe with her there."

Those words stopped Leo midstep. He leaned closer. "Mind explaining?"

Rick smiled, shook his head. "Talk to Neil."

Leo turned away. His gaze moved to the closed curtain.

"I'll make a deal with you . . . If you can't fall asleep on your own, I give you enough to take the edge off so you can." The nurse was negotiating the pain medication with Olivia.

"I'm fine."

"Your vital signs say differently. Sleep is the best thing for you, and you can't sleep if the pain is too intense."

"I don't want the fog."

"Small amount . . . I promise. You'll wake up in the morning feeling so much better."

Silence made Leo wonder what was happening behind the curtain.

When the nurse left the room, she stopped long enough to mutter, "That's one stubborn woman."

Rick chuckled.

Leo walked in.

The coughing had taxed her. Those eyes lost some of their luster, her skin had paled.

"Better?" he asked when their eyes caught.

Her smile was fleeting and not convincing at all.

"Why not let the nurse give you something?"

She shook her head.

"Do it for me."

"The guy I flirted with is asking for a favor?"

"I see the tired in your eyes, a little will help you sleep." For a second he thought she was wavering. "You have a lot of people looking out for you here."

That wavering drifted away. "Like the man outside. The guard."

Leo looked over his shoulder at the empty doorway.

"The doctor told me I'd remember day-to-day things. Like driving a car or how to use a computer, just not the details like passwords or addresses . . . or who I am. And one thing I know is that man out there is here to either protect me or protect people from me. And since no one has said I'm in police custody, I'm going to assume the former. In which case, I know something . . . that I've obviously forgotten . . . and that information needs protection."

Leo blinked several times. *Holy shit.*

"And I see by the expression on your face I've concluded correctly."

Leo sunk into the chair at her side. "I have to add smart and beautiful to your list of attributes."

"You're flirting again . . ."

He lifted both hands in the air, felt heat in his cheeks. "Guilty. And inappropriate in light of everything."

"It's okay. Refreshing, actually. But for all I know, I'm married." Her face rejected the thought. "If someone was missing me, they would have come looking by now, wouldn't they?"

Leo thought of Neil and everyone involved with him, all working together for her at that moment. But how they couldn't say a thing to her. Not yet. "You could have come to Vegas for a quick weekend."

"Alone?"

"Maybe for work. And maybe you're not due home for a few days?"

She chewed on that for a full minute. "Dr. Everett said I have dissociative amnesia. He thinks because of the shooting. That my mind can't process the assault, and it's protecting itself by hiding the memory and those around it."

"Did the doctor say how long it would last?"

"Hours, days, weeks, months . . . He said my memory could come back quickly or in slow chunks. But sometimes people like me will never remember the events leading up to the shooting, or the shooting itself."

Leo pulled in a deep breath. "You were facing the street. My back was to the shooter. You saw something, because you reached for me and told me to get down." He nodded toward the door. "The security is for you. We don't have an ID on the shooter, and there is always a possibility that the people involved will . . ."

"Want to eliminate an eyewitness." As she said the words, a glaze settled over her eyes.

"I don't want you to worry about that."

"You don't have control over my emotions or thoughts." All humor was gone from her face.

Leo sighed. "We are going to protect you. Get you through this and make sure you're safe."

"Someone was shooting at *you*," she concluded.

"Most likely," he admitted.

"And I got in the way. That's why you're guarding me. A random person on the street in a shooting would be left on their own. But a federal agent . . ."

Very smart and beautiful.

"Why are you in Vegas?" she asked.

"A case." Her silent stare prompted him to continue. "Somebody did some bad stuff and my partner and I were here for the trial." And since the reason Leo was in Vegas was the same reason Olivia was in Vegas, he couldn't help but wonder if the conversation would prompt a memory.

Instead, she had the same blank look on her face when someone asked her what her name was.

"Then you stop to get my name, and I got shot." Her words were a string of emotionless noise. Monotone. Cold.

"I'm sorry."

"Now who is the one with the limited memory? Your apology is futile."

Maybe so, but he wanted to scream it until she heard it.

"I believe I've had about all the new knowledge I can take for one day," she told him.

He took his cue to stand. "I'll be back in the morning."

She pressed a button on the bed and lowered her head.

Outside the room he stopped at Rick's side. "I assume Neil is still at the hotel?"

Rick smiled. "I'll tell him you're on your way over."

It was time to get more answers.

CHAPTER EIGHT

The rocks were scalding and jagged. Each step more painful than the last. If only she could breathe, then maybe she could control the pain.

"Breathe through the pain. You know that's what you have to do."

Tears stained her cheeks.

"Stop crying, you weak piece of shit."

It hurts.

"Get over it. And walk. What are you going to do, lie there and wait for the Grim Reaper to come and carry you?"

She took a step, and another, refusing to look up into the vastness of nothing. Nothing but fire, rock, and pain.

Her eyes opened, and with them her lungs pulled a sharp inhale.

The room was dark.

And hot.

Something wasn't right.

"Nurse?" She cleared her throat. "Nurse?"

~

Neil's words swam in Leo's head as he sat across from his boss, pushing the plan.

"Olivia is a highly skilled operative, if she starts coming out of the amnesia and thinks someone is a threat, there is no guarantee how she'll react. With my location, and my people, she'll be safe."

"Define operative," Leo had told him.

"I can't do that."

"Can't or won't?" He knew there was something Neil wasn't telling him. "Your choice."

Their conversation had been short. One where Leo asked questions and Neil avoided the answers.

In the end, Neil gave him an ultimatum. "You convince your superiors that my protection program is far greater than theirs, complete with doctors, nurses, and armed security, and that your people should focus on finding the shooter, or whoever paid the shooter. Or . . . Olivia will disappear, and you'll never see her again."

"Not only are they invested, they know the players. From Mykonos, to his cousins, uncles, the two-bit grunts that do the dirty work. Yeah, we could brief the marshals, but why bother?" Leo asked.

Brackett stared. "Where would they take her?"

"No idea."

"That won't work. We need to know."

Leo had seen that expression on his boss's face before. It said *nonnegotiable.*

Fitz kept silent at his side. She knew what was being said.

"I have vacation time I haven't used," Leo started. "I spent nearly a year of my life undercover on this assignment . . ." Months pretending to be someone he wasn't. His personal life on hold. "I'd like to take that time now."

Brackett leaned back in his chair, arms folded. "What are you suggesting?"

Leo leaned forward. "Sign this off to me. I'll stay with the witness. Along with Neil's team. You get what you want, and the two people that were shot at disappear until we can guarantee their safety."

Brackett glanced at Fitz.

Time ticked and ticked . . . and ticked.

He sat forward. "I want weekly updates."

Leo felt a lion's smile spread over his face.

"This better not have anything to do with your dick, Grant," Brackett warned.

Leo shook his head and repeated Olivia's words. "For all we know, she's married with two kids and a dog."

"If that's the case, someone is bound to look for her. In the meantime, keep her alive."

Leo stood, shook his hand. "I will."

~

Durango, Colorado, was a quintessential western town nestled in the southwestern corner of the state. The mountainous terrain was perfect for the team to hide in plain sight. The summer months were filled with tourists, people that came and went, most of them just passing through. An old narrow-gauge steam train was a major attraction, carrying passengers up to the small town of Silverton, where the population was anywhere between four and five hundred people. That population doubled and sometimes tripled in the summertime when the train was running. All of those passengers started their journey in Durango. A town as small as Silverton would be a place the team would stick out. In Durango, however, that was not the case. Not that the team planned on spending much time in the city itself. With summer sliding into fall, they arrived at the perfect time to blend in. It would take a while before winter brought in the skiers, and tourism was winding down.

The vacation cabin rental boasted over five thousand square feet on nearly twenty acres of land and sat far enough off the main road that no one would accidentally veer down the private driveway.

Neil drove the SUV from the small private airstrip they'd flown in to. Leo sat beside him with Olivia in the back seat. Behind them, AJ and Sasha followed in a four-wheel-drive Jeep.

The nurse he'd hired was already at the cabin, and Lars and Isaac were putting the final touches on the surveillance system that would be monitored from miles away.

They hit a bump in the road, and Neil immediately looked in the rearview mirror to gauge Olivia's expression.

If she hurt, she didn't show it. Though every mile they traveled, fatigue settled on her face.

The doctor had taken the chest tube out and followed up with a chest x-ray two days later before okaying her to travel on an airplane. The slight fever she'd spiked the day the tube was supposed to be removed ended up causing a delay and worried everyone that they'd have to postpone the transfer. And with Navi on the move and the sentencing hearing less than a week away, Neil wanted her as far away from Vegas as they could get but still be a short plane ride away.

"How are you doing back there?" Leo asked her.

"Never better."

Neil eased up on the gas.

"No, really. I'm fine. Not to sound like a child, but how much longer?" she asked.

"Ten minutes to the turnoff, then we're on-site," Neil informed her.

She nodded and continued to look at the passing landscape.

Neil couldn't help but wonder if anything looked familiar. He knew she'd spent several years in Germany, but he didn't have a lot of information on the woman before that time. And after, well . . . he could only speculate. Her history had been erased long before she was shot.

As they moved toward the gate, AJ drove up first, jumped out, and opened the manual fence. Much as Neil would have liked an automated gate, the homes that had them were in more densely populated areas. That didn't stop him from securing sensors that let those inside the house know the gate was opening. There were trip wires, electronic and physical, closer to the house. He'd be sure and spend some time with Leo outside before he left.

AJ moved faster down the road while Neil stayed mindful of the patient white-knuckling it in the back seat.

She needed time to heal.

The doctor had joked, telling her to avoid gunshots, car accidents, or bar fights for at least a month.

None of which were off Olivia's radar when she was in her right mind.

The docile woman staring out the window would have no problem avoiding drama.

Olivia . . . not so much.

~

I've seen trees. They're pine trees.

The smell reminded her of Christmas. How was it she could *remember* the holiday, but not a single one with her in it?

Every bump in the road was a knife in her side.

She wanted to look at the bandage on her chest but didn't desire drawing attention from the two men in the front seats.

She'd been under a microscope for days and looked forward to time alone.

A proper shower. What she would do for a shower.

Neil pulled the car up to what had to be one of the largest log cabins in existence. When she'd heard *cabin*, she assumed something small and easy to manage.

That was not what he stopped the car in front of.

"Wow," Leo said for both of them.

"I'm sure it will be comfortable for everyone," Neil said before opening his door and moving to hers.

Outside the climate-controlled car, she took her first step with Neil close by. He didn't reach for her, but somehow she knew he would if he had to.

Leo, on the other hand, walked around the car and took her elbow like she couldn't manage without him. Something about the gesture felt off, but she didn't know why.

He'd only been helpful the whole time she'd known him.

"Doing okay?" he asked.

She took a deep breath. "Only hurts when I breathe."

She wasn't sure, but for a second she thought Neil laughed. Since the man barely cracked a smile, she must have been mistaken.

The home appeared to have two entrances, one on the ground level, the other, larger one requiring a flight of stairs.

She wasn't about to admit that she appreciated Leo's arm when she started stepping up. Nearly a week in a bed took a toll on her body. And as much as she wanted to stop and take in the grand vista of trees and forest surrounding the cabin, she was hyperfocused on that shower and a bed. One she could collapse in and sleep for a year. Maybe then her memory would come back, and her life could return to normal.

Inside, Sasha and AJ were talking with two other men, both of whom stopped when she stepped inside the spacious room.

Big furniture, leather accents, with massive logs holding the whole thing together. Huge windows shot up twenty feet taking in the view, with a vast porch that stretched the length of the house. The living room opened to a kitchen and dining area that looked like it seated eight. "This is crazy," she said softly.

"There are enough rooms for everyone," Neil pointed out.

She turned away from the windows and found everyone staring at her.

"Hello," she said to the new faces.

"I'm Lars," the older of the two said with a slight wave across the room.

"Isaac," the shorter one wearing glasses added.

"I'm . . ." This was getting old. "Jane Doe, happy to meet you."

Both men seemed to wince at her introduction.

Sasha stepped around the giant sofa and tilted her head to one side. "You remind me of someone I went to school with." Sasha glanced at Neil, then back. "Her name was Olivia."

Olivia blinked a few times, noticed all those eyes on her . . . the microscope dialed in.

"I like it," Leo said. "It's better than Jane Doe."

"You don't look like a Jane," Lars told her.

"Olivia," she said aloud for the first time. Then she shrugged. "You have to call me something. Might as well be Olivia."

Again, everyone seemed to hang on whatever she was going to say next. "Which room is mine?"

The question had everyone moving.

Heavy footsteps preceded a woman half jogging down the stairs from the floor above. "Is our patient here?"

Olivia turned toward the woman. "That's me."

"You look haggard."

"Great." What was she supposed to say to that?

"Sorry . . . I'm Pam, the nurse." She had to be in her sixties, short gray hair, wiry . . . thin.

"I'm a . . . Olivia, I guess. They all just named me," she told her.

Pam narrowed her eyes, looked around the room. "Are you okay with that?"

"It's a name." *Just a name.*

"Well, Olivia . . . you've got to be tired."

"It's been a long day."

Pam nodded toward the stairs. "Let's get you settled. You up for a shower?"

Olivia sighed. "I'd kill for a shower."

Someone behind her laughed.

CHAPTER NINE

"Holy shit . . . not one spark of recognition. How is that possible?" Isaac asked. "The woman tied me up and put me in a cell . . . How can she forget that?"

Leo turned to Isaac. "She what?"

Neil stared at his colleague.

Isaac closed his lips. "It was a case. A joke."

AJ sat in one of the overstuffed chairs. Sasha took up position on the armrest with his hand on her leg. "Not even her name. It's hard to believe."

Sasha sighed. "It was only a matter of time before one of us slipped and called her Olivia."

The close-knit group would keep anything Leo wasn't supposed to know to themselves. He'd just have to whittle away at them, one at a time. "So, what's the plan?" he asked, looking at Neil.

"We work in shifts," he said, lifting himself up from the couch and walking away. Everyone stood and followed. They took a back stairway down to what looked like in-laws' quarters. The living room furniture had been pushed back, and a set of portable monitors were set up like a workstation.

Cameras had been placed around the inside and outside of the house, and all the feeds funneled into the monitors.

Isaac sat at the chair and started typing. "I'll show you a shortcut of commands," he said, looking over his shoulder at Leo. The feed from the living room brightened and then faded when Isaac moved to another one. The camera he was highlighting was one just outside the door of a bedroom.

Leo saw a shadow, then Isaac turned on the audio.

"You're sure you don't want something for the pain?" It was Pam's voice.

"There are cameras in every room except Olivia's and this one." He pointed to the bedroom off the living space where they were standing. "And all the bathrooms."

"I would think Olivia's room would be the most important," Leo said.

Lars started to laugh. "Yeah, well . . . when she gets her memory back, I don't want to be the one to tell her we watched her sleeping . . . or saw her naked."

"She'd kill us," Isaac added.

AJ shrugged in agreement.

"I'm sure she'd understand," Leo suggested.

Sasha lowered her eyes and shook her head. "You don't know her. Don't think the woman you're seeing here is the real person. It isn't. And Olivia wouldn't kill you, she'd remove your balls and make you eat 'em. Then if you're lucky, she'd kill you."

Lars moaned, shifted his hips a couple of times. "Thanks for the visual, Sasha. We can always count on you."

Leo couldn't help but think Lars believed Sasha's joke.

She had to be kidding.

Isaac pointed to a monitor with an aerial view of the property. There were red lights dotted in a dozen places. "Trip sensors. Red means they're live. If they're off, they've been cut, or something is in the way of them talking to each other. They work in pairs. If they're blinking, something has disturbed them. They need to be manually reset."

Neil glanced at Leo. "You and I will take a walk before it gets dark."

"We've been here for two days. There's a lot of wildlife out there, so remember that. When the trip sensors go off closer to the house, the lights turn on and the audio sensors enhance." Isaac brought up a video.

Leo peered closer. It looked like the outside by the driveway, and it was pitch black. The lights clicked on, and a few raccoons stood up, looked around, and then lumbered off. "If they keep coming back, we might have to do some target practice."

Neil walked toward the other room. Inside was a bedroom, but so much more.

He opened a closet to display a significant amount of firepower. ARs, AKs, several pistols, two shotguns, and a couple of rifles that Leo couldn't identify. "Do I even want to know how many of these are illegal?"

"It's Colorado," AJ said. "People are less itchy here."

Yeah, sure . . .

Neil moved the closet door to the other side to display vests, both for protection and for carrying ammunition and magazines. "Audio," he said, pointing to a stack of headgear. "Channel six."

Leo remembered the first time he'd seen Neil. He and one of his staff were all but jumping out of the rafters of a warehouse dressed for war. Someone on his team kept Claire from a bullet to the head by making a kill shot of their own. Leo looked around the motley crew and wondered which one of them had taken that shot. Neil had said it was him . . . but something told Leo that Neil would take blame, or credit, to take any heat off his people.

"This is one hell of a setup," Leo finally said.

"She's one of us," Sasha said, as if that's all that mattered.

"How long have you known her?" he asked.

Sasha stared at him as if he were an idiot. "A long time" was all she offered.

Neil closed the closets. "Let's take that walk."

~

Neil waited until he was well outside of the audio feed to start talking.

It was a story he'd repeated with nearly every recruit on his team. One that spelled out just enough facts to let a new employee understand what they were all about and why.

"When I left the Marines, I thought I'd be able to go back to a normal life. But when a war is still playing in your head, that war is around every corner. I started all this as a bodyguard and driver for my now brother-in-law." Neil offered a rare grin. "Blake shits money in his sleep. The man can't make a bad investment. I followed his lead. Invested, got a decent return. Was lucky enough to win his sister over."

"I've seen your wife. You're a lucky man."

Neil warmed just thinking of Gwen. "She's not as fragile as she looks. She's put up with me for nearly twenty years." He kept walking. "Slowly, through time, this team fell together. Too amped up after being military grunts to see things the way other people do. And too skilled to give up the parts about the service they loved. Big part of our job now is keeping people safe and oblivious to the stupid in the world. Celebrities, politicians, businessmen and women with deep pockets. I have this team and another one in Europe. And on the outside, that's what we are . . . what we do. But you know we do more."

Leo knelt down and picked up a stick lying on the forest floor. "Undercover agents tracking down a Russian mob ring selling kids . . . yeah, I know you do more."

Neil nodded. "Some of our intel might not be gained in ways that your boss would approve of."

Leo shrugged. "I know that, too."

"Then you'll have to respect when I, or my people, avoid your questions."

"You can trust me, Neil. I'm sure Claire would vouch for me." While Leo was playing undercover teacher, Claire was playing undercover student. Only for two different departments. He thought the world of the woman.

"She has. Many times. Our secrets aren't just for us, they're for you."

"I'm not following."

Neil took a deep breath. "What happens if you overhear or obtain information you can't sit on?"

Leo stopped, turned to Neil. "You're the good guys."

"I like to think so. But we don't call 911. We call each other."

Leo stayed silent, digesting what that implied.

"We didn't wait for your people when that scumbag held a gun to Claire's head. We all know she wouldn't have made it if we had," Neil said.

Yeah . . . maybe Leo didn't want to know all their secrets.

Just Olivia's.

Or maybe he didn't.

"I take it Claire's situation wasn't unique."

Neil closed his mouth and stared.

"I allowed you to come here because I do trust you. I also saw something in your eyes that told me you weren't going to take no for an answer."

"Got that right."

"Good. So now that we understand each other, let me tell you why she's really here. And this is for you, not your boss."

"I'm listening."

"None of us are in a hurry for her to get her memory back. In fact, if I could stop it from ever happening, I would. But since the doctors believe it's only a matter of time, I want to make sure that when it does return, she has healed one hundred percent. That her body is ready to jump out of an airplane and land on someone's back when her chute doesn't open."

"That's pretty hard-core."

"It's not far from the truth." Neil wouldn't be surprised if Olivia had taken that leap at some point in her life and lived to tell about it.

"Why?"

"If someone hasn't already said this, I'll let you hear it from me. The moment Olivia knows she is Olivia . . . you won't see it . . . you won't sense it . . . she'll just be gone. And it may be years before she contacts me again . . . if ever. And I like sleeping at night. I want to know that we gave her the best chance of survival. You may never know what she saw the night she was shot. She absolutely won't tell you for the purpose of going after the person who shot her."

Leo's expression dialed in on that. "She doesn't call 911."

Neil started walking again. "When you report in to your boss, we have a secure line. Give your phone to Sasha when we return so she can shut down all trackers."

He'd turned off his phone the second they arrived at the airport.

"None of that is enabled," Leo told him.

"Just give it to Sasha." Neil found the first set of sensors. "Let me show you how this works."

~

Olivia jolted awake.

Her feet tingled from the echoes of her recurring dream.

The room was dark with the exception of a small nightlight plugged into the wall between the bed and the en suite bathroom.

They'd given her the master bedroom, complete with a fireplace and access to one of the patios surrounding the house. The log home would have felt heavy if not for the tall ceilings and windows.

She stretched and turned to look for the time. Only there wasn't a clock on the nightstand or the wall. She supposed a home like this was meant for holidays, and staying on any kind of schedule became irrelevant when trying to relax.

Her gaze gravitated toward one of the many windows in the room. Outside, the moon shed light on the trees as it descended on the horizon.

The room must be facing west.

Which meant the early morning sun wouldn't blind her.

"Why do I even know that?" And what did it matter?

She tried closing her eyes and heard her stomach.

"I'm starving," she whispered to herself. She'd fallen into bed after her shower and Pam's doctoring. The memory of someone checking on her and the smell of food were there, but sleep was more important.

And now it was God only knew what time, and Olivia's body was reminding her that she hadn't eaten since the stuff they passed off as food in the hospital.

She moved the covers back and slowly climbed out of bed.

Her muscles still ached, but she was happy the stabbing pain had eased considerably. Maybe everyone would stop asking her if she wanted pain meds. Just thinking about them made her brain fog up.

I'd rather feel pain than nothing at all.

A pair of slippers sat on the side of the bed, a bathrobe flung over a chaise lounge. They had thought of everything.

Even clothes.

The drawers had jeans, T-shirts, sweaters, leggings . . . a pair of hiking shoes, all-weather boots, and runners. Even underclothes . . . and everything looked like it would fit. Olivia was pretty sure she had to credit Sasha for the outfits. Whoever these people were, they were thorough.

Olivia couldn't help but wonder what she normally preferred in terms of style. She didn't look at the pants and wish for a dress or see the black leggings and think she'd never wear that. They were clothes. Cloth that served a purpose.

Forcing her thoughts away, she pushed her arms into the bathrobe, careful to not make too many fast movements and encourage discomfort in her chest. And then decided against putting on the slippers. She'd rather feel the stairs under her feet, even if the floor was cold.

The house was asleep . . . or the people inside were, in any event. She moved quietly through the hallway, past a TV room on the third floor, and down the stairs to the main floor.

At the bottom of the stairs she saw the shadow of a man in front of the window watching the same moonset she had up in her bedroom.

She looked closer.

It was Leo. He and AJ were similar in size and shape, only Leo's hair was shorter, his shoulders maybe an inch wider.

Olivia stared.

He was wearing a pair of lounge pants, the kind some men wore to bed and others stripped down to after a long day.

No shirt.

A slow smile spread over her lips.

Leo worked out.

Those slightly-wider-than-AJ's shoulders were sculpted like Michelangelo's statues. His waist tapered to an ass she couldn't help but think matched the rest of him. The fact that he was in a house full of people but was walking around without a shirt meant two things . . . it was the middle of the night and he didn't expect anyone to be up . . . and Leo slept naked. She would bet money there weren't any boxers or briefs under those pants. Her thoughts led to him dropping the pants before climbing into bed and grabbing them when he needed a quick run to the kitchen or bathroom.

She felt her breath fall from her lips a little faster, a little warmer.

Attraction.

The word floated in her head as if what she was feeling in her belly was more than hunger. Or hunger of a different kind.

She closed her eyes and forced the word, and the heat, out of her head.

Not the time.

Not the place.

Diverting her eyes, she took a couple of steps toward the kitchen.

Because Leo still hadn't heard her, she softly cleared her throat.

He jumped and pivoted quickly.

"Sorry. I was trying to be quiet," she told him.

His shoulders relaxed when he saw her. "You succeeded." He looked at the path she'd just walked.

"I woke up hungry." She found a light switch, turned it on, and dimmed them to match the evening.

"No one wanted to wake you for dinner, but there is a plate for you." Leo moved past her and into the kitchen. He opened the fridge and reached inside. "We all thought you needed to sleep . . ."

He kept talking, but his words didn't register. Mr. FBI had the perfect amount of hair on his chest.

An image of her fingers raking over his pecs settled in a comfortable position in her brain.

Leo turned, a plate in his hand, the light from the refrigerator casting him in a silhouette. He stopped talking and moving . . . and his eyes met hers.

Chemistry. The moment when attraction hits both people at the same time.

Her gaze moved to his chest, then back up . . . slowly.

Leo closed his eyes, shook his head, and blew out a quick breath. "I should, ah . . . put a shirt on."

That's a damn shame.

But she didn't suggest otherwise. Instead, she removed the plate from his hands and walked to the microwave. "Thank you."

His footsteps followed him out of the room and rapidly up the stairs.

By the time he returned, her food was hot, and she was getting comfortable in one of the bar chairs at the kitchen counter.

Once there, she realized she was missing water and started to get up.

"What do you need?" Leo asked.

"Water."

Once again he moved to the fridge. The silhouette still nice, just not as distracting. "Sasha insisted on having sparkling."

"That would be perfect," she told him. "I think I prefer that."

He twisted off the cap and set it down.

"Is there a glass?"

He stopped for a moment, smiled . . . then headed to a cupboard. He removed a tall wineglass and placed it in front of her.

"Thank you."

She picked up her fork and looked at the plate of food. "What exactly is this?" she asked.

"It's meatloaf. Pretty good, too."

Olivia was sure she'd heard about meatloaf but couldn't recall ever eating it. She sliced a small bite off, gave it a quick sniff first, then put it in her mouth. Ground beef, spices . . . almost like a savory hamburger patty only with gravy. "Not bad."

Leo pulled out a chair beside her and sat. "That's what I thought. Apparently, it's Isaac's specialty. Since we're taking turns cooking, I have a feeling we'll be eating this once a week."

A forkful of potatoes was next.

One taste and she wanted to spit them out. "Oh . . . my." She looked at her fork. "Potatoes?"

"The kind from a box."

"Potatoes in a box? Is that possible?"

"Instant mashed potatoes. That doesn't sound familiar?"

"Sounds awful." She wiped her fork on the side of the plate and went back to the meatloaf. "Tastes worse."

Leo smiled and watched her eat. "Interesting," he said at one point.

"What's that?"

"You hold your fork in your left hand."

She looked at her hands. "That isn't right?"

"No . . . it's fine. A preference, I guess."

She took another bite, feeling the edge of her hunger starting to fade. "I don't know any of my preferences." Her words paused, her thoughts drifting. "Isn't that crazy? Like this meal. I know I've eaten a hamburger but can't recall this. The oatmeal in the hospital . . . I ate it, knew what it was, and knew I had tasted better. But when and where I'd eaten oatmeal before . . . I have no idea."

Leo tilted his head to the side. "That must feel awful."

"Frustrating." She closed her eyes, left her knife on her plate, pinched her thumb and index finger together, and brought them in front of her face. "It's right there. I think it's all right there, but I can't seem to sift through the files to find it." She opened her eyes, dropped her hand to her lap. "When we arrived here, I smelled the pine trees, thought of Christmas lights and snow but couldn't remember one single Christmas."

"The doctors said it will come back."

"They also said the memory loss is a protective thing. What if I remember and something awful is there?" She looked up when Leo stayed silent.

His eyes were razor sharp, his lips pressed together, and his breathing had picked up.

Distress and worry oozed from him about something she'd just said.

He blinked. "It isn't every day you get shot. That would prove difficult for most people to process."

She couldn't help but conclude he was thinking something else when those words came out.

Or maybe she was just imagining things. Everything and everyone was unfamiliar. Maybe the emotions weren't right either.

"Clearly I'm not going to remember anything today," she said as she picked up her utensils.

"Want my advice?"

"Sure." She took another bite.

"Let it go. Don't think about it. Just do what feels right and don't question it. And when things start to come back, talk to me. Maybe I can help."

"Easier said than done."

Leo laughed. "Yeah, it sounded like a load of shit as I was saying it."

Olivia laughed along with him. The movement in her chest caught just a little, and she placed her free hand on her side.

"Sorry," he said.

"It's okay. It's better, actually. Much. Maybe the fresh mountain air will help."

"It can't hurt." He leaned back in his chair and appeared to catch himself staring at her and looked away.

"What time is it?" she asked.

"One in the morning."

She lifted a forkful of green beans to her mouth. "What are you doing up?"

He rubbed the back of his neck. "I don't know. Considering the handful of hours I've slept in the past month, I should be facedown in a bed for a week. But I heard a noise and had to look." He turned toward the windows across the room. "Then I saw the moon and started asking myself . . . *When was the last time I stopped to look at the moon?*"

Olivia turned in her chair to see the last of the moon slip behind the horizon. "It is beautiful."

Leo hummed, his eyes slid to hers.

Her chest warmed.

Yup . . . chemistry. A tiny snap of air.

She directed her attention to her plate, took one last bite, and then pushed it away.

"That's better than I thought you'd do," he said.

"Food is fuel. You don't overfill a gas tank or you'll just make a mess."

"What about pizza? Everyone overeats pizza."

She smiled. "A proper Italian pizza, maybe." An image flashed in her head. A small outside table with an entire cheese, basil, and tomato pizza sitting in front of her. She closed her eyes, chased the scene.

Nothing.

"Are you okay?" Leo leaned forward and placed his hand on her arm. "You're trembling."

"For a second I thought I remembered something. But it's gone." And a pulsing in her temple threatened to blossom into a headache.

He ran his hand over her arm through her bathrobe. "It's going to be okay."

She covered his fingers, and that snap of air became physical energy at the simple touch. Even that . . . she knew what it was but couldn't identify the last time it had happened. She squeezed his hand gently and broke the connection. "I appreciate your assurance." Even if she knew it was speculation at best. There was no way he could predict that things would be *okay*.

She lifted her plate and started to get up.

"Let me."

"I'm sure I can . . ."

"Next week. When laughing doesn't cause you to wince and walking up the stairs is just as easy as walking down."

She let him have the plate and watched his backside as he turned away with it and emptied what she didn't eat into the trash.

Stop looking at his ass.

Olivia stood, pushed her chair in. Even that movement took effort. She needed to build some strength.

In the morning. She'd start tomorrow.

Leo turned the water on in the sink.

"Thank you for the company," she said.

"Anytime."

She took a few steps from the kitchen. "Try and get some sleep, Leo."

He looked up. "Good night, Olivia."

She huffed, the name sounding so odd to her ears. "Good night."

CHAPTER TEN

Neil sat back in the desk chair, his arms folded over his chest.

Sasha stood beside him, eyes taking in the footage he'd brought up for her to view.

"Are you seeing what I'm seeing?"

A touch . . . a smile . . . and just enough ogling when the other one wasn't looking to clear any doubt of what was going on. It was like watching one of those women's movies Gwen insisted on dragging him to a couple of times a year.

"Should we stop it?" Sasha asked, her eyes glued to the footage that kept playing.

Lars had caught the interplay between Leo and Olivia from the night before and made sure to bring it to Neil's attention first thing in the morning.

Neil shook his head. "I saw the look on Leo's face . . . but now it's clear it's mutual. I say leave it. Maybe encourage it."

Sasha turned her back to the monitors, leaned against the desk, and crossed her arms over her chest. "Are you turning into a matchmaker in your old age?"

He'd deny that to the grave. "Maybe this will give Olivia a reason to stay."

Sasha nodded toward the screens. "This is sexual."

Doesn't all attraction start that way? "Tell me in a week if you feel differently."

"There's a reason she's alone. You know it. I know it. Everyone here but Leo knows it."

"I'm more concerned with Olivia losing her humanity than Leo ending up with a broken heart. He will survive. She might not." Neil pushed back from the desk and stood.

Sasha didn't argue, which told him she agreed.

"I won't encourage it."

That, he was okay with. "Then encourage the others to leave them be. Give them time . . . alone."

"A wee bit manipulative, MacBain," she accused.

"If there's nothing there, nothing will happen."

Sasha was a beautiful woman when she smiled. "When is your flight?" she asked.

He looked at the time. "Three hours. I'll be back next week, give you and AJ a break."

"We told you that wasn't necessary."

"You and Olivia are a lot alike. The more you're around her, the more likely she's going to notice similarities. Her questions may lead to her memory returning too quickly."

"We don't know that."

"We don't *not* know that."

Again, no argument.

"You're doing the right thing here," Sasha said. "Maybe not the matchmaking part . . . but taking care of her."

"Claire could have ended up like her . . . or you."

"There isn't a day that goes by that I don't remember that."

"Then you know why we're here."

"We all do."

Neil smiled and left the room.

~

"Stop fidgeting."

"I'm not."

Pam glared with a stink-eye stare that had Olivia holding her breath and standing still.

"There." Pam eased back, looked at her handiwork.

"It's only one hole," Olivia told her.

Pam stared in the mirror. "One hole. One soldier at a time."

Olivia let her gaze shift. "When did you serve?"

Pam's eyes caught hers in the reflection. "A long time ago."

"You're too young to say that."

"I'm twenty years older than you."

Olivia felt a smile on her lips. "Considering I don't know how old I am . . . that's safe."

Pam chuckled. "I'll take a bullet wound any day over a bomb. A hole . . . so much easier than a dripping mess of bone and flesh with no skin to pull it together."

That was a visual Olivia would take some time to get over.

And from the look in Pam's eyes . . . yeah, her, too.

"I'm sorry," Olivia found herself saying.

Pam blew out a breath. "Long time ago."

"Still affects you."

She shrugged. "And you don't remember what you did last summer."

For reasons Olivia couldn't name, she started laughing.

And laughing.

"Touché, mademoiselle."

"I think we're going to get along just fine."

They descended the stairs together.

The *crew*, a term Olivia had coined for the lot of them, had gathered around the kitchen. Someone said something about the temperature of the flame for the eggs being prepared on the stove, and someone else questioned to what level the bacon had been cooked.

"Good morning," AJ said from his perch in one of the many chairs in the open living room.

"Morning," Olivia greeted him. Her eyes moved around the room, did a quick inventory.

Lars and Isaac were wrestling in the kitchen in an episode of "I know more about cooking than you do."

Neil sat in one of the high counter chairs, a duffel bag at his feet.

Sasha and Leo were both absent.

"Where are the others?" she asked, really only interested in Leo.

"Sasha's in the surveillance room, and Leo is doing his best Sleeping Beauty impersonation," AJ told her.

Pam left Olivia's side once she'd cleared the last step of the stairs. She moved into the kitchen as if she was now the boss. "Is this going to be a daily thing with you two?"

"Bacon should be close to burned, right, Neil?" Lars asked.

"I'm staying out of this." Neil gave Olivia a sideways glance. "How did you sleep?" he asked her.

"It's very quiet here," she said.

"Everywhere is quiet compared to Vegas," Lars said.

"And dark," Isaac added.

Olivia only had the trip from the hospital to the airport to compare. And she'd been so busy watching Neil and Leo as they escorted her, she didn't think to look out the window. The men had a laser focus on everything going on around them and the car as if they were truly worried someone was going to jump out at any second and shoot her again.

Of course, the lead vest they'd put on her before leaving the hospital would have clued her in to the threat even if they'd said nothing.

She looked at the bag on the floor at Neil's feet. "Are you leaving?"

He offered a single nod. "I'll be back in a week. Sooner if I'm needed."

"I doubt it will take this many people to keep me safe."

Isaac started laughing, then seemed to catch himself before turning around and going back to preparing breakfast.

"I thought the same thing," Pam said as she removed juice from the refrigerator.

"If you knew the players, you might think differently."

Olivia moved to stand beside the kitchen counter. "Who are the players?" she asked Neil.

He paused and weighed his words. "A large international family. People that don't like going to jail."

"Does anyone like going to jail?" Pam asked.

"I've been avoiding it for years," AJ said from the living room.

Isaac and Lars stopped arguing about the bacon long enough to laugh at AJ's statement.

Olivia found herself staring at AJ, a tilt to her head. *Is he serious?*

"Time to eat."

She was shooed out of the kitchen when she attempted to help. After pouring herself a cup of coffee, she took a seat at the table and let the crew serve her.

From what she'd been told, Pam was the only newcomer. But you wouldn't know by watching her interactions with the others. The bacon debate continued, the easy banter telling Olivia that this group had a long history.

She'd been told they were a private organization that helped the feds and local police from time to time. And since they were invested in Leo, and she'd been with him when she was shot, Neil's team had taken on the task of keeping her safe.

If she was a burden, she didn't see it. They all appeared to like each other's company and acted as if relocating to remote areas with complete strangers was a weekly occurrence.

Olivia ate in silence and soaked in their individual mannerisms.

Neil said very little but did smile on occasion. He spent most of his time watching her and pretending he wasn't.

AJ passed the plate full of toast to his left, the way he moved suggesting he had a gun strapped to his side. Not that she could see it with the light jacket he wore. The knowledge and absolute certainty of that fact caught her unexpectedly. Once she realized that, she started to look for signs of who else in the room was armed.

Neil . . . his weapon was behind his back.

Pam? No. She didn't have a firearm on her.

Isaac had his sleeves rolled up, his shirt tucked in. No.

Lars wore utility pants, and she counted one gun and two knives on him.

Pistols . . . So where were the rifles?

Olivia's eyes shifted around the living room, scanned the open kitchen.

Pantry.

Behind the dining room hutch.

Why did they hide them? Did they think the sight of a gun would cause some kind of PTSD?

Considering the circumstances, that was likely.

"You're not hungry?" AJ asked, causing Olivia to turn her attention away from the weapons and back to her plate of food.

She picked up her fork and filled it with eggs. "Distracted," she said.

That's when she realized that everyone at the table had their forks in their right hands.

Her thoughts returned to the conversation the previous evening with Leo.

"A preference . . ."

As if just thinking his name somehow summoned the man, Olivia heard Leo's footsteps descending the stairs before he came into view. "I thought I smelled food."

"Last one to the table does the dishes," Isaac teased.

Leo stopped at the coffee pot before finding an empty seat across from her. "Morning," he said with a smile.

"Finally found yourself facedown in that bed?" she asked. He looked rested, a fresh shave . . . his hair slightly damp. His weapon was in the same position as Neil's.

Why did her mind pick that up?

"A late-night conversation seemed to do the trick."

"Glad I could help."

Isaac used a piece of bacon as a pointing stick. "What did you think of the meatloaf?"

"Surprisingly good."

Isaac puffed out his chest.

Lars rolled his eyes.

"But if I find the box of potatoes, I'm likely to burn it." She politely smiled and chewed her eggs.

"They're easy," Isaac insisted.

"They were hideous."

"Do you cook?" he asked.

"No." Her denial was instant and felt right. "It's a potato, how hard can it be?"

"I vote you make the mashed potatoes," Isaac decided.

She set her utensil down. "Challenge accepted."

~

"Keep an eye on her," Neil told Leo. They stood in the driveway, the driver's side door of the SUV open.

"We will," Leo said for the others.

"*You.* You're the only one in this group she doesn't know. And Pam, but I didn't hire her to protect her. The more time Olivia spends with the rest of us, the more likely she'll remember things."

Spending time with the woman was not a hardship.

"I won't let her get shot twice," Leo assured him.

Neil extended his hand to shake. "I have Claire and the others working on Navi . . . see if we can find a link."

"You and I both know it's there."

"Then we'll find it."

Neil climbed into the car and drove away.

Leo walked around the perimeter of the house before taking a back stairway up to the main floor. The wraparound porch was a nice touch. The house sat up on a small knoll and looked out to a valley with a mountain range in the distance. He had a feeling he'd be spending a lot of time outside watching sunsets and stars.

Which didn't suck.

"Are you from this area?"

He heard Olivia's voice before he walked around the front of the house to find her sitting in a deck chair, her legs kicked out in front of her . . . Pam at her side.

"No. I live in LA, like everyone else here."

"Lots of traffic," Olivia said.

Leo hesitated.

"Have you been there?"

"I think so. It's a bitch not knowing for sure."

"You're not missing much. Busy city, traffic like you said. I prefer this," Pam said.

Leo stepped closer. "Best seats in the house," he said as a greeting.

Olivia smiled up at him. "My private nurse said I need fresh air."

"You do."

Leo took a vacant seat. "Your color is better today," he told her.

"It's amazing how good you feel when a member of the hospital staff isn't sticking a needle in your arm every morning at five a.m."

"Hospitals are no place to rest," Pam said.

They all nodded in agreement.

"Do either of you know when this area gets its first snow?" Olivia asked.

"No idea, but we can find out."

"I'd like to get a feel for the place before then. Take a few walks," she said.

Leo thought that was a reasonable request.

Pam, on the other hand . . . "Veto on walks in the woods for a couple of days."

Olivia looked at the woman as if she were crazy.

"That evil eye isn't going to work on me. The altitude is higher here, the ground uneven, and a few days ago you needed a hole in your lung to breathe. Up and down the flat driveway is enough for you."

"And never alone," Leo added.

"I have a feeling the logic the two of you are using is only going to work on me for a short time."

He didn't like the sound of that. "Never alone, Olivia. Neil has done everything he can to ensure that no one knows we're here, but . . ."

Those green eyes found his briefly, then turned away to stare at the landscape. "I don't have a death wish. I do, however, have a desire to build my strength and be independent."

"You're independent now," Pam assured her.

"As evidenced by the fact that one of you is at my side every time I walk up or down the stairs."

Leo smiled at Pam. "She has us there."

Olivia sat up, placed her feet flat on the ground. "You have fifteen minutes to decide who gets to hold my hand on my morning walk. I plan on taking another after dinner, so be warned."

"Olivia!"

"Yes, Pam?"

The two of them stared each other down.

Pam rolled her eyes. "I knew this assignment was too good to be true," she muttered, a smile on her face. "Meet you out here in fifteen." She left the two of them alone.

"Are you always this stubborn?" he asked.

"I think so. The opposite feels uncomfortable. Much like holding my fork with my right hand." She paused. "Every day I feel that much closer to remembering who I am."

Leo's stomach churned. "That's good," he lied.

Olivia stood. "So, you're up for a walk? I mean, you're the one with the gun." She nodded toward the path Pam had just traveled to go inside. "She's making sure I don't hurt myself, and you're here to make sure no one hurts me."

Leo nodded. "Fourteen minutes and counting."

CHAPTER ELEVEN

Stubborn.

"I am stubborn," Olivia said to herself in the bathroom mirror.

Dinner was behind her, and even though she could put her head on her pillow and conk out for the night, she was determined to take a walk before the sun completely set.

Lifting her left arm to work a band into her hair took a huge amount of effort. Each muscle extending and contracting on her left side was sore. And when she thought about it, some were trying to mend themselves back together.

Once her hair was up into a ponytail, she used a washcloth to rinse away the look of pain on her face. She'd gone a whole day without one person asking if she wanted something for pain. She counted that as a win.

She grabbed a sweater, placed it over her arm, and left her room. At the top of the stairs, she took a deep breath, squared her shoulders, and intended to set a pace going down the stairs and not falter.

Five steps down she reached for the handrail and cursed the ache in her side. Why did a bullet to the chest cause her entire body to slow down?

She counted the last three steps in her head and paused when she reached the bottom. She closed her eyes and took a deep breath. Even that was painful. And in truth, it got worse as the day moved on.

"It's not a race."

Olivia opened her eyes to find Sasha standing several feet away, her knowing stare pinning Olivia in place.

She lifted her chin. "It feels as if it is."

"Push yourself too hard and you'll slide backward."

Olivia knew her words were meant to help, but that didn't stop her from justifying her actions. "I can't push my mind to remember a solitary thing. Pushing my body is my only option."

Sasha swallowed, looked away. "Leo is waiting for you on the porch."

No argument . . .

Olivia was liking Sasha more each day.

She passed Pam, who was sitting in the living room, a book in her hand. "You're not coming?" Olivia asked.

"What's the point? If I tell you it's time to turn around, you'll just ignore me."

Which had happened on their morning walk.

"Besides, if you can't make it back on your own two feet, he can carry you. I can't." She flipped the page in her book, never looked up.

Olivia wanted to laugh but settled for a smile instead.

"We'll be back before it's dark."

Pam looked at her watch, glanced up, then back to her book. "Stubborn."

Olivia walked past her and out the front door.

Leo stood talking to Isaac and Lars, the three of them laughing about something.

"Looks like we have a crowd," Olivia said when she approached them.

Lars nodded toward the opposite side of the drive. "We're on a mission. Two of the sensors keep getting knocked offline by raccoons."

"Try moving them up," she suggested. "Above the level of the animals."

Isaac cleared his throat.

"That was the plan," Lars said, the smile on his face fading.

Leo turned to her. "If you want this walk, we need to go now. If we're still out when it gets dark, I'm carrying you back."

Olivia narrowed her gaze. "You've been talking to Pam."

He lifted his hands in the air. "There are three women in this house, and two of them are ticked that you're doing this. I can piss off one of you or two of them. What would you do?"

Lars chuckled. "Have fun."

She moved ahead of Leo and took a good look at the second set of stairs.

"If you can't make it down, you won't make it back up."

Her eyes shifted to him, drifted to his chest. "I've seen you without a shirt. You're capable of getting me up these stairs."

"Now you're just using flattery to get what you want."

Without asking, she placed her hand on his arm and reached for the handrail.

She took her time and felt good at the bottom.

"Let's do this," he said.

She removed her hand from him and started walking. "I know I appear obstinate—"

"Are," Leo corrected her. "It's only been a week. And most of that time you were in the ICU."

"They kept me in the ICU for security. I'm pretty sure Neil bribed them for the room."

Leo stayed silent.

"We're simply going to have to agree to disagree on this," she finally said.

"Fair enough. But I'm your walking buddy. I'll be able to tell if you're getting better or worse from day to day where the others may not if they aren't out with you all the time. And you'll bullshit them if it serves you."

"You think I'm that conniving?"

Leo glanced down, then back to the road. "Yup."

She laughed. "You might be right."

The gravel under her feet crunched, the noise heavy in her ears. Why not a paved driveway? The homeowner spent a lot of money on the house itself.

But would Neil pick a house with a paved drive?

No. He would want to hear cars coming and going.

Olivia watched her feet moving. Why would she know what Neil was considering when he picked their location?

"What are you thinking?" Leo asked.

"Random thoughts. They keep coming out of nowhere."

"Memories?"

She shook her head. "Not memories. It's hard to explain."

"Try."

"Like this . . ." She reached behind his back and patted where he held his weapon. Smiled when she confirmed with a touch what she'd figured out earlier that day. "I never saw it, but I knew it was there."

Leo had stopped to watch her. "I am a federal agent."

She kept walking. "It's not knowing that you *should* have a gun on you, but that you did and where it was. Isaac has his in his cargo pants. Must be strapped in somehow, otherwise it would have been obvious. AJ has his here." She patted her left flank. "Lars . . ." She stopped, thought of him before he walked off to set sensors. "He's armed to the teeth. Why would I know that?"

"You're intuitive?" Leo didn't sound convinced by his own words.

"It's more than that. Pam walks up and down the stairs with heavy feet. She's a small woman, but her footfalls are like an elephant in my ears. Isaac and Lars are better, but Lars favors his right leg. I bet he's had an injury. And Sasha . . . I never hear her. That woman is stealth. It's more than intuition. It's knowledge that's ingrained."

"Maybe your other senses are heightened since your memory is missing?"

"You really believe that?"

"You have a better theory?"

"No." She hadn't thought that long or hard about it. She'd been spending too much time thinking of the facts as they dropped into her head.

She swatted away a mosquito and considered putting the sweater on if only to ward off any bug bites.

They walked in silence for a few yards. "You don't have to hide them."

"Hide what?" Leo asked.

"Your guns. They don't scare me."

Leo chewed on that for a few steps. "If we all walked around armed to the teeth, and someone from a neighboring property took notice, questions would come up."

At first, his explanation made sense, but Neil wouldn't choose a property with neighbors. At least not neighbors who were actually around.

Another mosquito moved in for blood.

Leo reached over, took her sweater from her hand, and held it out for her to step into. "You're not the only one who's intuitive. It's cooling off, the mosquitos are attacking, but it's hard to get into the sweater without hurting."

She accepted his help, eased her left arm in first. "Another week and the mosquitos will die off with the shift in the weather."

"You think so?" he asked.

"Yeah."

He pulled the sweater around her, let his hands linger on her arms. "Better?" he asked.

"Your hands are warm." So were his eyes. Trusting. Like a net at the end of a fall.

There it was, the rapid rise and fall of his chest, his eyes drifting to her lips. How would they taste? How would *he* taste? A feeling washed over her with the memory of what a kiss felt like, but not the who on the other end.

Then logic knocked on the back side of her brain. "Getting mixed up with your protectors is just as foolish as with your captors," she whispered. Not that her words stopped her from her next thought about the day's growth of beard that gave Leo an edge she liked even more than the clean-shaven look he started with every morning.

How would he feel on her skin?

Did he want to find out about her as much as she desired to learn about him?

Leo snapped his eyes away, dropped his hands to his sides. "We should head back."

Olivia took that as an agreement.

A few steps toward the house and she confronted him. "Are we going to ignore this?" she asked.

"You called it foolish."

"Am I wrong?"

"No."

"Yet you volunteered to escort me on my walks."

He kept his gaze forward. "That makes me a masochist."

Why did this feel like a challenge? "Are you afraid I might be married?" she asked him.

"Happily married women aren't walking around Las Vegas without a wedding ring," he told her.

She glanced down at her left hand. No evidence of atrophy where a ring had lived, no tan lines. "What about an unhappily married woman? Or maybe I have an awful boyfriend."

He snuck a glance her way.

She pretended not to notice.

"You don't strike me as a woman who would stay in any relationship she wasn't happy with. We can't even get you to stay inside and put your feet up. I don't see a man controlling your actions."

Part of her believed everything he said, and something else told her he was wrong.

"If there is a Mr. to my Mrs., he might want to show up soon."

"Oh?"

Olivia looked over at him, waited until he looked back before she spoke. "I'm starting to have some thoughts on how to spend the time around here." Without thinking, she licked her lips.

Leo blew out a very audible breath and forced his eyes away. "You're killing me," he murmured.

She couldn't say for sure if this was her normal behavior, but she wasn't going to deny it felt damn good and familiar. "You're too easy."

"I'm a man."

They walked in silence. The house and the valley below came into view.

Leo reached over and gently slid his hand over hers.

Her heartbeat rushed in her head.

The flirting felt familiar.

The handholding . . . not so much.

Not that she wanted to pull away.

~

"Does she have her memory back?"

Not *hello . . . how are you? How's the weather?* It had only been a week that they'd been in Colorado, and Leo's boss sounded as impatient as ever. "No, Brackett, her memory is still on the streets of Las Vegas where someone shot it out of her."

Leo was in the situation room on the secured line. Isaac sat in front of the monitors watching the most boring show on television.

Although Leo didn't want to invite excitement.

"Thought as much. Am I to assume there's no trouble?"

"We're good. And movement on Navi?"

"He left Vegas after the judge sent Mykonos away for forty years to think about all the bad things he's done."

"Out in ten for good behavior?" Forty years wasn't enough.

"Minimum twenty. They're appealing, of course."

Still not enough time. Only they couldn't pin down a manslaughter charge since the man who had killed the women that were with Marie ended up dead in his cell before he could stand trial. Crazy how the little guys never make it out alive, and the big bosses always do.

"We're interviewing all parties. Looking for who was watching the headlines and would have behaved differently should that bullet have hit you instead of the girl."

Leo thought about that a lot.

"Someone on the jury?" Leo suggested.

"Or the judge . . . maybe even the lawyers. But they aren't about to say a damn thing. We're digging. Looking for patterns."

"Whoever they were trying to make me an example to didn't get the message."

"Unless someone just wanted you out."

Leo had a hard time seeing that. He wasn't even a witness in the case. Though he did put a target on himself when he cornered Navi. In which case, Leo had no one to blame but himself. He knew the dirtbags he was dealing with. "Always a chance it was meant as a warning to me."

"That's not off the table either. Considering you didn't take the hit. These guys are professionals. They don't miss very often."

"How is Fitz holding up?"

"She asked for a raise . . . says she's working both of your jobs."

Leo laughed. The government didn't give two shits how hard you worked. Raises were mapped out from the day you took the job to the day you retired.

"So, she's fine."

Brackett laughed. "Talk to you next week."

"Sooner if I have anything."

His boss hung up, and Leo looked at the phone, then Isaac.

"What are the chances that this phone call wasn't recorded?"

Isaac reached over, pressed a button on his computer.

Leo's and Brackett's voices replayed the conversation for several seconds before Isaac shut it off.

"It's not about trusting you. You wouldn't be here if Neil had any doubts. It's about taking his intel and putting it with ours. Adding scenarios, removing others."

"When is that happening? This scenario speculation you guys do?"

"Once Olivia is sleeping. Plan is to meet down here, video with Neil and the others. Swap stories."

The hair on Leo's neck pulled with irritation. "Was it also in the plan to clue me in?"

Isaac stared at the monitors. "Not my call."

"Yet you just told me about it."

"Was told to wait for you to ask. You earn your stripes with this group. Nothing's given for free."

"Olivia earned her stripes?"

"Oh yeah. In spades."

CHAPTER TWELVE

Olivia stood in front of the mirror wearing only a bra and panties. How was it possible that a week had passed since she arrived in Colorado and she was no closer to knowing who she was than the day she left the hospital?

She looked at her hair, which rolled midway down her back. Except for the chunk that had been shaved so the doctors could staple the parts together that split open when she'd fallen to the ground. She ran her fingertips along the edges of the scar she couldn't see. Hair prickled under her touch as it started to grow in. Rolling her head from one side to the other at night had woken her up more than once with the pressure on her sensitive skin.

She moved her fingers to the back of her neck, then around to her right collarbone. She hesitated and then moved back to the center of the bone.

A flash . . .

She'd broken it.

Olivia palpated the bone, could feel a slight bump. She immediately moved her finger to her left side and compared the two.

"No class until the doctor says you're clear."

The words were plain as day in her head.

She'd been young, or at least still in school.

But where was she and who was talking?

Olivia placed both hands on the rim of the sink and squeezed her eyes shut. "C'mon, damn it. Give me more than that."

No class.

Not allowed to go to class.

What class?

"What class?"

She tapped on the counter, trying to catch the edges of the memory.

"Bloody fucking hell!" She swiped her hand out, caught a cup and the toothbrush holder. Both went crashing to the ground.

Movement without sound flashed in her peripheral vision.

There was no thought, just action.

Her body twisted, and her left arm came up to swing through as her right hand moved in to punch whoever was in her personal space.

Sasha avoided the swing and ducked the punch. She came up with both hands in front of her, palms spread. "Hey . . . it's me."

Every muscle in Olivia's body was keyed up. Her skin was fire, her eyes laser sharp, and her heartbeat had gone from sixty to a hundred in two seconds.

"It's me."

The small space of the bathroom felt as if it were closing in.

Get out!

Get out!

"Olivia . . . take a deep breath. You're okay."

Footsteps pounded up the stairs, voices calling out.

"Olivia?"

"What's going on?"

"Everyone, back off."

The room slowly came into focus.

Her short breaths fought to overpower her.

Sasha stood an arm's distance away.

Leo was at Sasha's side.

All the others piled into the bedroom but stood far away.

"Slow, deep breaths," Sasha continued to coax.

That's when Olivia felt the pull on her left side. She looked down at the angry scar that had just started to feel better.

She put her right hand over her skin as if protecting it now would do any good. "Oh, God."

Pam pushed past Leo and Sasha. "Okay. All boys out," she demanded. "C'mon. Let's lay you down before you pass out." She pushed under Olivia's right arm as if she couldn't walk on her own two feet.

Though the first few steps suggested Pam had the right idea.

"Out!" she shouted when the men had yet to leave.

The room spun and heated. "I need to sit."

"Aw, fuck."

All Olivia remembered was Leo reaching for her as the world faded away.

~

"We're here." Leo's voice called her out of the fog.

Someone had placed a cold washcloth on her forehead.

She was on her bed, her feet propped up on pillows.

"Olivia?" Sasha stood behind Leo.

"I attacked you."

"It's okay."

Olivia tried to sit up.

"Oh, no. You lay right there." Pam had a blood pressure cuff on Olivia's arm and was blowing it up. "Give it a few minutes."

"I could have hurt you."

"Didn't come close," Sasha told her with a small smile.

"I needed to get out of the bathroom. You weren't going to stop me." She'd felt like a caged animal. "Why would I do that?"

Pam sighed. "Seriously. Calm down."

Leo stroked her right hand. "It's okay. It's over."

"I don't understand what happened . . ."

"I'm going to get you some ice water." Sasha moved toward the door.

"I am sorry."

"We're good. Let it go."

Olivia rolled her head toward Pam, looking for answers. "What's going on?"

"I'm not a neurologist."

"Don't give me that," Olivia chided.

Pam glanced at Leo. "Could be your memory trying to come back. Your body reacted instinctively. Hard to say."

"So I attack Sasha?"

"Did you remember something?" Leo asked.

Olivia looked down at her chest, realized only then that someone had tossed a sheet over her. "I broke my collarbone. When I was a kid."

Sasha returned with the water, and Leo and Pam helped Olivia sit up in the bed.

After a couple of sips, she relaxed against the headboard. Her side hurt like a bitch.

"You remember breaking a bone as a child," Leo redirected her.

Sasha sat on the edge of the bed and listened.

"I don't remember breaking it. I just know that it was broken." She took Leo's hand, guided it to her collarbone, and pressed his fingertips to the bump she'd discovered earlier. She grabbed his other hand, ignoring the sheet as it slipped to her waist, and pressed it on the left side. "Feel that?"

He nodded. "I do."

"I remember a voice . . . someone telling me that I couldn't go to class until it was better. The harder I thought about it, the more distant the memory felt." She sighed, let go of Leo's hand, and placed hers in

111

her lap. "I didn't see you walk in," she said, looking at Sasha. "Next thing I know—"

"I heard you yell. I came in."

Olivia glanced at Pam. "Is this what I can expect? Every time a memory sneaks in I'm going to pass out?"

"You were hyperventilating. Maybe next time a memory starts to emerge, sit down and slow your breathing. Call one of us."

She nodded a few times. "I should be happy I remembered something. My reaction was ridiculous."

"The brain is powerful. Don't underestimate your reactions. They're likely there for a reason," Sasha told her.

The ache behind her eyes started to spread to the back of her head.

She reached down and placed her hand on Leo's. "I think I'll skip this morning's walk. See if I can't get rid of this headache."

"That's the best idea you've had so far," Pam said as she removed the blood pressure cuff.

He lifted her hand to his lips, pressed a kiss to her fingertips. "Let us know if you need anything."

Leo and Sasha left the room, but Pam lingered. "How about some Tylenol?" she asked.

Olivia didn't respond. She simply adjusted herself in bed and pulled the sheet over her shoulders.

"That's what I thought," Pam muttered before closing the door behind her.

Who the hell am I?

The more she asked the question, the more afraid of the answer she became.

~

Clouds surrounded the log home, cocooning it in a dense shroud of moisture. The gray skies matched the mood inside the house.

Olivia's unexpected outburst had given everyone a stark reminder that her memory was going to come back, and when it did, her reaction may be just as unexpected as it had been in the bathroom.

The way Neil's team gave Olivia space showed Leo just how much room they needed to avoid injury.

She didn't emerge from her room until long after lunch. By dinner she was a little quicker to smile, but slower to move.

It was meatloaf night for the second time, and she insisted on making the mashed potatoes.

"You really don't have to," Isaac told her. "I'm sure we can manage."

"I don't welsh on bets or go back on my word. You make the hamburger thing, leave this to me."

Leo joined her at the sink and washed his hands. "I'll help you peel."

She gave him room and not an argument.

He counted that as a notch in the right direction.

"Did your mother make you help in the kitchen?" she asked him.

"My grandmother. My mom hates to cook. Nana, on the other hand . . ."

"Is she still alive?"

He turned the water on in the sink. "They both are. Nana lives in a retirement community, always talking about how she drives the widowed men crazy. Insists that she has at least one marriage proposal every six months."

"You grandma sounds like someone I'd like to know," Lars said from his perch in the living room.

Leo thought of his nana's smile and easy nature. "You might just be young enough for her," Leo suggested.

Olivia's laugh was the first one he'd heard all day.

"You'd like her. She says what everyone else is thinking and doesn't care who it offends."

"Best way to live," Isaac said.

Olivia hacked away at the skin of a potato with a vegetable peeler, and Leo used a small knife to do the same job.

"How old is she?"

"Eighty-two. Still has all her faculties . . . walks on her own two feet."

"So why the retirement place?"

"She says she needs people around, and if it wasn't for where she lived, she'd be bugging her family to entertain her. She's the woman that is first on the group bus to Vegas or when they go wine tasting in Temecula. She does a senior cruise once a year."

"Isn't *senior cruise* an oxymoron?" Isaac asked.

Leo nodded, finished with one potato, and moved to another. "She's enjoying her life. We should all be so lucky."

Just talking about his nana made Leo wonder about Olivia's family.

Who were they?

Did she even have a family?

Did any of them?

Or were they all like the toys on Misfit Island, odd, damaged, and alone?

A splatter of rain drew his attention away from thoughts of Neil's crew and out the window.

"I felt this coming," Lars said, staring at the rain.

"Oh?" Olivia asked.

"My right leg has been talking to me all day."

Olivia glanced up at Leo, a knowing smile on her lips. "When did you break it?" she asked.

"In the service."

Damn if she hadn't been right about the injury. Not that Leo had noticed any limp, even after Olivia brought it up earlier that week.

"Don't make it sound all heroic," Isaac teased.

"Are you suggesting Lars wasn't playing Superman at the time?" Olivia asked.

"I *was* flying through the air." Lars laughed.

"Jumping out of a plane on a training mission. Came in too hard." Isaac opened the oven and put their dinner inside. "Catch Lars after a few beers, you'll hear the story three different ways."

"That true, Lars?"

Leo enjoyed the amusement on Olivia's face as she learned the team's secrets.

"I only remember the story when I'm drinking," he told her.

"Be sure and add beer to the next run to the store," she said.

"No can do. Hard to play bodyguard when you're drunk."

Leo finished the last potato and rinsed off his hands. "We'll have to ask the questions when this is behind us," he suggested to Olivia.

She laughed. "I expect every one of you to line up to buy me drinks," she said.

"Is that so?" Isaac asked as he pushed his way into the space between Leo and Olivia at the sink to wash his hands.

"Well, yeah. Men have to buy me a drink before they see me in my underwear. The way I see it, you owe me."

Leo couldn't help but glance down below her chin.

Isaac kept his eyes straight ahead, his mouth shut.

Leo had seen more than enough to fantasize about, but he hadn't enjoyed it at the time.

"I'll buy you a few drinks, Olivia." Lars pushed off the couch and walked out of the room.

"I'll remember that," she called after him with a smile.

"Meatloaf will be done in an hour." Isaac backed away from the sink, turned toward the mess he'd made preparing dinner.

Leo leaned a little closer to her. "I don't think anyone really noticed."

"That's unfortunate. Apparently, I take care of this body."

That she did.

"You didn't notice?" she asked in a whisper.

Slippery slope, Leo.

"Nope."

"Hmm . . ." She walked behind him, removed the pot they were going to boil the potatoes in. "What color is my bra?"

"Black," he said without thinking.

"That is my cue to vacate the kitchen. Feel free to clean up my mess," Isaac said behind them with a dramatic slide of one palm against the other as if he was brushing away a fistful of dirt.

Once they were alone, Leo started to laugh. "You sure know how to clear a room."

She plopped the potatoes into the pot as it filled with water. "I didn't scare you off."

He wiped his hands on a dish towel, turning to lean against the counter beside her. "That's because I'm probably the only one that's been wondering what you look like in next to nothing."

"Not that you're acting on that." She turned off the water, took the towel from his hands, and dried hers.

"Which you are not making easy."

She laughed, looked down at the towel, and tossed it on the counter. "Busting your balls is the only time I feel normal," she told him.

"That's a recipe for disaster," he said.

He felt her fingertips as she reached out and brushed his hip.

Suddenly the memory of that black bra and slim waistline wasn't so fuzzy from the stress of the moment.

"Makes me wonder what else will feel normal."

She stepped into his personal space, leaned into him.

His cock jumped to attention. Damn thing was his truth serum.

Leo inched his gaze to her shoulder, then moved up to her chin, and finally those eyes he envisioned every night before he fell asleep.

This is a bad idea.

"No?" she asked as she dropped the hand she'd used to touch him. She sighed as if giving up and put space between them.

His hand shot out, stopped her from leaving.

Her eyes showed surprise when he reached for the side of her face and pulled her in.

Their lips touched with a physical spark, the kind that came from walking across carpet. Maybe that stalled their kiss, but something put it on pause, and they took a breath at the same time before he tilted his head and made sure she'd remember his kiss long after this moment passed.

She was soft in his arms as he folded her in. Those tempting lips opened slightly as if testing the waters.

He gave in, letting her lead.

A touch of her tongue against his retreated and then returned for more.

He released her hand and placed his own on her hip.

Hers fell on his leg, dangerously close to his erection. Not that he had any intention of doing anything with that other than giving it a cold shower.

No, this kiss was for her. Give the woman what she had all but asked for.

But the dig of her fingertips on his leg told him her raw need matched his . . . and that had to be curbed. Stopped.

He didn't know who slowed down their kiss, but they pulled back just enough for him to feel her rapid breath on his lips. "Feel better now?" he whispered.

She nodded. "Ah-huh." And then she shook her head. "You've been holding out, Mr. FBI."

"It's the right thing to do."

"I don't think I do the right thing very often," she said, looking up into his eyes.

Damn, she was sexy. "Now would be a good time to start."

She leaned fully into him, from knees to chest, pulled her lips away.

All the hard parts of him pushed into the soft parts of her.

The woman may not have the memory of where she'd learned to seduce a man, but her body knew exactly what to do. "The only reason I'm walking away is because my chest is killing me, and I don't want any distraction when we make this happen."

Her mentioning the gunshot wound had him placing a hand farther up her side, softly, as if he could make it better with his touch. "That bullet should have been in me."

"I don't want to hear you say that again."

"It's how I feel."

"Get over it." Her eyes searched his. "Now kiss me again."

He leaned down even when the neon sign flashed in his head.

Danger.

Danger.

Her hips pushed against his and snuffed that danger sign right to the depths of hell.

CHAPTER THIRTEEN

"I understand you had some excitement today." Neil's face came across just as stoic on a video monitor as it did in person.

Leo stood in the background as one of the monitors performed as a giant Zoom meeting. Neil was on one camera, and Cooper, Claire, and Jax were squeezed into another. Considering the newest members of the team all lived in the same house, it made sense. Clearly this group didn't mind late hours.

Olivia had stayed up past ten, and they hadn't assembled down in the situation room until eleven.

The monitors throughout the house would show any movement should she wake and decide she needed something that wasn't in her bedroom.

"Olivia had a memory flash, tried to marry her fist with Sasha's face," AJ told him.

Leo listened while Sasha relayed the facts to Neil.

"Old memories, then . . . nothing new?" he asked.

"Not that she's told any of us," Lars said.

"What about you, Leo?"

"Nothing I haven't shared." The intimate moments didn't need to be talked about. He couldn't help but look at the monitor that showed the interior of the kitchen. There was no way the household hadn't shared that with everyone.

Neil took his word. "Before we dig in, I want to remind everyone that while Leo is here, we have to respect his position and Olivia's privacy. And, Leo?"

"Yeah?"

"If I ask you to step out . . ."

He didn't like that. "I haven't earned my stripes yet . . ."

"Thank you for understanding." Neil nodded. "Let's start with Brackett."

Isaac cued up the conversation Leo had had earlier with his boss.

"Jax and I have been mulling this conversation over all day," Claire announced. "There isn't any logic to taking Leo out this late in the game . . . not for the sake of the lawyers. And since the judge didn't slap Mykonos with a 'say you're sorry and don't get caught doing this again' sentence, it's safe to say the judge hadn't been threatened."

"That leaves the jury," Lars said.

"Agreed," Claire said.

"If one or more of the jury members end up facedown in a river, we'll know we're onto something," Cooper added.

"Hey! Sensitive much?" Isaac said to the camera and nodded in Sasha and AJ's direction.

"Awww, fuck, AJ, I'm sorry."

Leo felt the weight of the room, and judging from the pressure, there was a lot to whatever was making Cooper apologize. "What am I missing?" Leo asked.

Claire said something in German.

Sasha responded in the same language, then turned to Leo. "I'll tell you later," she said in English.

Claire cleared her throat. "Okay . . . going back to motive. If not as a warning to those in the courtroom . . . that means it's personal. Leo, can you go over exactly what happened when you confronted Navi again? Maybe we're missing something."

He'd told Neil the details shortly after they discovered Olivia's identity, but he went ahead and repeated the story for the entire team. "There isn't much to tell. I followed him to the restaurant to see who he was meeting."

"Was there any intel on a meeting?"

Leo shook his head. "A hunch. Navi was too quiet. Perfect cousin standing by his family with a shut mouth and not so much as a glare? It didn't feel right."

"Who knew you were going to watch him?" Neil asked.

"No one. My partner and my boss were pissed when they found out."

"So . . . you follow him in. He's having dinner with a woman. Why did you approach him?"

"His bodyguards saw me. I could bow out like a coward or confront the man. Make sure he knew I was watching. I walked in, asked about the food, told him to have a good time, and I left."

"That's it?" Cooper asked.

"By the time I cleared the restaurant, Claire called and told me you had Navi Sobol covered."

"Olivia saw you. Called in," Neil explained.

She more than saw him, they all but ran into each other.

Right in front of the bodyguards. "Olivia was in the restaurant . . . walking out as I was walking in. I stopped her," he said, remembering the scene vividly.

"Why?" Sasha asked.

"I thought she looked familiar." Leo shook his head. "That's when Navi's bodyguards saw me. As Olivia was walking away."

A hush went over the room and the others online.

Sasha said something in German.

Claire and Jax both responded.

"English, ladies!" Lars said with a roll of his eyes.

"Leo wasn't shot," Cooper said for them. "Olivia was. A centimeter in the other direction and she'd be dead."

"So maybe Leo wasn't the target," Claire said.

Sasha shook her head, started again in German.

When no one insisted she speak in English, Leo couldn't help but wonder if the secrets he'd yet to earn his stripes to hear were being discussed.

"Or maybe Navi is a pushy prick and wanted to get back at me for interrupting his evening," Leo said, not willing to accept that Olivia was the one the bullet was intended for.

The alarm on the trip sensors went off, and everyone turned to look at the map. A second set in line with the first sounded off.

"Same two sensors. Neil, when you come, bring some silencers. I'm in need of a hat," Lars told him.

Leo stood, looked around the room. "Since it appears as if I'm about to get asked to leave, I'll go out and reset them."

"Take a radio," Sasha told him.

Leo grabbed one that sat on a charger and left the room.

He looked up the silent stairway and pictured the sleeping woman everyone was talking about.

Who the hell is she?

~

"There is the logical side of your brain and the emotional side."

Olivia sat across from a new doctor. The man had flown in with Neil for the sole purpose of following up on her healing process. After a thirty-minute physical exam, he now sat with her in the sitting room on the upper floor. Leo was beside her while Neil and Pam were across from them.

"The logical," Dr. Falconio said, "is what you're using right now. It's the knowing how to speak without having to learn the language again. It's cooking, driving . . . whatever your normal function is."

"Fighting?" she asked.

"Yes, fighting. If you were a boxer, you'd remember how to box, but maybe forget that you did it for a living. I once knew an emergency medicine doctor who hit his head in a skiing accident. While he was a patient in the ER, he couldn't remember his name or his profession, even though he was in his normal environment. He could read an EKG but couldn't recall why he knew how to do that."

"Did he regain his memories?"

"Yes. The trauma wore off and he went back to normal. But consider the emotional part of the brain. The part that is likely blocking you from remembering who you are or were the day of the shooting. Here you are walking down the street minding your own business and you see someone with a gun. There is an emotional component here that protects the brain. Over time there are triggers . . . like the strong reaction you had when you thought you were threatened. Emotion shot through your system, triggering logic to kick in."

"It wasn't logical for me to attack Sasha."

"It's no different from thinking you see something on the side of the road dart out, and you swerve to get out of the way. You striking out is like swerving out of the way. It was instinctive. Eventually you'll match your logical actions with your emotions, and attacking Sasha or anyone else won't be an issue. Severe head trauma often changes people's personality."

"The extent of my head trauma was a laceration and a headache."

Dr. Falconio shook his head. "The extent was a loss of consciousness, a concussion, and amnesia. Just because you didn't need brain surgery to fix the problem doesn't mean the trauma is less."

All this was nice information, but it wasn't answering her question. "How long is this going to last?"

"Until your brain is ready to accept the mechanism of injury without causing it more harm."

"That was a perfect political answer," Leo said at her side.

Dr. Falconio laughed.

"When your brain is damn good and ready," Pam answered for him.

Dr. Falconio pointed to her. "She's right. Physically, you're doing fine. Your lungs sound good, your wounds and incisions are healing. If you weren't here, I'd send you to physical therapy, start building strength in your left arm and upper body. But you can do those exercises without a professional. Work on you . . . the parts you can control. Maybe try some meditation, write down your thoughts and dreams. If you see a calculator and think you need to use it, use it. Maybe you were an accountant. A piano . . . play it."

She didn't see herself sitting at a desk, but she understood what the man was saying.

"One thing I do know is forcing the memories will only frustrate you. If you remember eating an ice cream at a lake, relax into the memory, but don't try and remember the lake, the day, or the people you were with."

Or who was telling her she couldn't go to class with a broken bone. "I'll try."

"In the meantime, if you have any questions, I'll leave my contact information. Feel free to reach out." He looked at Neil, then back to her.

"Thank you."

"You're welcome."

He stood and looked at his watch.

"Doctor?"

"Yes?"

"Is it possible that I won't get my memory back?"

"There are very few documented cases of permanent loss. Not in cases like yours. And considering you're starting to recall snips and pieces . . . I honestly don't think that is something you should spend time worrying about. Get your strength back." He glanced at Neil again. He signaled to Pam. "Let me go over some PT for her."

The three of them left her and Leo.

After they disappeared downstairs, he twisted his position and rested his arm on the back of the sofa. His hand gently touched her shoulder.

Her mind raced. When would she remember? This couldn't keep going. Every day she opened her eyes, she held her breath and waited. Waited for her brain to kick in and life to return to normal. One where she didn't look at the stranger in the mirror.

"That's not what you wanted to hear," Leo said.

She shook her head. "I want to circle a date on the calendar and know it will all come back."

"He did offer some practical advice. Start a journal. Work on your physical strength."

"I'm glad he said that. Maybe now Pam will lay off." She looked out the window behind them. It had been raining for the better part of the weekend. "When it clears up, I'm taking a hike. I have a feeling that will bring me closer to who I am than plucking away on a calculator."

Leo smiled. "Olivia . . . CPA. I can't see it."

She placed a hand on his knee and pushed off the couch. "I'm going to find a notebook, put it by my bed. If nothing else, maybe I'll write a book about my acid-trip dreams."

"Your what?" Leo stood along with her.

She thought of the hellish landscape and fire that always burned her feet. "Nothing."

He stepped closer, touched her hair.

Olivia looked at his hand, then him. "One kiss and you feel like you can touch me whenever you want?"

He lifted his eyebrows, a smile in his eyes. "I counted three. That last one might even be considered two in one."

It sure could. Mr. FBI knew how to lock her mind down and let her simply feel. The few minutes in his arms made her forget everything going on around her. Flirting with the man had been entertaining. Kissing him pulled her shoulders back and brought out a boldness that felt completely normal. "Stamina is a good thing," she said, teasing.

He placed his hand on the side of her neck, his intentions clear. "Maybe someday I'll show you what I can really do."

She leaned in, stared him in the eye. "Maybe?"

His eyes traveled to her lips.

She placed her hand on his hip as if inviting him. When he leaned in, she let her pinky trace the outline of his arousal before dropping her hand and walking away.

His growl was satisfaction to her ears.

CHAPTER FOURTEEN

Neil and Sasha walked in the misty afternoon while AJ drove the doctor to the airport.

"AJ and I aren't leaving," she announced.

Neil knew better than to argue with the woman. "What's your reasoning?"

She pulled up the edges of her coat, kept talking. "The collarbone break. Those happened all the time at Richter. It was a badge of honor when it happened to you. It showed you went at a sparring match hard or ignored the kick of a gun that was too powerful for you. If Olivia remembers Richter, she's a half a breath from who she really is."

The more he learned about the military boarding school they'd gone to, the more he wanted to return and burn the place down. Although he'd been assured they'd changed their ways, that didn't stop him from sending in one of his people from time to time to check.

"How does her remembering how she broke a bone equate to you and AJ sticking around?"

"I think we need all hands on deck. When her memory comes back, she'll bolt. But will she be pissed that none of us tried to help her remember and come out swinging, or will she slip away?"

Neil had thought of how Olivia would disappear on many sleepless nights. "What does your gut say?"

Sasha shook her head. "Before coming here . . . she'd be like this fog. Here one minute, gone the next. Now? After Leo . . . after eating meals with the group and joking with the guys about seeing her in her underwear? She's softer."

"That was the objective," Neil said.

"But . . ."

Neil glanced over his shoulder, waited for Sasha to continue.

"The feral look in her eyes when she thought she was threatened . . . the way she slammed into *kill or be killed*? That wasn't Olivia. Maybe it's who she'd become since we brought down Richter. I don't know. How often did you see her?"

"I didn't. We spoke over the phone. She refused to meet me in person. That didn't mean I didn't feel her watching me . . . us."

"What do you think about who she had become?"

Neil collected his thoughts before he responded. "I think you're right. Her voice grew colder, harder over the last year. But she was the one reaching out. She wanted the connection. She'll remember that when she's back with us."

"And if she doesn't?"

"We did what we had to. Eventually she'll see that."

"Eventually. But the gut reaction could be violent. And we'd do well to remember that."

Neil had considered that, too. "She wouldn't want to hurt any of us."

"She might not be in control," Sasha said. "That said, AJ and I aren't going anywhere."

~

Leo's shift at the monitors was blissfully short, unlike the rest of the team, who sat down in the situation room six hours at a time. He volunteered for a dinner shift while the rest of the group sat around the dinner table upstairs.

He watched and he listened.

And he started a journal of his own.

In order to determine who Olivia really was, he needed to find clues in the people who knew her.

He started with Sasha, a mysterious woman herself. Leo compared the two.

Both women were fit. While Sasha hadn't tried to fight her way out of a bathroom in her underwear, there was no mistaking the definition in the woman's body when she wore black spandex.

Which she did all the time.

But neither woman resembled a bodybuilder. More like a yogi who could do a handstand using only two fingers.

Leo already knew Olivia was an operative for Neil.

But not really part of the team.

Why?

He wrote a question mark on the page where he wrote his notes.

It wasn't for lack of the team wanting her. Look at what Neil was doing to keep the woman safe, the effort and time all of them were giving up.

Just watching them during dinner made Leo feel like he was watching a family.

Cut from the same cloth.

Neil, Isaac, and Lars . . . all retired military.

AJ . . . husband to Sasha, but how did he fit?

Of all the people in the house, AJ had been the most aloof. It helped that he and Sasha spent most of their time together. But Cooper had apologized after a reference to being facedown in a river. Sasha started talking in German.

Who had ended up facedown? Leo wrote the question and circled it several times.

Leo knew that Sasha and Claire had the same alma mater. Something elite in Germany, but that was the extent of what he knew. Claire accepted Sasha as an aunt, although he knew that was a self-proclaimed title and not given by blood. Claire was an orphan. Neil brought her in and treated her like his daughter. Something Leo and Cooper had spoken of a few times since it was Cooper's intention to ask Claire to marry him and he knew he'd have to ask Neil's permission.

Leo looked closer at the scene in the dining room, making observations. Sasha ate with her fork in her left hand, just like Olivia. Just like every European he'd met.

No one was missing Olivia.

The people who knew her were at the table eating dinner. Was Olivia an orphan as well? Was the school that Sasha and Claire attended a school for orphans?

Leo wished now he'd asked Claire more questions instead of catching a buzz with new friends the last time they all went out for happy hour.

Ultimately the question Leo asked himself many times over was . . . What kind of secrets could Olivia be hiding, therefore Neil and the others hiding for her, that Leo couldn't ignore?

Something unlawful, that was a given.

But what?

~

The weather was turning from wet to cold. The morning fog blanketed the cabin and valley below, and frost had already started to kiss the ground and windows.

There were two fireplaces in the house, one in the grand room and the other in Olivia's bedroom. Leo roped AJ into helping him split some firewood to add to their limited entertainment in the evenings.

The group had gotten into the habit of finishing dinner and pulling out one of the many board games the homeowner had stacked in a closet.

Neil and Sasha were making a run into town for supplies, Olivia and Pam were going through the physical therapy exercises the doctor had left behind well over a week ago, and Lars and Isaac were both in the situation room.

"Why the FBI?" AJ asked after they were in a few logs.

He was setting them up, and Leo was swinging the ax with the intention of trading off.

"I ask myself that question all the damn time," he said with a laugh. But since AJ asked the question and opened up the "get to know me, get to know you" questions, Leo elaborated. "Started out with a love for action flicks."

"Really?" AJ asked.

"Kid you not. There was always a theme . . . military heroes, cops, undercover agents . . . I told my parents I wanted to be a cop." He swung the ax, waited for AJ to push the split logs away and stack a new one.

"What happened to that?"

"Nana. 'Why the hell do you want to work that hard and get paid so little?'" Leo did his best grandmother impersonation. "Since she was the one footing the college bill, and I wasn't ready to go out and adult at eighteen, I went. Took a lot of different classes and eventually ended up with a degree that gave me the opportunity to get a job with the feds."

AJ set up a log, stood back. "Do you like it?"

He nodded. "I do. There's a lot of diversity in my fieldwork."

"Like pretending to be a high school teacher?" AJ asked.

"I tell you what . . . I liked that job." He took a moment to reflect on it. "Early in my career we'd had extensive training on school shootings and profiling potential at-risk kids that do that kind of thing. Some of the videos . . . the stories . . ." Memories of those videos swam in his head. The images . . . the carnage and misery left behind would rip any sane person in half.

"I can't imagine," AJ offered.

"It's awful shit. I found myself asking for casework at the high school level. I thought if I could stop just one kid, just one, from going there, I could go to my grave knowing I'd done something with my life."

"Putting Mykonos away should feel the same."

Leo pulled himself out of his thoughts. "Different, but yes. It does." He took a swing, handed the ax over, moved positions, and switched the subject back to AJ. "What about you? Were you in the military like everyone else here?"

AJ shook his head. "No. I hated all authority growing up."

"How did you end up with Neil?"

"Can't say that I work for Neil. Yeah, I help out when he needs it. Like the night you planted the bug to flush out Claire. I followed you home, gave the intel to Neil."

Claire had infiltrated the school Leo was undercover in, and after a few weeks he became suspicious of her and the people she spent time with. Leo had planted said bug without realizing that her team had cameras watching everything.

"Claire made a convincing teenager," Leo said. "She'd make a great agent."

AJ laughed. "She is . . . just for a different team." He lifted the ax overhead and brought it down hard.

"Is it safe to assume you met Neil through Sasha?" Leo moved the wood, pulled over another log.

"Yup." He didn't elaborate.

Leo stood back. "So if you don't work for Neil, what do you do for a living?"

"I dabble in some investigative endeavors."

Leo laughed. "Okay, Mr. Cryptic."

AJ didn't apologize or clarify. "Truth is, Sasha and I really don't have to work. I, too, had a grandmother. She had money. Sasha has a fair amount. So we pitch in when Neil needs a hand. It's philanthropic without giving away money."

Leo hadn't expected that answer. "Neither one of you are getting paid to be here?"

"Does that surprise you?"

Hell yes. But then he saw how this team worked. "I guess not."

"Why should the mafia be the only ones with extended families you'd do anything for?" AJ asked.

"Good point." Leo liked the concept, although he'd never seen a mafia-like family be anything but criminal. "So do Lars and Isaac get paid?"

"Oh yeah. Claire, Cooper, Jax. Neil has a lot of people on payroll. But if they all won the lottery tomorrow, they'd still pitch in."

Another log. Another cut.

"That's saying something about the boss."

"It's about the work, too. Bringing down Mykonos? Who wouldn't want to see a dirtbag like that get what he deserves?"

Leo peeled off his jacket when AJ handed over the ax.

"I have a question for you," AJ said.

"Go for it."

"I seem to remember a child's room in your decoy apartment. What was that about?"

Leo brought the ax up in both hands. "Part of the disguise. A single new teacher would likely socialize with his colleagues more than a bitter divorced man with a son. My older sister has a son. My nephew offered a lot of fodder for a single father. I kept a couple pictures of him on my phone when people asked."

"I thought it was strange that I didn't see any photographs in the apartment."

"You went into my place?"

AJ looked at the sky. "Not in a 'breaking and entering' kind of way."

Leo pinned him with a stare.

"Slightly wiggling a lock. Besides, we weren't sure you were legit at the time."

Leo smiled, swung the ax. "Nothing I wouldn't do."

"We know."

He laughed. "What about you? Do you have siblings?"

AJ paused. "Had. Sister. But she's gone."

Leo let the head of the ax rest on the forest floor. "I'm sorry."

"It's been a long time."

But not so long that AJ didn't have that look of grief in his eye. "I'm guessing this is what had Cooper apologizing the other night."

AJ looked at him. "Why do I get the feeling I've just been interviewed?"

Leo shrugged. "It's hard to be cooped up in the same space without information exchanging hands. I've determined a lot of things about all of you. None of which strikes me as irreversible criminal activity. If anything, it seems as if you all have justifiable reasons for your actions. Maybe someday my character will prove I'm worthy of knowing everything."

AJ opened his mouth right as the sound of a gunshot rippled through the air.

They instantly crouched and ran to the side of the house for cover.

Leo reached for his weapon as adrenaline shot through his system like wildfire. "Sounded like a shotgun," he said.

Leo took the lead and motioned for AJ to follow him back into the house.

A second shot echoed through the forest, the location of the weapon difficult to determine. Not that either of them wanted to stay in anyone's range to figure it out.

Leo pushed through the downstairs door, and they both scrambled inside.

Isaac stood at the bank of monitors scrolling through the feeds. "Where is it coming from?" Leo asked.

"All of our circuits are clear." Isaac pushed his glasses farther up his nose and started typing. They heard a third shot.

Leo's entire body stood on alert.

A noise from the floor above made him look up. "Where is Olivia?"

Isaac pointed to one of the cameras.

Olivia and Pam were in Pam's room, both sitting on the floor behind the bed and away from the windows.

Lars stood by their door, a weapon in hand.

Another shot.

"I don't think it's on the property," Isaac said, punching keys.

"Might be a local hunting off-season."

"Four shots?" Leo asked.

AJ lifted his hands. "Target shooting?"

A radio on the desk crackled, Lars's voice came through. "Any idea what's going on?"

A fifth shot and three sets of monitors set off alarms one after the other.

"Something is running fast," AJ said. He moved to the weapons room and grabbed a rifle.

Leo turned toward the stairs. "Better view up there."

Isaac lifted a hand. "Hold up."

The sensors around the house sounded, and a running deer dashed by one of the outdoor cameras.

Isaac pushed around AJ and grabbed a drone from a shelf. "I bet it's some yahoo screwing around."

They heard another shot, not any closer than the last.

Leo started to loosen his grip on his weapon.

Isaac turned on the drone and set it right outside the door. Back inside, he moved to the computer, pressed a few keys, and grabbed the remote for the drone.

The phone on the desk rang.

AJ put it on speaker.

"What's the situation?" Neil's voice boomed over the line.

"We're all safe," Leo started. "Six shots fired. Sounds like a shotgun. No evidence that they are aiming at us. Isaac is sending up an aerial view now. How far out are you?"

"Fifteen minutes."

The camera on the drone fed the center monitor.

The cabin quickly came into view. Isaac circled to catch anything close by.

The firewood and discarded ax lay right where Leo and AJ had abandoned them.

"The deer was running from the north," Leo said.

Isaac moved the drone in that direction.

The mist in the air accumulated on the lens, but not so much that they couldn't see the woods below.

Another shot fired, this one sounding farther away.

Leo kept his eyes on the images flashing by the drone.

Isaac held the drone in place on the edge of the property line.

"Can it go up any more?" Leo asked.

Isaac brought it higher, spun the camera.

A flash of movement caught his eye.

"There," Leo said, pointing at the monitor.

Isaac positioned the drone and focused the camera.

"Talk to me?" Neil said over the phone.

Leo had forgotten he was still there. "Looks like an old truck, a Ford," Leo told Neil.

Isaac zoomed in on the plate, and AJ wrote it down.

Abandoning the gun he'd grabbed from the closet, AJ sat at a computer and typed. "I'm sending the license plate number to headquarters now," AJ announced.

Leo and Isaac looked at the movement on the screen at the same time. Isaac reported as he moved the drone closer.

"Two males. Young, wearing green camo and shouldering shotguns."

Both men looked up at the same time.

Isaac snapped a picture.

"They see the drone."

Leo shook his head as the young boys started running toward the truck.

"Isaac was right. Looks like a couple of kids out shooting for fun." Leo put his weapon away.

Leo heard relief in Neil's voice. "Follow protocol. Sasha and I will return after we visit the owner of the truck."

When Leo left the situation room, Isaac was still following the truck with the drone, and AJ was talking to someone on Neil's team in Los Angeles.

Leo found Olivia and Pam halfway down the stairs with Lars at their side.

"Target shooting? Really?" Pam questioned.

"Or deer hunting."

Leo opened his arms to Olivia when she hit the bottom step.

She moved into them and rested her head on his shoulder. "You okay?" he asked.

"Surprisingly," she said, her voice even.

"Probably good this happened. Keeps us on our toes."

Leo hugged Olivia tighter before letting her go. "I'd prefer your bandit raccoons over gunshots."

"Me too," Olivia said.

The two of them looked at each other.

Although Olivia seemed calm, there was a twitch in her eyes, the way she was blinking, that told him she wasn't unaffected. "Let's make some coffee."

She agreed with a nod.

CHAPTER FIFTEEN

Olivia's feet sunk into the moist ground and made sucking noises as she stepped out of the mud. "There isn't one self-respecting animal that is going to come within a half a mile of us," she declared.

Sasha walked beside her, one of the rare occasions that the two of them spent any time alone. The local kids who had been out shooting for the fun of it had been found and reprimanded. Neil let the boys know that shooting on or near the property would result in charges in the future. He didn't want them suspicious of what was going on at the log home, but didn't want them coming back and getting caught in crossfire.

The excitement had lasted for quite a while. But eventually Olivia's daily walks resumed, and now she and Sasha were strolling through the forest without much care that they were going to get shot.

"We're not trying to be Cinderella and collect pets."

The reference wasn't lost on her, which was a nice change.

They walked a few more yards. "I think we're in for snow by the end of the week."

Sasha nodded. "Maybe sooner."

They passed a set of sensors, something Olivia had spotted on her first walk off the driveway path. "Those will have to be changed out before the weather shifts," she said, pointing.

"It's on the list. The men will get on it tomorrow."

That's good, she thought. Although after a snowfall they'd be able to see if anyone was walking around.

"Are you feeling stronger?" Sasha asked after several more yards.

"Yes and no. I'm doing the exercises and the pain is getting better, but there's a part of me that keeps telling me to do more." She looked up and saw a perfect climbing tree. "Like that. My head is telling me to get up there and look around."

Sasha nodded. "I understand that desire. Probably not the best idea for you right now."

"You don't think it's odd that I have a longing to climb a tree? I'm not twelve."

Sasha looked up. "The view would be better."

Olivia laughed as they walked past the tree.

"Tell me, why don't you carry a weapon?"

"Don't need it."

"You're not afraid someone could be out here watching? Someone with a gun?"

"If I thought someone was out here with a weapon pointed at us, we wouldn't be out here." Sasha's tone was even and without emotion.

That was fair. "Do you believe there is *anyone* looking for me? For Leo?"

"It's a possibility. Maybe when you get your memory back you'll lead us to the shooter."

"And if I don't? If I didn't see a face? How long does this isolation go on?"

Sasha shook her head, kept her eyes on the landscape in front of them. "We will deal with that when it happens."

"Waste of time speculating, I guess." Olivia reached down and picked up a long stick that had been on the ground long enough to lose all its foliage. She tested the weight and twirled it around like a baton a couple of times.

Sasha looked at her briefly, then diverted her attention.

Olivia used the stick to walk a few feet before abandoning it.

She heard Sasha sigh.

"I picked something up for you when we were in town," Sasha told her. From her coat pocket she removed a bag.

Olivia took it and glanced inside. And then she started laughing. "Is it that obvious?"

"Were you trying to be discreet? Because if that's the case, you suck at it."

Olivia folded the edges of the bag that held a box of condoms and put it in her pocket. "Leo's a good man."

"But he's still a man, and eventually he's going to take you up on your offer," Sasha pointed out.

She knew that, too. "It's reckless."

"It's human. And when all this is behind us, you won't want complications."

"Which is your way of saying that Leo and I are temporary." Why did that sound like nails on a chalkboard?

"Do you feel it's more?"

"I don't know. I have nothing to compare it to. I know I've seduced men, but can't see a single face. I know the mechanics behind using these condoms, but couldn't tell you the name of whoever popped my cherry. Do you have any idea how frustrating that is?"

"No. On the bright side, you block out any of the bad sex you've had."

Olivia laughed. "I think that's the first joke I've heard come out of your mouth."

"I'm serious."

And that was hysterical.

"If it's more than *just sex*, you'll know it," Sasha said.

"Is that how it was with AJ?"

Sasha hedged. "I was definitely using him for sex."

Yeah, sure. It was more than that. "And then . . . ?"

"He challenged me. Intrigued me. In my head, I told myself it was only sex. You don't have to have amnesia to not be in control of your emotions."

This was more of a conversation than Olivia thought she'd ever have with the woman. She liked it. It started out dry and awkward but now felt like an honest exchange. "You two look tight."

"We are. Caring for someone is always a risk. But the best things in life are on the other side of fear. I never thought I'd say those words, let alone believe them. But between AJ and this team . . ." Sasha smiled briefly.

"You didn't believe in love?"

A quick shake of her head. "Wasn't how I was raised."

Silence stretched in front of them. "It doesn't feel normal to me. The seduction, yes . . . that feels, well, good."

"I hope so," Sasha muttered.

They both chuckled.

"But the other parts. He holds my hand, Sasha. Sometimes just one finger as we're walking. At first I was . . . 'What the hell is this?' Certainly someone has held my hand before. Why does it feel so awkward?"

"Maybe they haven't? I'd had my share of sex before I met AJ, and the only handholding was in the moment."

"I hadn't considered that."

They reached the edge of the property and turned around.

"I didn't expect this conversation with you," Olivia admitted.

Sasha nodded in agreement. "That makes two of us."

~

Olivia sat in an overstuffed chair, legs tucked under her with a notepad in her lap.

Leo was on her right, taking up the edge of a sofa, a laptop perched on his knees.

To his right, Isaac worked on a crossword puzzle.

Neil scowled with a computer in his lap. Whatever he was working on was not bringing him joy.

The others were scattered throughout the house.

Or maybe Sasha and AJ disappeared in an effort to not be disturbed with a stash of condoms of their own.

The afternoon conversation with Sasha rolled around in Olivia's head. It had been a long time since she'd had a heart-to-heart with a woman. Even without being able to quantify that, she knew the conversation with Sasha was rare. It didn't matter that she didn't remember her life before someone in an SUV drove by, pointed a gun at her, and squeezed the trigger. Deep inside where her body knew her past, her soul knew where she'd come from . . . that part of her knew that the Sasha moment was unique.

So Olivia sat on a chair in front of a roaring fire with three men she hardly knew, one she wanted to know better . . . and wrote in a diary.

Even that felt unique.

But writing down her thoughts was helping them form.

And she wrote down everything.

Neil was pissed. Whatever he was doing on his computer . . . whatever conversation he was having was causing stress deep in his veins.

Isaac vacillated between bored and amused. Every once in a while, he'd concentrate a little harder and become amused again.

Leo . . . The man was harder to read. How was that possible? Shouldn't the man whose tongue she had had in her mouth come in loud and clear? He was working on something. And whatever that something was he was contemplating . . . it was frustrating the hell out of him.

And because Leo was the glitch in her system, she started with Neil.

"Do you want to talk about why you're growling at your computer?" she asked.

He looked at her . . . hesitated. "Gwen just told me Emma has been asked to the winter formal."

Isaac started laughing. Slowly. A sharp staccato that indicated pure joy.

"And?" Leo asked.

That question was met with a death stare.

"She's too young," Neil said.

"She's in high school," Isaac reminded him.

Another death stare.

Olivia scribbled the note . . . *protective of his own.*

"Have you met the boy?" Leo asked.

"No."

"When is the dance?" Olivia asked.

Neil typed on his computer and paused.

They all waited, breath held . . .

"Three weeks. Gwen is talking about dresses."

Again . . . Isaac started with the short bursts of laughter.

"What's the problem?" Olivia asked. She knew the problem. Daddy wasn't ready for his little girl to have big-girl dates. But she asked the question anyway.

"You wouldn't understand."

Olivia retreated. The man wasn't ready for the next thought. Dates led to kissing . . . kissing led to sex.

She glanced at Leo.

He smiled her way.

"Russian World War II gun?" Isaac said, waving the crossword puzzle in his hand. "There's a *k* in it."

Olivia laughed. "There's a *k* in every Russian word."

Isaac lifted the book of puzzles in his hands. "It's a weapon. Mosin-Nagant is the only Russian World War II gun I know."

"Tokarev," she said.

Isaac put his pencil to the puzzle and smiled.

Olivia looked down at her notebook. Several seconds ticked and she looked up.

The weight of the room fell on her.

Her first eye contact was with Leo.

Something inside his eyes clicked.

Isaac moved quickly back to his puzzle, his index finger pushing his glasses higher on his nose.

Neil blew out a breath.

Something was there. Tickling. "Tokarev. It came in both a pistol and a rifle. Semiautomatic rifle. But the bolt-action Mosin-Nagant . . ." Statistics played in her head like it would on a documentary. War weapons. Russian, German, American.

They were all there as if they had been all the time.

She stood, her notebook tossed aside, and she marched toward the dining room hutch where she knew a rifle was hidden.

She grabbed the AR-15 from where it had been stashed and put it on the island in the kitchen.

Once there it took less than fifteen seconds for her to clear the chamber and disassemble the gun, leaving it utterly useless.

She stood looking at the shambles and pieces of a weapon that could remove every heartbeat from the room.

And she started to shake.

How did she know this?

She closed her eyes and tried to capture where she'd learned what she'd just done.

When she looked up, all three men stared.

Neil's expression was stoic.

Isaac's concerned.

Leo's . . . confused.

She left the fieldstripped weapon where it lay, returned to the living room, grabbed her notebook, and left without a word.

In her room, she tossed her notes on the bed and walked into the bathroom. Leaning on the edge of the sink, she found her reflection in the mirror.

Every single thing that had "come" to her in the past month was just like the AR. Knowledge without reference. Where had she learned to pull apart a gun she couldn't ever remember seeing in the past? How did she know the name of a World War II weapon, let alone one made in Russia?

Who the hell was she?

Seconds ticked into minutes, and all she could do was stare at her reflection. A sharp rap on her door brought her back. She turned the water on cold and splashed her face in an effort to wake herself up.

She patted her face dry, moved into the bedroom, and opened the door.

Leo stood on the other side. "Are you okay?"

She shook her head and turned away from him, leaving the door open.

He followed her in, closed it behind him.

After crawling up onto her bed, she tucked her legs in and retrieved her notebook. "How did I know how to do that? And why do I know about Russian war guns?"

"What do you remember?" he asked instead of trying to answer her questions.

"Guns." She closed her eyes and envisioned weapons of all shapes, sizes, makes, and models. "There is a list a mile long in here," she said, pointing to her head. "All the calibers and capabilities. Which ones are reliable and which ones would be better off used as a kickstand on a bicycle. None of that information was there twenty minutes ago."

Leo attempted a smile. "This is good. It means you're remembering."

"Weapons?" she asked. "Okay, if I was an agent like you, maybe that makes sense. But . . ." Wait . . . was she? "Am I?"

"A federal agent?" he clarified.

145

She nodded.

"No. Not unless you're really deep undercover."

"So . . . maybe."

He sat on the edge of the bed, shifted a knee so he faced her. "What do you know about the FBI?"

Olivia pulled her thoughts inward. "You investigate crimes, terrorism, civil . . . organized crime, obviously. Threats to the United States, foreign and domestic, right?"

"Yeah. Can you think of any specifics? Something that would indicate you're working undercover?"

She sat up a little taller, thinking for the first time that maybe she was onto something here. And Leo wasn't completely disregarding her train of thought.

"Let's look at the facts." She opened her notebook and looked over her notes. "I was in Vegas. Wasn't carrying a purse or any identification. No one came searching for me." She glanced up. "If I was undercover, all of that fits."

Leo placed a hand on his chest. "If I went missing, my department would investigate. Hospitals and morgues would be the first things they check."

"Yes, but how much time would you have before they realized you were gone? You check in every week here, but . . ."

He shrugged. "There are times the assignment keeps you silent longer, but weekly check-ins are more common."

"Is anyone looking for me now? We're going on nearly two months since I dodged the reaper."

Leo cringed. "I don't like when you say it that way."

"It's true. I'm lucky to be alive. I know that. And I'm strangely at peace that I was shot. Almost as if I was expecting it. Doesn't that sound like something you'd say?" she asked. "If you woke up in the hospital and Neil was looking down at you . . . 'You were shot, next time duck faster,'" she said in a lower voice in an attempt to sound more like Neil.

Leo slowly started to nod. "I can't deny what you're suggesting."

She pointed to the closed door of her room. "What I just did out there, with the AR. I have weapons training."

"Do you remember shooting a gun?"

She blinked several times. "No, but I know I have."

"I'm trained in firearms, but I know nothing about what the Russians carried during the war," he admitted.

"But I would bet there are plenty of people in the FBI that do."

He shifted his position, and she could see his mind working through her suggestions. "Not impossible."

"I attacked Sasha. Punching, blocking." Olivia's thoughts shifted to her walk earlier that day. "And when we were out today, I picked up a stick. Just a stick . . . but after I tossed it on the ground, I kept thinking I could use it to defend myself."

"That's a skill set I don't have," he said.

She leaned forward, placed a hand on his knee. "I think I might be onto something." And for the first time, the fog felt as if it were lifting ever so slightly.

"There might be a different explanation."

She smiled. "But we can't rule this one out." She wondered if there was a boss out there wondering what the hell happened to her. That thought stilled inside her. Like a dead end. "Do we ask your people if they're missing someone?"

"My department has been trying to figure out who you are since this happened. We came up completely empty."

She patted his knee. "If I was undercover, that would make sense."

"Yes, but eventually there are breakthroughs," Leo said. "Very few people go undetected in this world."

Something about this felt so right. And then she had a sobering thought. "If I'm right about this, then maybe you weren't the target, and I was all along."

"I'm not prepared to release that guilt quite yet."

Olivia couldn't help but smile. "Let me guess, you're Catholic."

He shrugged. "Only on Sunday when my grandmother is looking."

"Leo, this feels right."

He covered her hand with his. "I don't think it's going to be long before it all comes in clear."

CHAPTER SIXTEEN

Leo left her alone when she stopped talking to him, retreated into her notebook, and started writing down a long list of weapons and her knowledge about them.

What he saw of that list was downright terrifying.

He wanted to confront Neil, make the man level with him. But as she was ticking off all the ways she mimicked an undercover agent, Leo was ticking off a list of his own.

She was an operative. She worked for Neil. She knew about Navi and the case. Neil did not want Leo to know her true identity because why? Because Olivia wasn't as innocent as the others? And how innocent were the others?

He'd looked up AJ Hoffman and found out why the man bucked authority as a child. AJ's father was a politician, an ambassador to Germany. As Leo followed that bouncing ball, he uncovered a family photograph along with names. And an obituary for Amelia Hoffman, who had been found facedown on the bank of a river. As Leo dug, he found that someone had been arrested for the murder in Germany, but the who or why wasn't on any public database. The fact that Neil's team didn't want to discuss it with him suggested it was connected to Olivia somehow.

Did she know something about AJ's sister's death?

If Leo could remotely tap into the FBI database, he could get the answers. But that wasn't possible with the current setup they were using. Not without being detected, which would defeat the purpose of staying off the radar.

But the big question after today was what Olivia had uncovered herself.

Maybe the shooter wasn't aiming at Leo.

And if that was the case, Neil and his team suspected it all along. In fact, they implied she had been the target, but Leo refused to see it.

So who would want Olivia dead?

Navi?

Did the man even know Olivia was in play?

If not Navi, or someone on Mykonos's side, then who and why?

And this was where Leo and Neil were in the same position. Neither one of them knew for sure who the shooter was, or who hired them.

But in order for Leo to find that answer, he first needed to know exactly who Olivia was.

The action flicks that had prompted his path to the FBI had started to spin in the back of his head. Reminding him that sometimes the good guys were the bad guys. And the bad guys did good things. And wasn't that the fine line Neil and his people treaded? And if Olivia was a part of the team, but at arm's length . . . had she crossed that line? And, and, and!

Leo moved to the window in his room and peered into the darkness, his mind racing. Neil asked the team to respect Leo's position and Olivia's privacy. If Olivia did in fact cross the line, and Leo was told about it . . . then him staying silent about said line meant he grabbed her hand and jumped over that line with her.

Even though he didn't want to be put in that position, he knew he was going to work overtime to uncover every last detail of Olivia's past.

It was hard to imagine her as anything other than what he was seeing right then. A resilient, caring, sensual, confident woman who intrigued him first with her looks and then with the sheer mystery of what made her into the person she was. And yes, the chemistry was driving him straight to a cold shower several nights a week.

There wasn't a lot of privacy in the house, which was probably a good thing. Especially now that Olivia was no longer convalescing and starting to thrive. The looks she cast his way, the teasing touch when she didn't think anyone else would notice . . . the sensual, playful side of the woman had Leo looking forward to every morning and every moment with her.

Since their initial lip-lock in the kitchen, they'd all but abstained from physical touch.

Well, except that one moment where he'd pressed her up against a tree in the woods while they were alone on a walk. So much heat and friction . . . they were both breathless when they stopped and stared into each other's eyes.

Her breath was heavy on her lips . . . swollen from his kiss. "You're making it hard to resist," *she whispered.*

"Me? You're the one dragging your foot up my leg under the dinner table."

A proud smile washed up her face. "I like watching you try to keep it together."

He pulled her hips flush with his, enjoyed the spark in her eyes with the contact. "I think you're trying to make me choke on my food."

"We're both consenting adults . . . Why again are we resisting what's going on?" she asked.

The answer for him was easy. "I don't want to hurt you."

She glanced down at her chest. "I think I'm past that."

He placed his hand on her face, made her look at him. "You don't know who you are, and the last thing I want is for you to have any morning-after regrets."

"The more I get to know you, the less I feel that's possible," she whispered.

"The more I get to know you, the more important it is for me that you're in the right place when this does happen." He'd be a fool to think it wasn't going to.

She teased him with her hands. "I'm not opposed to tying you up."

Why did that excite him?

"I have a feeling it won't be the first time I've tied up a man."

"You're a dangerous woman."

She leaned up, her lips close to his. "I'm worth the risk."

Leo shook the memory from his head.

He removed his cell phone from his back pocket and opened up his photos.

Olivia had stopped and picked up a pine cone on their walk back, and Leo snapped a few pictures of her. When she caught him, he turned the phone around and took a picture of the both of them.

They looked relaxed. Considering what had brought them together, the image felt like such a contradiction.

"We look good together," he'd told her.

She accused him of being sentimental. Something no other woman before her had done.

He'd likely have plenty of time to ponder the why of that at another time.

But for now, he needed to determine who the woman was behind the picture.

~

"Even I can't steal any more of your money," Pam told Neil, her duffel bag next to his by the door.

"I'm happy to keep you on longer."

Olivia watched the two arguing over her.

"You needed me for two weeks tops. And even that was a stretch. It's been a hell of a lot longer than that. I'm flying back with you." Pam didn't give him any room for argument. She turned to Leo and opened her arms.

Leo stepped in and hugged her goodbye. "Take care of her."

Olivia laughed. "*Her* can take care of herself."

Pam scowled over Leo's shoulder at Olivia.

She moved on to Isaac, who hugged her briefly, patting her sides. "Much as I tried to fatten you up, it looks like I failed."

"Maybe the next time," she teased.

When Pam turned to Lars, her smile was a tad softer, and their hug lasted a little longer. She said something in his ear that none of them heard, and then Lars locked his lips to hers.

Olivia's jaw dropped, unable to look away.

How had she missed this?

Pam stepped back. "Call me when you're back in town, sailor." She turned away, and Lars patted her ass.

"What the . . . ?" Olivia started.

"Oh, shut up," Pam said. The older woman pulled Olivia into an awkward hug and let go quickly. "You know how to get ahold of me if you need me, you stubborn bitch."

"You loved every minute of it." Olivia glanced at Lars. "Apparently more than I realized."

Pam's humor softened. "Take care of yourself. And always remember that there are people out there who care about you."

Olivia felt a strange pull in her chest. "Thank you. For everything."

Pam shook away whatever emotion she was starting to show and turned to Neil. "Let's go, big guy. I hate snow, and this place is about to get dumped on."

"Did you say goodbye to AJ and Sasha?" Isaac asked.

"We're all good." Pam picked up her bag. "Till next time," she said before heading out the door.

Neil grabbed his bag. "I'll be back in two days."

Isaac's short staccato laugh had all of them chuckling. The reason Neil was leaving in the first place was to meet the guy who wanted to date his daughter.

"Try not to threaten the boy," Lars told Neil.

Isaac's laughter grew.

"Neil doesn't have to say a word," Olivia teased.

He drew in a breath, let it out slowly. Neil's eyes fell on her. "You know how to get ahold of me."

Not that she needed to, with everyone else in the house. "You'll be back so soon we won't have a chance to notice you're gone."

He glanced at Leo and then left.

Isaac's laugh became contagious. "That poor kid."

Olivia moved to Lars's side and nudged her shoulder to his. "What was all that with Pam?"

He shrugged, looked between her and Leo. "Some of us are better at hiding what's going on than others."

Isaac just kept laughing as he walked away.

The sound of the SUV pulling out of the driveway brought Olivia to the window. She was going to miss the cantankerous, pushy woman. But she had been given her phone number and could see herself reaching out at some point.

Leo walked to the front door and grabbed his coat. "I'm going to bring in some more firewood."

"I'll help," Lars offered.

"I'll curl up on the couch and be a girl," she said.

Lars laughed. "I never thought I'd hear you say that."

Olivia found herself blinking several times at his words. Something about the way he said them . . . or maybe the words themselves.

Leo opened the door, and a rush of freezing air blew in.

Pam was right. Snow was coming.

Olivia welcomed it.

The quiet, peace, and cleansing of the landscape.

She was ready for a change in seasons.

~

Not again.

Blistering pain burned Olivia's bare feet. The craters dug into her skin by hell's surface were so deep that the sound of her own blood and flesh sucking against the fire and brimstone deafened her ears.

Somewhere in her mind, her conscious self was telling her to wake up. That the pain would go away if she just opened her eyes.

But it felt as if some kind of drug was weighing her down and stopping her from so much as turning her head.

The sound of the fire crackling, the smell of her flesh . . .

"Where are my goddamn shoes?"

She looked down and stared at her left hand.

Dangling from the tips of her fingers was a pair of sneakers.

The sight of them crushed her. All along . . . they'd been there all along and yet she walked all over hell without them on her feet.

She lifted them to eye level and started to cry.

With each tear the shoes melted from the heat of the fire, dripping . . . one oozing inch at a time.

"No!"

"Over here."

A voice called behind her.

She turned to find a line in the surface where hell disappeared and cold stone and wooden cases filled with books took its place.

It had been there all along. Only one foot in the opposite direction and she didn't have to have the pain.

"C'mon, Olivia. We don't want to get caught."

The voice belonged to a boy.

Young, energized.

"Take your shoes off so no one will hear," he told her.

She looked at her hands, her shoes nothing but bits of plastic melted together. One foot in front of the other, she made her way out of the fire, her feet sloshing on the polished floors of the library.

"We're going to get caught," she said. But she wasn't speaking in English.

"Only if you keep talking."

Then a hand slammed over her mouth, and she tried to scream.

CHAPTER SEVENTEEN

Leo had made a habit out of sitting in the room on the upper floor surrounded by bedrooms.

He would wait for the light under Olivia's door to turn off, and then give it a good hour before heading to bed himself.

Neil's words about how the woman would leave the second she gained her memories were a constant threat. *"You won't see it, you won't sense it . . . she'll just be gone."*

The thought scared the living hell out of him.

He cared for her.

Probably more than he should. But his brain and his heart were in the middle of a war, and his dick was taking sides.

He closed his laptop, set it aside, and stared out the window. Snow had started to fall right before the house quieted for the night. Bets were placed on how much would accumulate before they woke up in the morning.

Leo imagined Olivia lying down to make a snow angel. Entirely too soft for her, she'd much more likely be hiding behind a tree with an arsenal of snowballs ready to catch you as you walked by.

He smiled into the image, and then he heard her.

Olivia shouted from her room.

Leo jumped up and over the sofa and was at her door in seconds.

He pushed it open, heard footsteps behind him.

She was alone, in her bed . . . asleep.

A rush of words he couldn't understand came out from the obvious nightmare.

Isaac looked over Leo's shoulder.

He lifted a hand, realizing the threat was only in Olivia's head. "I've got this."

Isaac sighed, turned to the camera facing them in the hall, and shook his head. "We're good."

Leo moved into the room and closed the door behind him. He moved to the edge of her bed and sat at her side.

"Olivia?" he whispered.

Her hands were clenched, brow furrowed. Her words sharp. At first, he thought she was just muttering gibberish, then he recognized the sounds.

German.

Olivia was speaking German in her sleep.

He placed a hand on her shoulder. "Olivia? Wake up. You're having a nightmare."

She thrashed.

He said her name louder, and the next thing he realized, her hands darted up, straight to his neck, and he was on his back on the floor with her hovering over him.

Leo grabbed her wrists and squeezed out her name. "'Livia."

Her eyes were stark-raving wild. And he was having serious difficulty breathing.

Something snapped inside of her, and her hands jolted off his neck almost as quickly as they'd clasped on.

"Oh my God."

The door to the room flew open.

"What the hell is going on?"

Isaac's image at the door cleared through the fuzz in Leo's brain.

"I'm sorry." Olivia pulled her hair back, looked at his neck. "Did I hurt you?"

"Leo?" Isaac said.

Sasha and Lars had joined the party.

"I'm okay," he coughed. "She woke up confused."

"Olivia? Are you all right?" Sasha asked.

Olivia's chest rose and fell with rapid breaths. She sat back, her body still straddling Leo's. "I'm fine."

Not that she sounded convinced.

"Leo?"

He dropped his hands to his side. "I'm good. We're good."

"Okay, boys. Show's over." Sasha ushered the others away and closed the door.

Olivia shifted her weight off his body. Her butt hit the floor, and her back moved to the side of the bed.

"What is wrong with me?"

Leo pushed himself up until he was sitting beside her.

He noticed a bottle of water on her bedside table and reached for it. Once the water went down the right pipe, giving him some assurance that nothing inside was broken, he returned what was left to the nightstand.

"I scared you. It's okay."

"It's not okay."

"Maybe it's not normal . . . but it is okay."

"I was dreaming."

"It sounded more like a nightmare. I heard you from the other room and came in to check. When you didn't wake up right away, I nudged you."

She leaned her head back, closed her eyes. "I was in hell. Burning flesh and piercing rocks. And then I was in the stacks at school. We were trying not to get caught. Then someone came behind me and put a hand over my mouth. And then I'm kneeling over you trying to break your windpipe."

He reached over and clasped her cold hand in his. "Just a dream."

"I could have hurt you."

"You didn't."

She squeezed his hand back. "I could have."

Yeah . . . Leo would never underestimate her ability to lay him flat if she wanted to.

"What are the stacks?" he asked, picking apart her dream.

She sighed. "The bookshelves in the library. We called them the stacks." Olivia held her breath, looked at him. "Oh my God, Leo. I remember the library at school. There was a boy. It was late . . . everyone was asleep. We went there to make out."

"Was this a dream or a memory?" he asked.

She blinked several times, something he'd started to notice more and more as she was searching her thoughts. Almost like a blinking cursor on a computer letting you know it was ready for its next command.

"Both . . . I think."

"You called the library the stacks. Why?"

"The shelves were massive, floor to ceiling. The library was huge. Not Harry Potter huge, but vast. Old. The smell of old books and oiled wood. And fire."

"That sounds more like a bad dream."

She nodded. "The fire, yes. That dream is the same every time, but the stacks and the boy . . . that felt familiar."

"Do you remember his name?"

She shook her head.

He held his breath. "What about the school?"

She placed her fingertips on her head. "It's right there. So damn close."

He released a breath. Frustrated for her, but thankful at the same time. *If she doesn't remember, she won't leave when no one was looking.*

Her hand fell on top of his.

She smiled and climbed back over on him, her legs straddling his. "I do remember my first kiss." She wore a T-shirt and panties . . . and nothing else.

His body was uninterested in her words and much more excited about the weight of her resting on top of him.

"Is that so?" he asked.

"It was wet and sloppy."

Leo relaxed his grip and rested his hands on her hips. "Did you give him a second chance?" he asked.

She blinked a few times. "I don't know. Probably not."

For whatever reason, that made him smile. "Do it right or move along?"

Both her hands came up to his neck, gently this time. "I am sorry." She leaned forward and kissed where she'd placed her hands.

"Did you mean to try and hurt me?" he asked, knowing the answer.

"No."

"Then your apology isn't necessary."

She stopped kissing his neck long enough to look him in the eye. "Stealing my lines?"

"Maybe."

She inched over, kissed the other side.

The soft slide of her tongue brought the spark in his belly he'd grown to expect any time they'd touched before.

His fingers dug into her hips when she grazed her teeth on the edge of his ear.

"Your kiss isn't wet or sloppy," she whispered.

"I guess that means I get another chance." He turned his head, and she was right there, leaning into him.

Her lips were hot, open, and she pressed into him as if she could absorb him with a kiss.

His hands fanned inside her T-shirt and up her bare back, careful not to touch the scar she'd recently obtained. Did she even notice it anymore? Would he ever be able to hold her and not think about her lying on the dirty streets of Las Vegas? He wanted to take all that pain away. Give her something in return. Maybe this was it. This moment together. He had no power to resist her, not like this with her squeezing her thighs into his hips as they kissed, his erection painfully pressing against the zipper of his jeans.

He wanted to touch more . . . feel more.

And sitting on the hard floor was not going to work for what he wanted to do for her.

He dropped his hands to her hips and started to lift her off.

"We're not stopping," she demanded, her breath hot on his cheek.

"Not unless you tell me to."

She smiled and moved to her feet.

The very core of her was eye level, her panties outlining her sex.

He heard her chuckle. "What are you looking at, Mr. FBI?"

He leaned forward, placed his mouth on her through the thin material between her legs.

Olivia stopped laughing, her hand falling on top of his head.

He reached for the soft globes of her butt and pulled her closer. The scent of her, the heat . . . he wanted more of this.

Her knees buckled just enough.

Leo pulled away, kissed his way up her body as he stood. He stopped at her navel and let her shirt fall back down.

"Are you sure about this?" he asked once he was standing over her.

"I think we've danced around this party long enough . . . don't you?"

There was no way this was going to end well, but he couldn't stop himself. No, he didn't want to stop himself. This beautiful, vibrant woman . . . the person he knew right then, was diamonds and light and asking to be touched. Whoever she'd been before didn't matter.

They both had a past, and she knew no more about his than she did about hers. So what did it matter?

"You're beautiful," he told her.

"You're stalling." She reached for the button of his jeans.

He shook his head, turned her around so her back was to the bed. "No. I just want you to know that this means something to me."

That teasing smile dimmed, just a little, and her eyelids started to blink. And then she sighed, reached for his face. "I don't remember anyone I've slept with."

He liked that. "Do you think you're a virgin?" At first he thought it was a joke . . . then he paused.

Olivia looked at him and they both started chuckling. "No," they said at the same time.

A gentle nudge and she was lying flat on the bed, her hands stretched over her head. "Not too wet, and not too sloppy."

She laughed.

He dropped to his knees and pulled her to the edge of the bed, inched his hands up her thighs, and tugged at the panties that had been in the way and tossed them on the floor. "Hello, beautiful."

Olivia opened and he moved in.

~

The first orgasm slammed into her so hard and so fast she saw stars.

She hadn't been lying when she told Leo that she didn't remember any man she'd had sex with, but as her body shuddered under the talent of Leo's tongue, she knew orgasms like that were rare.

Leo looked at her through the frame of her legs. His smile said it all.

"Proud of yourself?"

"Yes, ma'am, I am."

She needed to catch her breath. "You have too many clothes on."

He reached behind and pulled his shirt off in one movement. He used his shirt to wipe the moisture from his lips and tossed it to the floor.

The man made her feel so alive. Sexy, yes . . . wanted . . . absolutely. But alive. While she didn't quite understand the meaning behind that, she didn't think it was common for her.

Olivia sat up on her elbows to watch him undress.

Oh, yeah . . . her initial assessment of the man still panned out. As he dropped his pants to the floor and kicked off his shoes, his erection said, *Hello, how can I serve you* while standing at full attention.

Full being the key word.

"Nice," she muttered.

He placed a knee on the bed.

"There're condoms in the drawer," she told him.

His eyes lit up in surprise.

"Sasha thought we might need them."

He laughed, reached for the nightstand. "Very thoughtful of her."

He removed the box, looked it over, and ripped the cellophane from the package. He dumped the contents on the bed, picked up one of the smaller sizes and tossed it over his shoulder.

Olivia laughed.

He went through a few more before finding one that would actually fit. "I'm going to have to have a talk with AJ." He set the condom aside and crawled up the length of her body. He captured her lips and pressed her back into the mattress.

The weight of him was a continuous, sensual delight from his knees to his mouth. His hand traveled up her side and tugged at her shirt. "Can I?"

She found the question odd until he pulled it from her shoulders and looked at her. He leaned forward and kissed the outside of the scar she'd have for the rest of her life. He moved to the second one on the side of her chest where the doctor had placed that tube to help her breathe.

Fascinated by the way he was being so careful, she stared.

He looked up, his smile soft. "If I do anything that hurts you . . ."

"You're not hurting me," she told him. Except for that tiny pull in her heart she didn't want to name.

He moved past her scars and pulled one nipple into his mouth.

All the parts of her that had simmered started firing up again.

She raked her fingernails down his back, over his ass, and reached around front. His cock was pressed against her leg, and she stroked what she could at the angle they were in.

He wiggled his hips, giving her better access.

"Hello, Mr. FBI."

He chuckled over her breast, caught her flesh in a soft bite.

She squirmed.

"Do that again," she told him.

He did.

He kissed, nibbled, and stroked every part of her, exciting and prolonging her pleasure with the process. She followed his pace, kiss for kiss, fondle for fondle. Many times she felt the need to rush, wanted to roll him onto his back and take control, but then he'd find another part of her that he hadn't cared for, and she was right back to arching into his touch and enjoying all the sensations he was bringing out in her.

Everything he was doing felt so new, unique to him . . . to them together.

And when they finally couldn't wait any longer, she reached for the condom and opened the wrapper.

She helped him roll it on and invited him in.

Leo reached for her hands, intertwining their fingers, and slowly sunk into her body.

It was like she couldn't breathe, the feeling was so complete. "So good, Leo. This is . . . you are . . ."

He was smiling a fool's grin when she opened her eyes to look at him.

He brought their joined hands to his lips and kissed her fingers. "We are . . ."

Slowly, he made himself comfortable.

Inside, her body trembled, each pass harder to control than the next.

Leo's lips found hers, his tongue mimicking what his body was doing. Her legs wrapped around his waist, giving him a better angle, placing him exactly where she wanted until rational thoughts just stopped swimming in her head and all she could see was the finish line. She guided him . . . faster, slower . . . right there. Until she was calling his name and flexing every internal muscle she possessed.

Once again she dropped her hands to her sides, lax in his care.

"Very nice," she heard him say.

Her eyes opened, she looked down. The man was still rock hard and inside of her.

She took that as a challenge.

A flick of her hips and a tuck of his shoulder and she had him on his back. "Okay, Superman . . . it's my turn."

She sat up tall, welcomed his hands on her breasts, and started to ride.

"Aww, fuck," he muttered, his eyes rolling back in his head.

CHAPTER EIGHTEEN

They'd made love for hours, took a late-night shower together, and laughed and played like two teenage kids without a care in the world.

Leo ate up every second.

They tiptoed down the hall to his room to get a pair of lounge pants before sneaking into the kitchen to refuel. He'd started a fire in the bedroom fireplace, and they watched the snow falling outside.

It was past three in the morning when Olivia finally settled into his arm and started to close her eyes. "Are you sure you want to sleep in here? I might have that dream again."

He pulled her close, wrapped a hand around her waist. "I'll take my chances."

He kissed her, watched her eyes flutter a few times, before she placed her head on his shoulder and allowed her body to rest.

And he watched her.

The dying fire in front of them, her breath gentle and steady on his chest. He wanted this to last so badly, he felt something inside him break.

Maybe Neil was wrong.

Maybe she wouldn't leave.

Maybe the feeling inside of him was inside of her and she'd want to make it work.

Finally, his brain couldn't hold on any longer and he fell asleep in her arms.

~

She woke with a start. An unfamiliar weight beside her.

The night's events flooded in, and the steady ache in her body from being thoroughly satisfied, repeatedly, sang in her head.

"Leo," she whispered.

Her eyes fluttered open to find him sound asleep.

Memories of orgasms and never-ending kisses . . . laughter. Teasing and playful moments. Soft moments where emotions she didn't think she knew snuck in.

Olivia felt utterly stuffed with the feel of the man. And not just sexually. Yes, he'd done all that . . . but more.

So much more.

She flexed her toes and, careful not to wake him, inched out from under his arm to use the bathroom.

Her reflection in the mirror caught her attention. Her hair was a mess, her eyes shined, and there was a significant love bite on her right breast.

Leo took direction well.

After splashing water on her face and brushing the morning breath from her mouth, she retrieved her T-shirt from the floor, put it on, and grabbed her bathrobe.

Leo hadn't moved a muscle.

She silently made her way downstairs, smelled coffee before she got there.

Sasha stood in front of the largest window of the great room, staring out.

"Oh, wow." Snow had dumped. A good foot covered the ground, whitening everything in sight.

"Good morning," Sasha said. The woman sipped her coffee. "I'd ask if you slept well, but everyone in the house knows you didn't."

And for whatever reason, Olivia started to laugh. "I'd say I'm sorry, but I'm not."

Sasha lifted her coffee cup in the air without looking back. "Touché."

Olivia rolled her shoulders and went straight to the coffee maker. "Where is everyone?"

"AJ's on the monitors, and Lars and Isaac are clearing snow off of sensors and making sure the generator is running for if we lose power."

The sheer amount of snow suggested a power outage was a *when* and not an *if*. "Are the monitors even necessary at this point? No one has come looking for me yet."

Sasha pulled her attention off the snow and turned to her. "Doesn't mean they won't."

Olivia wasn't about to argue. She'd been thinking this whole setup was overkill for a couple of weeks. But since she still didn't know her real name, she let it be. It wasn't like she had anywhere to go.

"Any word from Neil? Did the kid survive meeting Daddy?"

"Talked to him this morning. He avoided the conversation."

Olivia laughed. "Sounds like a Neil move."

"He loves his girl. Can't fault him for that." Sasha took a seat at the kitchen counter.

Olivia leaned against the island, enjoyed the dark-roast caffeine as it slid down her throat. "Will you and AJ have kids?"

Sasha cleared her throat. "I'm not sure I'm cut out for babies."

Olivia had a hard time picturing Sasha in mommy mode.

"We did talk about adopting someday. Older kids. The forgotten ones."

The image of a yard filled with children of all ages flittered in Olivia's head. They were laughing, yelling . . . wearing uniforms and throwing snowballs and talking with thick accents.

"Olivia?"

She shook her head and returned to the conversation.

"Are you okay?"

"Yes. Sorry. The snow has me thinking about Harry Potter . . . of all things." She blinked a few times. "Adoption, huh?"

Sasha stared, eyes searching. "I'm not getting younger, and the thought of a parasite living inside my body makes me a bit uneasy."

Olivia laughed. "If that's the reference you use, then it's probably best you adopt."

"As AJ keeps telling me."

The sound of a door hitting a wall upstairs had them both jumping.

"Olivia!"

Leo was yelling her name.

"Olivia?"

She put her coffee cup on the counter and started toward the stairs.

Leo saw her from the top and stopped dead in his tracks. He'd pulled on his pants but left his shirt behind.

"What's wrong?"

He dropped down on his ass right there at the top of the stairs and placed both hands on his knees as if trying to gain control.

Olivia walked up and knelt in front of him. "What's wrong?"

He grabbed her hand.

Leo was trembling, his eyes wide with fear. "I thought you were . . ." He blew out a breath.

"You thought I was what?"

He shook his head. "You weren't there when I woke up. I thought you were gone."

"Where would I go?"

There was serious stress in his eyes.

He was really upset. Her mind pushed at her, knocking. "Leo. I'm right here."

She stood, bringing him to his feet with her.

Leo looked beyond her at Sasha, who stood at the bottom of the stairs, watching.

"Apparently we both have a hard time waking up rationally," Olivia teased.

He reached for her. His hug felt as if it was the last time he'd see her.

She wanted to assure him she wasn't going anywhere but hesitated. Something about the moment felt off.

Really off.

He kissed her briefly. "I'm going to shower."

"I'm going to finish my coffee."

With a kiss to the top of her head, he walked away and disappeared into his bedroom.

Olivia laughed it off as she made her way back into the kitchen. "You make love one time and the guy loses his shit," she said to Sasha.

"One time?"

"Were we really that loud?"

Sasha drank her coffee and didn't answer.

~

Leo let the water rush down his face, pulling with it the adrenaline that had been surging throughout his body from the moment his eyes had opened and Olivia was gone.

"Fuck," he said under his breath.

He felt like there was an hourglass glued to the table, and when the last grain of sand slid down the tiny hole, it would all be over. There was no way to tilt the glass over, stop the train . . . avoid the crash.

And he would crash.

He knew that now. Making love to her was what poets write about. It was a give and a take and a give again. The look on her face when she dissolved under his touch . . . that image would fuel him for years.

Time was ticking, and he knew it wasn't going to take long for everything to crash in. He had to uncover her secrets so he could assure her that no matter what they were, they could figure it out together. Obviously, Neil and his team wanted to help her as well. She had to see that. Accept that.

His dreams had connected several dots about where she came from as she slept in his arms. She spoke in German, talked about going into a library at night. He had some questions for Sasha. Questions he didn't expect she'd answer, but he'd ask anyway.

Leo finished his shower and dressed.

When he made it to the kitchen, Olivia had left and was taking a shower of her own.

Sasha and AJ were in the kitchen talking to each other in hushed tones when he walked in.

"'Morning," he said, making a beeline for the coffee maker.

"You okay?" AJ asked. "Sasha told me what happened."

"I'm fine." Yeah, right . . . like they couldn't see past that. He poured a cup of java, turned. "Olivia was speaking in German last night . . . in her dreams."

Sasha's gaze flashed to his. "Did she realize it when she woke up?"

"No." He put the cup to his lips. "I'm going to tell her."

"Don't."

Leo knew that would be Sasha's order.

"That's where you know her from, right? Germany?" He kept his voice low, listened for the hot running water in the cold pipes to turn off.

Sasha and AJ looked at each other.

"From school. Boarding school, right? The kind where kids will sneak into a library once everyone has gone to bed to drink or get laid?"

"What did she tell you?" Sasha asked.

She didn't, but you just did.

"When you told her that you knew a girl in school she reminded you of, and her name was Olivia . . . that was the truth. You both went to the same school." Leo put his cup aside, looked at AJ. "And your father was an ambassador in Germany. Maybe you went there, too."

"Leo," AJ said on a sigh. "Trust me when I tell you, you don't want to follow this path."

He shook his head. "No. That's where you're wrong. That woman means something to me, and in order to keep her safe I need to know what or who could be after her."

Sasha lifted her chin. "You no longer think that bullet was meant for you?"

"I don't know that. But I will find out one way or another."

He picked up his cup and started toward Olivia's room. He wanted to spend every second he could with her.

"Leo?"

He turned.

"Be careful," Sasha said before heading toward the downstairs surveillance room.

AJ stepped forward when his wife was out of the room and paused. "She's not capable of loving you back," AJ warned.

Was it love?

He was so screwed. "You're wrong about that."

"I'm not."

"You underestimate her," Leo said.

AJ shook his head. "That is the one thing nobody in this house does."

CHAPTER NINETEEN

"We'll go outside, get bone cold, and then come back in and warm up." Olivia lifted her eyebrows and licked her lips, making sure Leo knew exactly how she'd like to be warmed up.

"We're going to have a snowball fight, aren't we?" Leo was sitting on the edge of the bed slipping on a warm pair of socks.

"I'm not twelve."

"That wasn't an answer."

She turned to leave his room. "Downstairs in five."

Damn, the day felt good. It shouldn't, considering how little she slept the night before. But she was energized. Bouncing out of her skin with restless energy. And with the clouds threatening to give them more snow, now was the best time to get out in it.

She bundled up with a knit hat that covered her hair and ears, a scarf that cut the cold around her neck, and ski pants and a water-proof jacket Sasha had picked up the last time she'd gone into Durango.

With all her layers in place, she worked her way downstairs, putting on her gloves.

"Grab some wood when you come back up," Lars told her from where he sat next to the fireplace.

"Too cold for you out there?" she asked.

"I'm with Pam on this one. The cold is for the birds. It's nice from in here, sucks out there."

She sealed up all the open parts of her outfit to ward off the chill and opened the front door. "You're missing out."

Lars waved her off.

Once outside she walked to the edge of the porch, closed her eyes, and sucked in a deep breath. Her cheeks instantly felt the chill in the air, and her lungs enjoyed the cold. She loved snow, she realized. The smell, the soft texture . . . the way it gave the earth a chance to slow down, both in nature and in people.

The door to the house opened and closed. "It is chilly," Leo said as he walked up behind her, his arms wrapping around her in a hug.

"It's beautiful."

"Okay, my snow bunny . . . what do you want to do?"

"Let's walk. Make fresh tracks."

"And the snowballs?"

She took him in over her shoulder. "Someone has a fear of snowballs."

He took his gloved hand, placed it in hers. A feeling that no longer felt awkward and in fact would be missed if it wasn't there.

Their snow boots did a good job of digging in and not letting them slip. "Sasha and the others have really made sure we have everything we need," she said.

"It's much better than what the feds would have come up with."

"You mean the witness protection program?"

"Yeah. You'd be safe, but the temporary housing isn't nearly as nice."

She pictured a subdivision home in the middle of nowhere. "What about the long term? How do your people set that up?"

They walked slowly on the trail, which was only outlined by fallen branches and rocks barely visible beneath the snow.

"I don't work directly with the federal marshals on long-term placement. But they do give witnesses new identities, a place to live, a chance at getting a job so that when the federal funding is gone, they can make it on their own."

"So the money does go away after a while."

"Every case is different, but in most cases, yeah."

"So eventually Marie will be on her own?"

Leo looked over. "The case from Vegas?"

"Yeah."

"How did you know her name?"

Olivia shook her head. "I heard one of you say it. Sometime after we first arrived here." Although she couldn't remember who or in what context.

"Marie will be fine."

"That's good. She's too young to not have a full life after what she's been through." She looked ahead, saw a low-hanging branch laden with snow and smiled.

"Who told you about the case?"

Olivia shrugged, her attention dialed into a new mission. "What is that?" She pointed to something on the ground beneath the tree branch, let go of Leo's hand, and picked up her pace to get in front of him.

"What is what?" Leo asked when he arrived.

"I think it's an animal track. Maybe a deer or something with long legs."

He pointed away from her. "There's more over there."

She turned away and Leo reached up and pulled on the branch, cascading snow all over her.

"Ohhh!"

"Deer tracks, my ass. You're sneaky, Olivia, but—"

She did not give him a chance to finish his sentence. She reached down, cupped her hands, and tossed a mound of snow right in his face. He hadn't shaved in two days, and the snow stuck to his chin like Santa Claus.

She laughed deep in her belly.

"Oh, it is so on," he said, laughing when he bent down to deliver a human snowplow of his own.

She ducked his first attack and ran, not getting far with a foot of snow making it difficult to lift out of it. Reaching down as she went, she rolled snow into a neat little ball, turned, and took aim.

He was ready with ammo of his own.

She found a tree, took cover. "You know the difference between you and me?"

"What's that?" Leo's voice was close.

"I'm not afraid to get hit."

She cleared the tree with three snowballs ready to go.

Only he wasn't there.

Then she felt a splash of snow on her butt.

She turned and fired at Leo as he retreated laughing.

They went at it until she felt breathless and warm from the effort of running, dipping, and weaving in the snow.

She knelt behind a tree, Leo stood behind another one, both of them rounding perfect balls to hurl at each other.

When was the last time she'd had a snowball fight?

The early days at Richter. When life was still innocent. The memory brought a smile.

Olivia stopped cold.

Richter.

Images flashed in her head . . . memories. Snowballs and stolen kisses in the stacks.

Words flew at her in languages she hadn't remembered until that very moment.

Richter.

The boarding school that turned her into what she was.

The school that stripped her of a life she could never have.

A life of snowball fights and laughter.

It was all there. Every dirty detail of her past.

How had it been missing when it was all right there?

Sasha, who she'd had in a few classes, but didn't really get to know until they'd beat the shit out of each other in Amelia's apartment. And AJ, Amelia's brother. Neil, Isaac, Lars . . . all of them.

All of them knew who she was all this time. None of them said a thing.

Olivia fell to her knees, her eyes lifted toward the sky, which had started to drop snow on them again.

She was not safe there.

They were not safe with her there.

Nausea built in her throat.

Get out.

Run.

Run . . .

Yes . . . all of that.

Her brain screamed and her heartbeat leapt out of her chest, ready to follow any direction or run and hide. But she needed a plan.

A plan that was already forming in her head.

"You don't stand a chance, beautiful lady," Leo called, laughing from behind his tree.

Olivia placed a hand on her chest, felt a sting of tears in her eyes. She cleared her throat. "No way, Mr. FBI. I'm locked and loaded." It hurt.

All of it.

She reached down, grabbed a fistful of snow, and rubbed it in her face. The cold snapped her backbone into place.

With hands filled with snowball ammo, she pushed away the images of the people on the other end of the scope and stepped out from behind the tree.

～

They stumbled into the mudroom, sloshing snow with every step.

They eventually called their fight a tie and let the new snowfall drive them inside.

Leo helped her out of her snow gear and accepted her help when he worked his way out of his.

He tossed his stuff to the side, and she carefully hung hers up to dry.

"Time to get started on that warming-up stuff," he said, coming behind her and kissing the side of her neck.

"An excellent idea," she said. "My shower is bigger than yours."

With an invitation like that, he followed her out of the mudroom and up the double flight of stairs to the bedrooms.

"Did you remember my firewood?" Lars asked from the chair he'd claimed since breakfast.

"Exercise is good for you," Olivia said as she walked right on by.

Leo pointed toward Olivia.

Lars grunted and unfolded from his perch.

Once in her room, Leo pulled her into his arms.

Her lips were there, offering . . . trembling. "You're still cold," he said after a quick kiss.

"Freezing."

He reached for her shirt, she reached for his.

They made it to the shower, but unlike the night before where every touch was slow and thought out, this time the buzz from the good-natured snowball fight sparked them in an entirely new direction. The water was just warming up, and Olivia had dropped to her knees, taking him into her mouth.

He'd never been so turned on and so ready to explode in his adult life.

Leo tried to pull back, attempted to slow them down. But no. Olivia wouldn't have it.

Considering their condom supply was limited, he supposed this was probably a better option.

When he warned her of his release, she kept going, taking all reason from his brain.

She looked up at him, smiling.

"Happy with yourself?" he asked, mimicking her words from the night before.

"Yes, sir. I am."

Such a dangerous emotion swelling in his chest.

He helped her to her feet and kissed her. He found the soap and made use of his hands, touching the edges of her sex until she hummed. With her back against the wall of the shower, he lifted one of her legs until one foot was up on the shower bench, giving him much more room to work.

The feel of her hands on the back of his head as he pleased her felt like heaven. He found all the spots he'd discovered the night before, and new ones that drew out her cries. And when she was tipping over the edge, he sucked her in a little harder and heard his name on her lips.

Later, with steam still filling the bathroom and both of them wrapped up in towels, he kissed her, slowly this time.

Just a kiss.

"What was that for?" she asked when he pulled away.

"A promise," he said.

Her eyes did the flickering thing they often did. Blinking. "What promise?"

"That I will always show you how you make me feel."

She blinked. "I-I think you just did that."

He smiled. "That was the exclamation point." He kissed her briefly. "This is the promise."

Olivia sighed and stifled a yawn. "Well, Mr. Promises. I'm going to shoo you out of my room so I can take a nap. Someone kept me up all night."

"I could use a nap."

She laughed, turned back toward the bathroom mirror, and pulled a brush through her wet hair. "If you stay in my room, there won't be any napping."

"You do have a point."

She slapped his butt through his towel as he turned to walk away.

Leo gathered his clothing they'd littered all over the room and gave her some space.

CHAPTER TWENTY

Olivia spent the first twenty minutes of her nap with her legs folded to her chest, head resting on her knees.

She knew this would be the last minute of peace she'd have.

And it was spent calculating and planning a route in her head. There wasn't any time to consider the past two months. She'd have a lifetime to remember and pick apart every detail.

That is, if the man who'd tried to stop her from breathing didn't return to finish the job.

And there was no reason to believe he wouldn't. Another layer of proof that she couldn't live a normal life.

Ever.

Couldn't cultivate friendships like the one she'd had with Amelia. AJ's sister was the only person Olivia tried to love as a friend, and now the woman was dead.

Just like everyone else in the house would be.

Then there was Leo. Goddamn it all to hell. How much had Neil told him about her?

Not everything. Or maybe she was wrong. Maybe Leo was the double agent guy doing what he could to take her off the streets. Ensure that she couldn't hurt anyone else.

The thought left almost as quickly as it came.

There was no way he would have tangled with her, in bed or otherwise, if he knew what she was.

The memory of him screaming her name that morning, and losing his shit when he thought she was gone, was real.

Neil had warned him, and Leo realized it was only a matter of time.

Olivia wished there was a way to stop what had to happen, but there wasn't.

Which meant that Neil was expecting her exit. But he wouldn't let her go without that fatherly lecture. Not that she had one of those.

A father, that is.

Neil would give her shit, try and talk her out of it.

Sasha would lay logic on Olivia.

AJ would tell her Amelia would want a different life for her.

And Lars and Isaac . . .

Emotion clogged her eyes. A new, annoying-ass byproduct of getting shot.

Olivia Naught did not cry.

It was not allowed.

She did not want to care for these people. Because with that came a need to protect and avenge them.

Then there was Leo. She couldn't go there. The hole was already growing and threatening to consume her. There was no time for any of that.

Olivia pushed off her bed and did a room sweep.

She knew about the audio feed and cameras in the hall, but hadn't had the knowledge in her head to look for more in her room.

Until now.

When her sweep came back clean, she was happy to know she wouldn't have to abuse the people who had made sure she was taken care of all this time.

She opened the dresser drawers and pulled out what she'd need.

It wasn't until that moment that she realized Sasha had more than just shopped for Amnesiac Olivia . . . she prepared Richter Olivia to make her escape. The dark knit cap and scarf were down in the mudroom drying, but their white sisters waved from the dresser. Camouflage for the snow. Black if the snow hadn't fallen. White snow gear, dark outerwear, layers with serious weather protection. She set what she needed aside and would get the rest on her way out.

Olivia dressed in warm, loose clothing as she had every day she'd been in Colorado and paused as she looked down at her bed. The memories of her nightmares surfaced. Hell and burning had been with her for years. The nightmares themselves had never changed since the first time she placed a bullet inside of someone's skull.

They were her prison, a nightly reminder of the evil she was.

~

The fire was roaring. The snow had stopped falling. And the evening routine was in full swing. Isaac was in his room, resting before his shift, Lars was in the surveillance room, and AJ and Sasha were cozy in a love seat.

Olivia rested her feet in Leo's lap at his request.

She left them there, because Amnesiac Olivia would allow him to rub the arch of her socked feet the way he was doing while he worked on one of Isaac's crossword puzzles.

Olivia held Leo's computer, the screen angled away from the others in the room.

"Anything coming back to you?" AJ asked.

Olivia faked a smile. "Well . . . I have determined that Leo looks up way too much porn on this thing."

Leo stopped rubbing and leaned over. "I do not."

She laughed. "Gotcha."

"Giving a woman your computer is like giving them the key to your front door," AJ warned him.

"His bedroom doesn't have a lock. Not that I'd need it anyway," Olivia said.

"Oh?" Sasha glanced over, obvious suspicion in her gaze. Seeing it now, Olivia realized Sasha had sent that look many times over the past two months. Probably searching for the moment Olivia knew more than she led everyone else to believe.

"Nothing opens a door faster than telling a man you're naked on the other side."

Leo purred.

"See?"

Sasha returned her attention to the fire.

Olivia plugged away on Leo's computer. She placed trackers and hacks . . . things that would give her access to what he was receiving and sending. Much as she didn't like the deceit, she needed to protect herself. And him, if need be.

"When can we expect Neil back?" Olivia asked.

"His pilot said he could fly tomorrow."

As she suspected. "Are we any closer to finding out who shot me?" Her questions were rhetorical. Ones that said, *See, I still don't know who I am and need your help.*

"We'll find them," Leo assured her.

No, they wouldn't.

But she would.

"I'm sure everyone is going to want to get back to their normal lives by the holidays."

"You're remembering more bits and pieces every day," Leo reminded her.

"I suppose."

"Any memory of the firearms training? Where you obtained it and why?" AJ asked.

Sasha tilted her head, hands in her lap, eyes glued to the fire.

Olivia could see the woman listening . . . if that was possible.

"No." Olivia finished what she needed to do on Leo's computer and closed it up tight. "This is a waste of time," she told him, handing it back.

"It will come," he assured her.

She looked at the time, counted down the minutes.

The lights in the room flickered off, but the space stayed lit because of the fire. A collective sigh went over the room.

"That was predictable," AJ said.

Leo slid her feet off his lap and stood. "Time to switch it all over," he said.

AJ took the hint and got up with him.

Olivia watched Leo's back as he left the room. He was a good man and deserved someone better.

"Are you okay over there?" Sasha asked.

Olivia kept her gaze soft. "Leo is falling hard," she told her. Amnesiac Olivia would be open and honest . . . naive about such a statement.

"What about you?"

Amnesiac Olivia and Richter Olivia started arguing in her head. "I can't let that happen until I know who I am. It's not fair to him."

"When that happens, he'll be here for you."

"In the meantime, we're going to need to do a condom run. Mr. FBI is packing a three fifty-seven and not a twenty-two."

Sasha hummed. "That is good news indeed."

"Yes . . . yes, it is."

~

"I'm kicking you out before you fall asleep." Olivia's statement was a warning.

One of her legs was stretched over one of his, their breath returning to normal.

"Why is that?" He traced the skin of her arm, enjoyed how her fingers curled into his chest as they talked.

"I felt hammered today."

He chuckled. "I would hope so."

"Tired," she corrected herself. "And if you stay in here, I'm likely to roll over and jump back on . . . and we're out of your size, Mr. Big Guy."

He didn't exactly stock up before taking that initial plane ride. "I've proven there are other ways to please you."

She purred with a sigh. "Yes. But . . ." She lifted her ear from his chest, looked at him. "I'm not afraid to tell you I'm exhausted. I need to build up to these all-day sessions."

If her words weren't enough, she covered a yawn and cuddled back into his arms.

"I get the hint." Even though he hated the idea.

She sighed. "I have Sasha doing a drug-store run tomorrow."

Leo kissed the top of her sleepy head. "You have to love a woman who makes sure her needs are met."

He felt her eyelashes flutter on his chest.

Within twenty minutes her breathing evened out and her eyes had closed.

He didn't want to leave. After ten minutes of internal debate, he slowly slid out from under her and smiled in silent satisfaction as the hand that had been on his chest fisted into the space he'd just vacated.

"Good night," he whispered before letting himself out of her room.

~

Olivia physically put her fist in her mouth to stop the sound that wanted to erupt with his departure.

This was the emotion she'd avoided her entire adult life. And it threatened to engulf her. Just like the hellish landscape of her dreams.

She lay there, wide awake, and waited.

Hours passed, the time of the surveillance room shift had come and gone, giving Lars a chance to fall asleep and Isaac a chance to become complacent.

She prepared herself with layers of clothing under her bathrobe and put into motion everything she had to do.

One last lingering look at the bed and the memories she'd made in it, and she walked out of her private world and in front of the cameras where others could see her.

She tiptoed into the kitchen, as she had many nights, and went to the fridge. She poured a glass of milk, meandered to the living room, and picked up the remote for the TV no one ever turned on.

She shook her head for anyone who might be watching her movements and set the remote back. Five . . . four . . . three . . .

By the time the generator kicked off, she stood at the edge of the stairway looking down.

Before Isaac could stop cussing about the generator, she was standing over him, her bathrobe dangling from her fingertips.

"Hello, Isaac."

She knew what he saw.

Richter Olivia was there, wearing what any cat burglar would. She dropped the robe, reached behind, and raveled her hair up onto her head.

A red security backup light illuminated the space, but otherwise, the room was dark . . . the monitors useless.

"You don't have to do this."

"Don't make this harder than it has to be." She motioned for him to stand.

"Olivia . . . we—"

"Stop talking."

He knew better than to tangle with her and stood.

"Turn around."

"C'mon. Aren't we past this? I'll just let you go, you don't have to tie me up."

Less than two minutes and he was on the sofa, a gag in his mouth, his hands and feet bound together. She felt bad this time but knew someone in the house would realize the generator wasn't running and come and check.

"I am sorry about this," she told him.

He rolled his eyes.

She opened the supply room door and went straight for the weapons she needed. Only two, and just for the short journey to where she had her stuff.

She pushed aside a field bag and saw her duffel. The one she'd stashed in the hotel ventilation system in Vegas. A quick look inside and she found her fake IDs and two wigs. In addition, there were two stacks of currency. Hundred American dollar bills and euros.

And a note with her name scribbled on the envelope.

Neil.

But now wasn't the time to read what he had to say.

She shouldered the bag, checked her watch.

"Tell him not to look for me," she instructed Isaac. And because she really did feel bad about tying him up, she placed a kiss to his forehead before walking away.

She exited through the mudroom, slipped into the still damp ski pants and jacket, and then went into the garage. There was a motorcycle, which would be suicide in this much snow, a Jeep, and a truck.

She yanked enough cables off the truck and the bike to slow the chase, opened the garage door, and fired up the Jeep.

There was a flicker in one of the upstairs windows of the completely dark house, telling her someone had watched her escape.

Sasha.

The others would have sounded an alarm.

She ignored the useless tears she didn't think she was capable of shedding as the silhouette of the log cabin disappeared in the moonlit background.

CHAPTER TWENTY-ONE

She's gone.

Leo had woken to Sasha's words, spoken from the doorway to his bedroom.

He'd jumped up and run to Olivia's room. Other than an unmade bed, the space hadn't changed.

Even though Sasha told him he was wasting his energy, he'd jumped in the truck as soon as AJ wired it back together, and the two of them followed the tracker Neil had put on the Jeep.

Olivia had abandoned it in Durango.

In the front seat AJ picked up three more bugs, devices placed in the lining of the ski gear, the duffel bag she'd grabbed, and the butt of the AR.

"She found everything," AJ told him.

Hours later, Leo stood over her bed with the only note she'd left behind.

Thank You!

That was it. It wasn't addressed to anyone, and yet everyone seemed to feel that was enough.

Fuck that.

It wasn't enough for him.

He should have just fallen asleep in her bed and she'd still be there.

The others in the house gave him room.

While Leo was trying to piece together what had just happened, everyone else worked together, packing up the house, removing the cameras, microphones, sensors, and alarms.

He heard the heavy footfalls of Neil as he ascended the stairs and came to stand beside him.

"When did you get here?" Leo asked.

"Just now."

It was hard to talk. "Where did she go?"

"I don't know."

"Will you look for her?"

"I will keep an eye out for her, searching is a waste of time and resources."

Leo shook his head and moved to her dresser. "The hell with that." He removed every single item he found, shook it out, and moved to the next. "People don't just disappear."

"Sometimes they do."

Neil's even tone and matter-of-fact words spoken as if they were the gospel hit Leo's last nerve.

He was right up in the man's business, eye to eye. "Fuck that! All of this, everything done here, was nothing more than a charade. It never had anything to do with keeping someone from shooting me, or her, again, was it?"

Neil didn't budge even with Leo shouting in the man's face. "Partially . . . in the beginning."

"When did you determine that there was no longer a threat?"

"Two weeks in."

Leo's nostrils flared with every tortured breath he drew. One where the air didn't have Olivia in it.

"I told you Olivia was here to heal. That never changed."

Leo searched Neil's face. "Then why me? Why keep me here?"

There was a flicker in Neil's eye, something that told Leo he was right to ask the question.

"You served a different purpose."

Leo had had just about enough of Neil's cryptic shit to last a decade. "Open your fucking mouth, MacBain. I have no problem getting bloody to help you find your words."

Neil's mouth didn't open.

Leo fisted his right hand.

"To prove to Olivia she still had a heart and a reason to live."

Leo looked over Neil's shoulder and found Sasha standing in the hall.

"What?" Some of the fight came out of Leo's tone.

Neil relaxed his shoulders, turned to the side.

"Olivia has been broken for years. This . . ." Sasha lifted her hands to the walls of the house. "This gave her an opportunity to experience a different life. You, and what the two of you shared . . . well, it's not my place to label any of that. The Olivia we witnessed here is not the woman you met in Vegas. Maybe now that she has been both, she can see a different life for herself."

"If you believe that, then why would she leave?"

"Reaction. Her normal mode of operation. What she's always done." Sasha's expression said her words were obvious. "She needs to regroup. Find her center."

He could have been that center.

Lord knew she was becoming his.

"You think she'll be back," Leo said.

Sasha didn't commit. "If I were her, I'd find the shooter. I'd learn who hired them and why."

The thought of Olivia going after the person who shot her . . . alone . . . made him want to vomit. "And then?"

"Depends on the information."

Leo looked up at Neil, who had remained silent during the whole exchange. "You think she'll remove the threat."

They were both silent.

"You really believe she will kill them."

Silence.

"Ahh, fuck." It was one thing in the heat of a battle, yeah . . . that's what they all trained for. But to find the shooter, or whoever hired them, and just pull the trigger. Premeditated and not within the laws of justice. "I can protect her. The FBI can take care of this."

Neil shook his head. "The FBI will not protect her when they learn who she is."

"Who the hell is that, MacBain?"

Sasha said something in a language Leo did not understand and stepped closer.

"Olivia and I did go to the same school."

"Sasha," Neil warned.

She lifted a hand, ignored him.

"The same as Claire." Sasha looked at Neil. "Nothing you haven't figured out." Her eyes moved back to Leo. "Richter was . . . is . . . a boarding school. When we were in attendance, this military school operated quite differently than it does today. Some of us, the orphans, those that showed aptitude, were pushed harder and given more incentives to learn languages, perfect our weapons training, hack computers."

Neil crossed his arms over his chest and scowled. "Why are you telling him this?"

Sasha glared at Neil. "Because he loves her and will discover these facts. While searching, he may end up leaving a trail straight to her. None of us want that."

Leo blinked past Sasha's label of his feelings for Olivia and moved on. "All of these skills made Olivia a better operative. So what government does she work for?"

Neil stepped out of the way and let Sasha continue.

She turned back to Leo, took a deep breath. "None of them. I have no doubt that was what she was told when she signed up. That there was a covert arm of British intelligence, maybe the CIA or even the FBI. And in your search, you will find that these legitimate organizations did in fact recruit students from Richter. But they weren't the only ones picking the cream from the top of the vat. There were others. Ones who acted as benefactors for orphaned students and manipulated which employment those students chose. One of these benefactors attempted to recruit me. I was older, had been away from Richter for a half a dozen years, and understood exactly what he was asking of me."

The picture was coming in clear. "Which was?"

"Do what they say, when they say, no questions asked."

"Anything?"

Sasha looked him straight in the eye. "Anything. Infiltrate, collect data—"

"Kill?" he asked, not wanting to hear her answer.

"Anything," Sasha said slowly.

Leo took a few steps back and sat on the edge of the bed.

"The truth is, none of us know exactly what Olivia is guilty of," Neil told him.

So much bile rose to meet the back of his throat. "Murder."

"Most assuredly," Sasha said without hesitation.

Something Leo had guessed all along.

Silence filled the room like thick and heavy fog.

"Olivia escaped this employment seven years ago," Neil told him.

"How can you be sure? You said yourself she isn't on your payroll. Only called in on occasion."

"The man who employed her is dead."

Leo's gaze snapped to Sasha. "Did she . . . ?"

Sasha shrugged, as if the answer was *maybe*. "He died in prison. Apparent suicide."

"You don't believe that."

Sasha once again said something in a different language, this time sounding like Russian. She rolled her eyes. "If someone forced me to kill innocent people, or even the guilty, and then held my life hostage to be his bitch, I would not hesitate."

It was then that Leo saw in Sasha that same look of determination Olivia had in her eyes right before she pulled him to the ground in Vegas.

"Only Olivia did," Neil said. "She was given a chance to take this man out. But we were there, witnesses and guilty by association. All he suffered at that time was a beating Sasha delivered and a gunshot wound to the hand. The wheels of justice started to roll, but he was dead before trial. That death could have been on Olivia's hands, or another like her. Could have been whoever paid him. We will never know."

"Nor do we care," Sasha added. "She wanted out, disappeared, and eventually reconnected with an old school friend, Amelia, AJ's sister."

All the dots started marching in line as Sasha spelled out the facts.

"When Amelia ended up dead, Olivia blamed herself."

Leo ran both hands through his hair. "When a suicide bomber changes his mind, it isn't his life he is threatening, it's his family."

"That would be us. Even if she doesn't like it," Neil explained. "I wanted her to see, feel, touch, and taste that connection with people here. Let her know that we can care for ourselves. That living in fear isn't living and there is another way."

"But then someone shot her," Leo said. "Is there a price on her head?"

"We don't know. The man who all but owned her is dead, and she only reported to him. That doesn't mean someone else out there doesn't have a grudge. Or someone may have obtained information to try and pull her back in," Neil pointed out.

"If she saw the shooter and recognized him, she'll find them. If she didn't, she'll assume the bullet was for her and avoid us . . . you . . . to keep us safe," Sasha added.

"I can keep myself safe," Leo said. As if he were a child telling a parent he could climb the stairs all by himself. There was always an element of danger and the unknown in his line of work. It had never deterred him from the job before.

"If it helps at all, none of us believe her to be a mercenary. She is lost and alone and needs to find her balance before she can believe any of what she found here to be true and worth fighting for."

Leo looked at his hands, envisioned them in Olivia's. "So I'm supposed to just wait for that to happen?"

"She'll reach out when she's ready."

Yeah . . . Leo didn't see himself waiting. But they were right. As with any branch of government, worldwide, they would extract as much intel as they could and only then determine if you still needed to be imprisoned for your crimes. Pledging the FBI would take care of her was a promise Leo could not keep.

"You're still going to look for her, aren't you?" Neil asked.

"Damn right."

"Then do it at my headquarters. I have two of Richter's top hackers on payroll," Neil said, and then he glanced at Sasha. "And one who does it for free."

"She cares about you," Sasha said after a moment of silence.

"She left."

"Which proves she cares."

Leo looked between Sasha and Neil. He didn't take their trust and honor lightly. "What the hell am I going to tell my boss?"

Sasha laughed, turned to leave the room. "We have that figured out. I'll go over the details on the plane home."

~

"Would you like me to top off your wine?"

Olivia looked up at the flight attendant who stood over her with a bottle of chardonnay in her hand. With more than seven hours remaining in her flight, she knew the effects of what she allowed herself to drink would wear off before they landed. "Yes, please." She was running on less than three hours of sleep. She was hoping the alcohol would help her fix that.

The cubical-style business-class seating kept the other passengers from watching her without being obvious.

The short red wig and tinted contacts changed her look dramatically from the woman who'd been throwing snowballs less than two days before. She pulled out her thick Russian accent and still spoke English to those around her.

She'd abandoned the Jeep in Durango, and *borrowed* a car parked on a residential street. From there she drove to Denver and left that car where it would easily be found and returned to its owner. She then backtracked on a flight to Seattle.

The next flight she booked was with a passport Neil had no knowledge of. First stop was Chicago, and now she was destined for Paris. From there she'd obtain a car and drive the rest of the way.

But for now, she breathed.

Even if it was painful.

The flight attendant refilled her wine, removed her meal tray, and disappeared.

The envelope with her name written on the outside had tiny tears on the edges. One for every time she considered opening the letter and then decided not to. Not until she was on the international flight and couldn't change her mind.

She took a generous sip of her wine and opened the letter.

Olivia,

If you're reading this, then you're gone. We will be sorry you felt you had to leave, but none of us thought you'd stay. I can assure you that this team has, and is still willing to, take an active role in helping you move beyond your past. You don't have to do this alone.

I will not personally search you out. But the same can't be said for our mutual friend. For what it's worth, I never revealed the truth to him. Though by now I'm sure he's figured much of it out. I will tell him what I must to keep you safe, no more, no less.

If your safety is at risk, there will be a yellow ribbon on my front door . . . any and all of them.

You know how to contact me.

Don't hesitate.

N

A thick knot of emotion balled in her throat.

So many memories flashed in her head. When he walked into the ICU room and looked down at her.

"Do I know you?"

"I'm hard to forget."

Yet she had forgotten him.

Even the name Olivia didn't click into line until she was knee deep in snow and out of breath from playing like a child.

The vision of Sasha handing her a box of condoms and claiming when this was all over, she wouldn't want complications, circled.

Isaac's plea to not be tied up, that she could just leave . . .

Lars telling her he'd be happy to buy her drinks since he'd seen her half-naked.

They all knew, this whole time, and they simply played house until her memory came back. All of them knowing she would leave without a proper goodbye.

Olivia looked at Neil's note again.

All that sacrifice of time and safety . . . knowing she would vanish.

She stared out the window at the setting sun, blinking as that information processed.

Leo.

She fought back tears just picturing him.

Mr. FBI . . . sleeping with an assassin.

By now he knows. And to think they were both talking about the possibility of her being some kind of glamorous double agent. A spy for the good team. A 007 type that would be celebrated in secret circles.

She finished her wine and pressed the button for the attendant.

What a fool.

Both of them.

They should never have started anything.

"What can I get for you?"

Olivia picked up her empty glass. "You don't happen to have a bigger glass back there?" she asked.

The attendant shook her head and smiled. "I'll come back around and keep it full."

For seven years no one had come for her. She heard rumors herself, that she was dead. A rumor Geoff Pohl circulated to keep face with those who paid him. A missing operative was a dead operative. She had no doubt the man had put a price on her head. Which was why he was dead.

She reached for the notch on her chest where the bullet had gone in.

The face of the gunman, his voice . . . his name echoed.

Someone from her past knew she was alive. The question was, How many others did with him?

Her wine arrived.

Olivia folded up the letter from Neil, her intention to burn it at the first opportunity. While names weren't implicated, she wouldn't keep it for sentiment.

No . . . she had a job to do.

Because when killers try to kill their own kind, they know the score. It was time to even it.

CHAPTER TWENTY-TWO

Brackett sat across the desk from him, leaning back in his desk chair, a pen twirling in his fingertips.

"Domestic violence."

"That's what she said." Leo wore a suit for the first time in two months. He didn't know what pinched more, the tie . . . or the shoes. Both reminded him that if he wanted to keep his job, he'd have to deliver this story to his boss and make it believable. "She was trying to get away from him, made it to Vegas. She'd only been there a couple of days. Wore a wig so he wouldn't recognize her."

"Did she say he was the one who shot her?" Fitz sat to Leo's right, her low-heeled shoe tapping on air as she digested Leo's information.

"No. But she believed he was responsible one way or another."

"She didn't tell you her name?"

"No. We told her we could help her, get her someplace safe. I thought she was turning to our way of thinking. I was about to call in, snow dumped, and the power went out. Without the uplink Neil set up, phone calls don't work."

"Where were you?" Fitz asked.

"Outside of Durango, Colorado. Mountain cabin. A big cabin. Neil has some seriously deep pockets." Leo laced a chuckle into his narrative.

Brackett dropped his feet from where they were resting on the edge of his desk and sat forward, tossed his pen aside. "Two months and the shooter wasn't aiming at you."

"My access was limited up there to search out anything. No one down here found a link. Neil's people, they were looking. Is there anything new, something to suggest Janie wasn't the target?"

"Janie?"

"That's what we called her. Jane Doe . . . Janie."

"Ewhh."

"It worked." He wasn't going to mention Olivia. Not that she would be in any of their databases.

"Nothing new. Mykonos was transferred to his new home. His attorneys are trying to get him placed in a Martha Stewart facility, but so far that hasn't happened. Navi spent some time in New York before returning to Russia," Fitz reported. "Interviews with the jurors and attorneys didn't implicate anything."

Leo already knew that.

"I'm going to assume the victim is starting her new life . . . wherever that is?"

"That's what has been reported to me," Brackett told him.

"So where is Janie now?" Fitz asked.

"I have no idea." Leo pushed the image of Olivia out of his head and put the cardboard cutout image of "Janie" there in her place. He did not need his boss, or partner, clueing in to his feelings. "She took advantage of the power outage, drove the Jeep to Durango, and that's as far as we tracked her."

Fitz shook her head. "I suppose if I had a brush with death and two months of not knowing my own name, I'd take my husband's threats seriously, too."

"It's unfortunate. She's a bright woman, full of life. The second she remembered who she was, everything changed." Again . . . not a lie.

Brackett pushed out of his chair. "Nothing we're going to do about it now. Much as I'd love an arrest to attach to two months of my agent being in a safe house, we can't force people to testify. Not when they're the victims. Let the local police in Vegas know we're giving this back to them."

Leo stopped himself from showing too much excitement. "Will do."

The story filled all the holes. While slightly fabricated, the bottom-line truth was Olivia had been the one who was shot. The shooter likely was aiming for her in the first place, and she wasn't going to testify to put that shooter in prison. Until there was evidence to suggest otherwise, that was the story, and Leo was sticking with it.

Not that Leo was sugarcoating reality in his own head. He was crossing a line by not clueing his people in, but how big of a line, he wouldn't say. Right now, the victim was Olivia. And unless bodies of known assassins that could have been the shooter started piling up . . . Leo shook the thought from his head.

He stood when Brackett got to his feet. "Fitz will catch you up on what you've been missing."

Later that night, when Leo drove to his three-bedroom bungalow home in the hills of Glendale, he pulled into his garage and closed it before he got out of his car.

The second he opened the door into the house, the alarm buzzed. Leo disengaged the security system as he tugged at his tie. He turned on a hall light and moved to the kitchen. He went directly to his refrigerator, opened it, and immediately shut it again. The smell inside was off the charts. His time in Vegas was only supposed to be for the duration of the trial, with weekends at home. Only that wasn't how it panned out. And all the perishables in the house perished. Instead of a beer, which he knew would be stale, he turned to a bottle of whiskey.

He walked into his dark living room, a big window facing the street outside, and sat in his favorite chair. After toeing his shoes off and unbuttoning the top of his shirt, he sat back and sipped his first drink in over two months.

The fireplace was dark, the room was cold, there wasn't anything to eat . . . none of that was any different than it had been before Olivia, but all of it screamed at him now.

Where was she?

Was she okay?

Did she know she had ripped a hole in him with her departure?

Leo was a relationship guy.

In all his years . . . from his first high school girlfriend to the two in college and the one beyond . . . he didn't know how to play.

Then Olivia showed up in his life.

A connection.

He sat up, pulled his jacket off, and removed his phone from it.

He found her picture. She was smiling at him from over her shoulder. Her flirty smile. The one she sent him as she lured him into the snow and attacked him with balls of fluff and ice. He touched the image. He wanted to save her. It's what he did. All she needed to do was come back and give him a chance.

Leo put the whiskey to his lips, welcomed the burn as it went down.

The image of Olivia disappeared as his phone rang.

He cleared his throat before answering the call on speaker. "Hello, Neil."

"How are you holding up?"

"Been better." No reason to say he was fine, everyone in that house knew what Olivia meant to him.

"Yeah."

"Have you heard—"

"No. She hasn't contacted us."

Leo didn't expect a different answer.

"How did today go?"

"Everything is fine. Back to normal at the office." He didn't have to say his boss bought the story, it was implied.

The conversation paused. "I don't know how to say this without saying it," Neil started.

It wasn't like the man to preamble any conversation. "Never stopped you before."

"True. Your security system sucks."

Leo looked away from the phone and around the room. "Excuse me."

"Go to your front door."

"Have you been in my house?"

Neil was quiet.

Leo grabbed his phone, walked to his front door. On his porch was a large paper bag. "What's this?"

He grabbed it, took it to his kitchen, and looked inside. The smell of warm roast beef met his senses before he could open the Styrofoam container. Under the container was a six-pack of beer.

"Sasha predicted you'll get drunk tonight and thought food would make your morning a little better."

There weren't many times he was at a loss for words. "That was thoughtful. Thank her . . . thank you."

"About your shitty security . . . with your permission, I'd like to bring people over tomorrow and correct that."

"Neil—"

"You don't have outside cameras, lighting, or alarms. The garage is completely penetrable. And what happens when something goes off, someone calls you to ask if you left a door open? My housekeeper has a better system than you."

"You probably put her system in."

"Beside the point."

Leo smiled, opened the lid on his dinner. *Prime rib . . . nice.* "I was undercover for months, barely made it back here to make sure a pipe didn't break and flood the place."

"If Olivia shows up, it's not safe enough for her."

He looked away from the food, considered Neil's words. "Do you really think she will?"

"Impossible to tell. I like being prepared."

Leo grabbed a knife and fork from the drawer.

"I leave at eight in the morning. I'll put a key under the mat."

"That won't be necessary."

It felt good to laugh.

~

The beautiful thing about hiding in Europe when you spoke a half a dozen languages, and you weren't too short or too tall and your features were ambiguous, was that you could morph into almost any nationality, and no one questioned a single thing.

Olivia walked into the ING bank in Amsterdam, where she had an account. And she did so as a woman twenty years older and thirty pounds heavier than her.

The teller walked her back to the safety deposit boxes where she was left in complete privacy.

Olivia looked down at the box she hadn't seen in three years. There were a dozen of them littered around the world. Europe, Asia, South Africa, the Middle East, America . . . They were her social security.

Pohl had bankrolled many of the early boxes. Cash, identification, passports . . . weapons. Unknowingly, she'd used them . . . at first. Then she realized how easily he could keep track of her through the boxes, through their contents. Slowly, she emptied those he'd financed, liquidated the weapons . . . literally smelting them after each . . . well, after each assignment. And even when he didn't have her squeezing the trigger, if she used an ID he'd procured for her, she burned it. Found her own resource for new ones and perfected a dozen different identities to access them.

And in time she was harder to track until one day, many months after she'd allowed herself to have a friend again, she disappeared completely.

Amelia's death had devastated her. Somehow Pohl must have found out about their friendship, and he'd killed her as an example.

That's what Olivia believed until Sasha and Neil's team came into play.

For a year after learning the truth, that Amelia hadn't died because the two of them had been friends, but at the hands of the reigning power at Richter . . . Olivia realized that her disappearance, her accepted demise, had taken root. And once Pohl was eliminated, no one was the wiser.

That didn't stop Olivia from looking over her shoulder. Didn't stop her from sleeping light and living with the ever-close gun under her pillow as if it were a teddy bear she could curl up with at night.

Twice in the past seven years she'd tried to find legitimate work. Promised herself she'd eventually abandon the boxes altogether, leave the blood money where it was or acquire enough wealth that she could dump the contents in a charity bin for orphans and walk away.

After all, abandoned and orphaned children don't care where the money that feeds them comes from. God knows Olivia didn't question anytime good fortune came her way.

She'd been found at the age of five next to a woman who had overdosed in an abandoned building. It was assumed the woman was her mother, but it wasn't like anyone bothered with a DNA test to make sure. Olivia remembered next to nothing of those years.

She'd been placed in an orphanage in Munich and shuffled around like chattel. Almost how a dog gets moved from one shelter to another to avoid being put down.

After the third orphanage in Germany, she was moved to one in the United Kingdom . . . some kind of exchange . . . or so she was told. Now she realized that it was likely Pohl acting as an early benefactor to see how she would adapt and grow.

And adapt and grow she did. She abandoned her German accent as she learned English and excelled in the education that was offered. So many of the orphans around her were busy following a path that would leave them dead in a warehouse. Instead of joining them, Olivia found a better way.

Someone had whispered in her ear once, "This is the life you were given, not the life you'll lead. It's temporary."

Olivia believed it.

By the time she was ten, she was at Richter. She'd won the lotto.

"Richter will teach you skills so you never end up like your mother. This education is free to you. The award system will help set you up so when you leave Richter you will have money to start your life." Thousands of pounds were offered for every language she learned. Incentives for marksmanship, hacking computers . . . more money . . .

By the time she was fifteen, she'd learned that even if she found trouble, and there were times she did, Richter wasn't going to kick her to the street. She was placed in solitary, which was pretty close to what it looked like in the prison system. No outside contact, dark room, food, but nothing more.

A voice through the door always said the same thing. "If you're going to step out of line, don't get caught."

Another lesson.

Little did she know every lesson she'd learned prepared her for the lonely life of an assassin.

After Richter and years of isolation, Olivia found she liked people. And with every opportunity to find friendship or connection . . . she did. Then she witnessed their lives, their loves . . . their families. Their ambitions and desires.

And then her hellish nightmares smothered her in hot lava, laughing at her . . . calling her a hypocrite. How could a woman who'd stopped hearts from beating be anything but a monster? The people around her . . . if they knew, they would turn on her. Or worse, someone would use them to pull her back into a world she wished she could forget forever. So she pulled away . . . didn't allow any true connection to anyone.

All legitimate employment was pushed aside, and abandoning the money in charity boxes never happened.

She lived simply. No cars, no insurance, no trail. She rented a month at a time, moved around a lot. Her lovers were limited and never held on long enough for any real connection. As Sasha had pointed out, handholding in the moment was the only handholding that took place.

Olivia looked at her palms as the thought passed.

Leo.

She pushed aside memory lane and opened the safety deposit box. She removed three passports, all the cash and credit cards, and a handgun. From her purse, she removed the remainder of the cash Neil had given her, and the identification she'd used to leave the States, and folded them inside before closing the box and returning it to its place in the wall.

After exiting the bank, Olivia pulled up the collar of her jacket as she walked around the city acquiring what she needed. Cell phones, the kind one used as a pay-as-you-go customer. She went from store to store, buying one or two at a time until she had enough. She bought a laptop and an antitheft backpack that would keep electronics, bank cards, or cell phones safe from someone standing beside you and stealing your shit.

Which was what she did at her first opportunity.

A middle-aged couple stood in front of a sex shop display window, fascinated by the Eiffel Tower–shaped condoms. Olivia moved beside them and struck up a conversation.

"I love visiting Amsterdam for this very reason." She spoke English with her German accent.

"This is our first trip here," the woman said.

"Americans?"

"Yes," the man replied.

Olivia stood close to the woman, placed her hand in her pocket, and turned on the device that would detect any electronic strip in the woman's purse, including credit cards and identification, and recorded it for later.

"I have heard Amsterdam is often referred to as Europe's answer to Vegas. Is it?" Olivia asked.

The man was quick to respond. "No."

"Yes, it is," the woman countered.

"There aren't *coffee shops* with a pot menu on every corner in Vegas," he argued.

"You can buy pot there." The woman turned to Olivia, her smile big . . . like she'd been sitting in a smoke-hazed Amsterdam coffee shop for hours. "Pot is legal in a lot of places in America. It's only a matter of time before it looks more like this."

"She's right," the man said. "But the sex business is less in your face. If you want a peep show, you have to find a club and walk in. Nothing can be seen on the street, and prostitution is illegal everywhere."

"Is that right?" Olivia asked.

The woman giggled. "How would you know where to look at naked boobies?" she asked her man as she snuggled next to him.

"Yours are the only boobies for me."

"I think we should try that one." The woman pointed to one of the many condoms hanging in the store window.

The man smiled at Olivia. "If you'll excuse us. Looks like I'm gonna get some tonight."

"Have fun," Olivia called after them as they disappeared inside.

From there she found a crowded bar and ordered a drink. Within an hour she had three random cell phone numbers, two residing in Europe, one from the States, and the ability to move through those phones when making calls and go undetected.

On the walk back to her hotel, she dodged bicyclists that outnumbered the motorists four to one. She took her time along one of the many canals that crisscrossed the city. The streetlights were buzzing on and reflecting on the water.

Amsterdam was nothing like Las Vegas.

Sex was sold here openly from a window. Prostitution was legal and taxed. That didn't make it better, just . . . open. With competition and free trade, men like Mykonos didn't have nearly the same hold on the industry. Olivia wasn't stupid enough to think human trafficking wasn't walking past her right at that moment, but it wasn't the norm.

There were plenty of drunk and high tourists in the city, but there was a rich and sober economy there as well. Jobs that didn't center on gambling, sex, drugs, and retail. They were known for the fashion industry, shipping, tech . . . the city was filled with highly educated finance and business executives and their companies. And she would venture to guess that most of those inhabitants didn't frequent the red-light district or coffee shops any more often than a New Yorker walked in Times Square for the fun of it.

Olivia had always liked Amsterdam.

She blended there.

Was invisible there.

Back in her hotel room, she stripped her fake identity away, one layer at a time, and stood under the spray of a hot shower. When her thoughts turned to Leo, she purposely turned the water to cold until all she could think about was scrubbing the soap from her hair and getting out.

For hours she sat at the desk in her room, electronics spread out, the computer and uplink in place, and worked. Every moment since her memory returned, she had questioned how it was possible that all this knowledge could vanish. The languages, the legit technology skills, the hacking . . . infiltrating a computer, a cell phone. Disguise. She really was good at changing her appearance. She'd have to be, she realized, if she wanted to stay alive. It was amazing how big the world was and yet how small at the same time.

She had just started to believe that the world did think she was dead.

Her phone call to Neil, and the job he put her on, was a first step to finding some peace. She would take the money he offered and never reach into a covert safety deposit box again. But that blood money was going to keep her alive, and instead of avoiding it, she decided it was time to embrace it. Take the money she'd sold her soul for and put it to use.

Finally, somewhere after two in the morning, when her fingers couldn't type any longer and her eyes started seeing double on the computer screen, she backed out of the system she was in.

Olivia relocated a few feet to the bed and climbed on top of the covers.

She closed her eyes and took a few deep breaths, tried to still her mind.

Leo . . .

Was he still in hiding? Did he think the shooter was aiming at him? Did he hate her?

Now that he knew who she really was, did he think of her and cringe?

Not since her high school years had she felt the need to validate someone else's feelings about her. Because no one ever felt anything for her.

"I want you to know this means something to me."

He wasn't talking about the sex. Hell, she would have owned up to that early on had he taken her up on her offer. He was talking about them, together. It was as close to anyone saying they loved her as she had gotten in her entire life.

The "I love you, baby" in the stacks didn't count.

Amnesiac Olivia had to know if he hated her.

Richter Olivia justified the desire to reach out by saying he needed to know he didn't have to hide. That the shooter was aiming at her.

And since Amnesiac and Richter were both on the same yard line, Olivia crawled off the bed, retrieved her computer, and pulled it on her lap.

A few keystrokes in and she nudged Leo's computer.

If he wasn't online, she wouldn't see it.

She closed her eyes and pressed Enter.

He was there.

Or at least his computer was on and linked to the internet. She waited, holding her breath for him to do anything to indicate that he was in fact sitting in front of the screen.

The screen shifted to a search engine, and Olivia's heart jumped in her chest.

CHAPTER
TWENTY-THREE

A message from Neil said his crew was done and to call him before Leo tried to enter his own house.

For thirty minutes Neil walked him through the new system over the phone. Just the basics. Details would be explained on the weekend when Leo promised to be in Neil's office to make good on his search for Olivia.

There wasn't a care package for dinner, but there was a note on the refrigerator.

You're a slob, Grant. Clean this or throw it out . . . but for fuck's sake, put it out of its misery.

He pulled on a pair of jeans and a T-shirt with the goal of tackling the mess so it was safe to go to the grocery store and refill the thing. After two months of home-cooked meals, he looked at the deli sandwich he'd grabbed on the way home with disinterest.

What he really wanted was mashed potatoes.

He dragged his laptop to the small dining table and brought his bagged dinner with him.

After a couple of bites, he logged in to Amazon and started searching for a couple of kitchen gadgets he'd used at the cabin and found useful.

He walked away to grab a bottle of water and heard his computer ping with a message.

He twisted off the cap on the water and opened his chiming chat screen.

Hello, Mr. FBI.

Leo dropped the bottle. It hit the table, bounced off the chair, and fell to the floor . . . water spilled.

He scrambled to the keyboard. Olivia?

The second he typed her name, both messages disappeared like the invisible ink function on an iPhone.

"No, no, no, no, no!" He couldn't type fast enough. Are you there?

Yes.

The words disappeared.

He sat, ignoring the mess he'd made, or the water as it soaked into his pants. Where are you?

His words were gone in the time it took to read them.

Please don't go.

You were not the target.

Leo's fingers hovered over his keyboard. If he told her he knew that, would she then log off? If he argued, would she engage?

You don't know that. He pressed send and waited.

If I learn otherwise, I will contact you.

Panic rose in his throat. Her words sounded like goodbye. Don't go. Tell me you're okay.

His words vanished.

How can I get ahold of you? I can help you. Let me.

No response.

He pounded his fists on the table. She needed to hear him. How could he make her listen?

We deserve a chance.

Silence.

Leo swallowed hard. I love you. He pressed send, hated that he had to type the words he'd never said to a woman who wasn't family before.

The words faded . . .

Did she see them? Was she still there?

Loving me will only get you killed. I'm sorry.

He closed his eyes. It's a chance I'm willing to take. He pressed send, and a screen popped up. Message undeliverable. Address not available.

"Fuck!"

~

Forty minutes later he sat in Neil's headquarters with Claire typing away on his computer and Neil quizzing the conversation.

"Are you sure it was her?" Neil asked.

"She addressed me as Mr. FBI. It was a joke . . . kind of. Yes, it was her."

"The entire conversation. From the top."

"I asked her where she was."

Neil shook his head.

"Right, she didn't say. Then she said I wasn't the target. I told her she didn't know that."

"Did she counter you?"

"No. She said she'd contact me if she learned otherwise," Leo told him.

"So she doesn't really know. But she is actively searching for the answer," Claire said.

Leo agreed. "My thoughts exactly."

"Then what did she say?" Neil asked.

"Nothing. I panicked. Asked if she was okay. Told her I can help her." His breath was shaky. "I told her I loved her."

Claire stopped typing and looked up, eyes wide.

"She didn't respond," Neil concluded.

"No, she did. She told me loving her would get me killed. Then she apologized and logged off."

Neil turned away, walked to the other end of the room. "Okay, then. We have something to work with."

Leo didn't see it. "W-what do you mean? What do we have to work with?"

"First, she contacted you. That's not easy for her. And she did so in less than a week."

"That means she's thinking about you," Claire declared without looking up from the computer.

"And the feelings you have for her are mutual," Neil said.

"Ahhh, look at you tapping into your warm and fuzzy side," Claire teased Neil.

"I don't have a warm and fuzzy side . . ."

"Wait. Stop. How did you conclude that?" Not that Leo didn't like to hear that perspective.

"She apologized," Neil said.

"I heard her apologize several times in Colorado."

217

"That was the amnesia talking," Claire said. "Olivia would run over your leg with a car, get out, and ask what the hell it was doing there in the first place. Saying *I'm sorry* isn't in her wheelhouse."

Neil pointed to Claire. "Which means she's changed." He poked Leo in the chest. "That's all you."

Leo's head was short-circuiting.

Claire started singing. "Warm and fuzzy. Warm and fuzzy . . ."

"Zip it, Claire."

She chuckled.

Neil patted Leo's chest where his finger had poked. "Fair warning. Loving her can get you killed."

He had already concluded that. Didn't stop him from falling hard. He leaned against the desk where Claire was working. "I know."

"Now, the next time she contacts you—"

"We don't know that she will."

Neil waited for Leo to look up to start talking again. "The *next* time she contacts you it will be to convince you that what you had wasn't real. That she couldn't care less about you or any of us."

"To push me away."

"Yes. The more convincing she is, the more likely there's a threat. If she didn't care, she wouldn't call. So when she does reach out, try and get her on the phone. Listen for clues. Background noise, is she tired . . . is it day or night where she's at."

"And if I can't decipher any of that?"

"I'll place a recording device that activates when you turn up the volume on your phone or computer. You can deactivate by pressing it twice. Then we can pick apart the recording here," Claire informed him.

"I thought you weren't going to actively look for her," Leo reminded Neil.

Neil hesitated, as if he wasn't sure how to answer the question, and then decided. "I changed my mind."

"And how often do you do that?" Leo asked.

"When it's warranted."

Claire sat back in her chair and rubbed her hands together.

"Did you find something?"

"No. Clever bitch. I really need to know how she did this." She sighed. "I found the time the messages started and when they ended, but no data. No number, no computer ID. Nada. The disappearing ink is just brilliant. That's some *Mission Impossible* shit right there." She was clearly excited.

"Damn."

Claire turned back with a new fever driving her. "Now the question is, Did she activate your audio and video? I would have."

"Wait, you think she saw me, heard me when she was texting?"

Claire looked at him like he was an idiot. "Why would you have mono when you can have stereo?"

~

The last time Olivia stood outside the gates of Richter was the night she and Neil's team took down Pohl. She'd convinced Neil to take her with them for their sting operation and flush out Amelia's killer.

Olivia had every intention of putting a bullet in Pohl's head at the first opportunity. But when she'd seen how Neil and his people worked, she couldn't jeopardize his operation. If Pohl had ended up dead at that point . . . more questions would have been asked.

Seven years later and she sat perched in a tree with a pair of binoculars in her hand.

It hadn't snowed yet, but the bitter cold kept the students bundled in their uniform jackets and colorful scarves. It looked as if Harry Potter had made an impact on fashion at the school.

In the short conversations she'd had with Neil in the past year, he'd informed her that the dynamics had changed at Richter. That the military-style training was there but saved for the upperclassmen. The prison-like rules had been eased, and no corporal punishment was handed down. Which meant no time in a dark cell when you acted out.

The headmistress, Lodovica, was still serving time for child endangerment, and her lover was serving a life sentence for murder.

As Olivia searched the grounds of the school for familiar faces in the staff, she found quite a few. She had snapshots of the administration; some had been there when she was a student. Professors that saw holes in the leadership and rushed to fill them.

But how many of them liked the old ways? Did they know where the students had been farmed out?

Olivia was fairly certain Neil already had this information, but asking him to find a name was like drawing a line on a map to who had shot her. At that point it would be a race to find the shooter before Neil could. Olivia had already learned that hacking into Neil's system required her to be on the inside. And that was too risky.

Seven years ago, the information that would lead her to the shooter had been on campus, deep in the bowels of the school in a hidden room. Was it still there?

She doubted it, but needed to see for herself.

Over the course of the next few days, Olivia climbed a lot of trees, took plenty of pictures, and formulated a plan.

Getting inside was easier than it had been seven years ago. Yeah, she could have infiltrated at night, jumped the walls, dodged the cameras, hacked the system . . . but why bother?

A commercial laundry service used by the school was based twenty miles away. Obtaining one of their uniforms took up one evening, and perfecting her disguise took another.

With her car parked far away to avoid detection, and the laundry service truck on campus, she hopped over the wall to get on the school grounds. Once there, she worked her way to the backside of the dining hall and pushed open the door.

The sounds from inside instantly drove her to memories of her past.

Breakfast was in full swing. Noise from the kitchen where a small army of cooks were cleaning up one meal and prepping for the next. She shimmied past the dining staff and into the hall itself.

The smell of eggs, which never really tasted like eggs, and cooked breakfast meats made her pause. She opted for porridge most mornings when she was there, thinking the meat was too greasy and the eggs too wet or too dry.

Then there were the kids themselves. All ages from mid–primary school to college.

It was a school where rich parents tucked their children away so someone else could not only teach them but raise them. And the college students, at least in the past, were able to finish their university degree in three years instead of four.

And they were protected.

The school security kept the unwanted out and the kids in. But how had that changed?

"Excuse me." A boy, maybe ten years old, stood in front of her with an empty tray of food.

She was standing next to the return counter, where dishes were stacked on top of each other, and flatware went into their respective bins.

Olivia spoke in German, as most of the local staff did, excused herself, and moved away.

The first sack of laundry she found sitting in the hall she grabbed and walked with as she searched the perimeter of the hall. When she worked her way to the back, where a stairwell to the lower levels once resided, she was met with a brick wall.

She followed the wall around the corner, and the space where the dumbwaiters had been was also bricked in.

What did she expect? The lower levels were where most of the shady shit at Richter took place. That didn't mean the area wasn't still there, it just had a different access. Unless the space was completely abandoned, including the storage room where Sasha had found all the blackmail crap.

She lowered her head and turned away from the walls.

She'd find another way.

With her bag of dirty laundry, she moved to the service area, dumped it in the bin, and grabbed a clean sack.

She started to the youth dorm, searching for floor guardians, often teachers who had computer access in their rooms.

Students rushed around, their uniforms pristine, their innocence untarnished.

Sad that the world would show them that this was the best time of their lives. The part before reality crashed in and they were exploited for their talents.

Once Olivia realized that the supervisors' rooms were unlocked, and void of any computers, she switched her plan again.

The university dorm looked untouched.

The same color on the walls that weren't stone or brick. The same sconce lighting that made it impossible to see but easy to sneak around at night.

Without meaning to, she found her floor, the one where she'd spent the last three years of her time at Richter, and walked to the door of her room.

"They offered me a job!" Olivia bounced on her bed, excitement in her voice.

Amelia pushed her shoulder, her smile just as huge. "I told you that you didn't have anything to worry about. You're like the smartest person here."

"I'm so ready to get out of this place. I'm going to be able to travel and see the world. I'm going to sleep with exotic men and wear fancy clothes." She dropped her head on her pillow with visions of evening gowns and champagne dangling from her fingertips.

"Which company hired you?" Amelia asked.

That was the best part. "I could tell you, but I'd have to kill you," she said, laughing. She sat up almost as quickly as she'd flopped down. Her voice was nothing but a whisper. "Super hush- hush. It's some kind of secret society. I think it's run by the UN."

"I bet my dad knows about it," Amelia said.

"Don't say a thing to your dad. I shouldn't have even told you. I was told that if anyone found out I was working for them, I'd lose my job instantly."

Amelia frowned. "That's weird."

Olivia shrugged. "I don't care. It's my ticket out of this place. The money I earned with the extra language classes still won't get me a flat in Berlin for longer than a year. Now I can put that money away and add to it. I get to be an honest-to-goodness spy. Can you believe it?" She grasped Amelia's hands, and they both squealed.

"This calls for a celebration."

"I know where the key is to Charlie's locker."

Olivia placed her hand on the door as her memory faded.

The door opened and she stepped back. A young man, maybe twenty, seemed startled by her presence. "What are you doing up here?" he asked in German.

"I'm new," she told him in German as she lifted the empty sack. "Was told to gather the dirty."

The kid rolled his eyes. "We don't leave them up here, they're down the chute." He closed the door behind him and brushed by.

"That's no way to talk to your elders, Kellen."

The reprimand was in English and a very familiar voice.

Kellen turned back to her, placed a smile on his face that hadn't been there before. "My apologies, ma'am."

The kid walked away, leaving Olivia with Checkpoint Charlie standing three feet away.

CHAPTER
TWENTY-FOUR

Leo placed his report on Brackett's desk, tapped the file twice, and walked out of his office. The man was off for the day, but had wanted the file on his desk by morning.

So there it was, most of the details one hundred percent true, and a few were drawn a tad outside the lines.

It had been over a week since Olivia had reached out.

A week of leaving his computer on, his cell phone ringer on loud . . . and jumping anytime it rang. Even though he was distracted at work, his mind was never far away from wondering where she was and what she was doing.

Right now, the distraction came in the form of two new human trafficking cases. One that involved women being brought in from Southeast Asia to serve as anything from prostitutes to slave labor in the fashion industry. And the other involved the new management of a gang that had started finding their girls in the local youth centers.

Since Leo was well versed in teenager, he and Fitz were on point to create a relationship with the staff and teens at the Y and the Boys and Girls Club, and see if they could start narrowing down the playing field.

Fitz drove while Leo gave her directions to their first stop. At that moment, they were stuck in the ever-popular LA traffic. A complete stop on the 405 freeway.

"Why do we live here?" Fitz asked the rhetorical question.

"The weather," he replied, looking up at the gray clouds that would make the day dreary but wouldn't deliver any rain. It wasn't until the meteorologists started yelling *storm watch* that Los Angelenos considered grabbing an umbrella. Twenty percent chance of rain always meant eighty percent chance of nothing.

Heavy on the nothing.

"There's plenty of sunshine in other places."

"Florida has bugs."

The annual struggle of living in Southern California always included a discussion of sunshine versus humidity versus snow.

Although he didn't mind the snow.

Not when there was someone to share it with.

Damn, he missed her. He dug down into his Catholic roots and prayed to whoever was listening that Olivia was alive and safe. He also asked that she contact him soon. He and Neil's team needed something more to go on.

Apparently, when you were a retired assassin, the entire world was your office space. And Olivia had told the team nothing about her past. Making it impossible to track her.

Except there was one critical detail she'd told them years ago.

The man who'd hired an innocent girl and made her an assassin had recorded her first kill and held it over her.

Leo wondered what he'd done to make her take that first shot. Maybe he convinced her the head on the other end of the scope was evil in human skin.

Leo didn't know how it played out. What he did understand is the woman he'd fallen for was nothing like the killer Sasha and the others described.

"Okay, what the hell is going on in your head?" Fitz asked.

"What?"

"It's that woman, isn't it? Janie."

Even he knew to stick as much to the truth as possible. "I spent two months with her. So yeah . . . I'm worried about her."

"How did you spend those two months?" she asked, her eyes on him and not the stopped car in front of them.

"The house was filled with people."

"Ah-huh."

"And cameras and microphones. Seriously, there was no privacy."

"If teenage kids can figure it out, two grown adults can . . ."

He blew her off. "It's not what you think." It was so much more.

"I'm not Brackett, all right. I don't care who you sleep with."

"I never said I slept with her."

Fitz smiled and turned her attention to moving traffic. "You just did."

He moaned at her conclusion but didn't deny it.

"I'm sorry it's complicated and couldn't work. You deserve someone in your life."

"I'm sorry, too."

~

"Follow me. I'll show you where we collect the soiled laundry."

Olivia thanked him and kept her step just behind him. Her disguise added thirty years to her appearance, a longer nose and short salt-and-pepper hair. The glasses were an added distraction.

Checkpoint Charlie was Richter's version of a butler and hall monitor.

She glanced at him as they walked down the stairs. The man didn't seem to age. She remembered assuming his age to be in his sixties, but now that she was older, he still looked in his sixties. He spent most of his time at the front entrance to Richter as a literal doorman. Though he always had time to make it to the doors since there was a gate, keeping people out or announcing them when they arrived.

He was kind.

When students didn't have a family to celebrate a milestone with, he was always the one who offered something as a gift. Sometimes that gift was turning the other way when he saw something that would have gotten them in trouble with the headmistress. On Olivia's eighteenth birthday, he accidentally left his locker open, where he occasionally put a bottle of liquor or wine and made sure she knew it. He did that for a lot of students. Especially those that were truly stuck there.

Charlie opened the laundry room door and stood aside as she walked by.

"Danke," she said and looked around.

"It appears your colleagues beat you to it." Charlie spoke in English and closed the door with the two of them inside.

Olivia turned and found him staring.

She knew her jig was up.

If there was anyone who had the finger on the pulse of a home or business, it was the maid or the butler. And Charlie was bright.

"Why are you back?" he asked, his eyes searching her face as if trying to place her.

Olivia stood taller. "Do you know who I am?"

He moved his head from one side to the other. "It's a good disguise, but a bit thin, if you ask me. A man who watches you grow up always pictures what you will look like when you grow old."

Well, damn.

He sighed. "The world thinks you're dead."

Words she always liked to hear.

She pushed aside the uniform top and exposed the scar on her chest. "Not everyone."

He closed his eyes. "I'm sorry for that."

"I survived."

He shook his head. "Not the bullet. The resurrection," he clarified.

She was bummed about that, too. "I want the information from the lower levels."

Charlie chuckled. "Ahh, the lost treasures of the bowels of Richter. They do not exist."

"They do. I know people who have touched them."

He paused. "If there was, at any time, this information, it is now gone."

Bullshit. Richter had too many secrets to maintain.

"How many have come before me looking?"

"A few," he said.

"And were they like me? Did they have the same *employment*?"

"Some." He swallowed. "I did not know of the extent of Lodovica's crimes."

She wanted to believe him. "You know everything that happens on this campus."

"Eventually, yes. By then it was too late for many of you."

"But not all."

Charlie lowered his eyes. "A cross I bear every day."

"Then why did you stay? Why are you still here?" She removed the glasses that were no longer needed to shield her face.

"For you. And all like you. Those who come back deserve answers, and I do what I can to provide them."

"Then show me the files."

"What are you searching for?"

Again, Olivia exposed her scar and pointed to it.

Charlie caught on. His expression sobered. "The shooter was one of ours." It wasn't a question.

She gave one quick nod. "I need to know where—"

Charlie's hand shot up, stopping her.

"Don't tell me a name. Please. Just as I will never utter yours, do not tell me theirs." Pure distress crossed Charlie's face. That's when the man looked as if he might have aged . . . just a little.

She constructed her words as carefully as she could. "If I'm to have a life—any life—I must remain six feet underground. I need some direction to find the person that put a hole in me. There is no reason for the bullet to have been personal. I must find who hired them. I need to know who else knows I'm breathing."

At first, she didn't think Charlie was going to offer anything. And then he opened his mouth. "There is a place in Hungary. Budapest. A sanctuary for a night. A place where one might have a conversation without risk of another hole in their body."

She liked the sound of that. "Honor among thieves," she clarified.

"I doubt anyone there looks like themselves. I have mentioned this location many times in my tenure at Richter, and no one has called me a liar. So I must assume it exists and is useful. And since only a select few graduates of this institution are privy to such information, I must assume you would know people who partake in the occasional libation without risk of being shot."

This was perfect.

He told her the name of the pub and stood back.

She smiled at him for the first time. "Thank you."

"I do not deserve your thanks."

For whatever reason, she pictured Leo saying the same thing. "That may be true, but thank you anyway."

He stepped away from the door.

She paused at his side, placed her hand on his arm. "And you're lying about the lost treasure."

He looked her dead in the eye. "In order to protect the innocent, you must sometimes protect the guilty."

Again, Leo's image jumped in her head.

She leaned forward without thought and kissed Charlie's cheek before walking out the door.

~

The team was on point, working every angle they could to bring Olivia in.

How had this become his life? How had caring for others consumed so many hours of his day?

Neil sat in his home office watching his headquarters as his staff changed shifts.

Staff . . . Who was he kidding?

Claire and Cooper were on their way out the door, hand in hand. Neil was still getting used to the idea of his adopted daughter having an emotional connection with someone. Someone Neil had personally known longer than her . . . but that didn't weigh in. Claire was an innocent teen when they'd met. Too goddamn smart for her own good. A prime pick for Pohl, or anyone to come along and turn her into what Olivia was now.

The shift changed and Jax lingered.

In a half an hour, the alarms at the Tarzana home where Claire, Cooper, and Jax lived would indicate someone had come in . . . and that alarm wouldn't be set again until after Jax was home and everyone was safe. Jax staying behind at the office on a weekday meant she was letting Claire and Cooper have some private time.

Neil really needed to get over the fact that Cooper was having sex with Claire.

A noise behind him had him turning in his chair.

"Please tell me you're not spying on Claire."

Gwen walked into his office, a knowing smile on her face.

"I'm not spying on Claire."

Her laughter filled the room as she sat in his lap and blocked his view of his computer. "You're a bad liar."

He grinned. "I used to be really good at it."

The love of his life, his wife, the mother of his children, placed her lips to his forehead. "Why are you worried?"

He removed the glasses he only wore at home and tossed them on his desk. "She was on the case. A key element to how Mykonos went down. Olivia was shot while talking to Leo. I pulled Claire as soon as I realized there was a bigger threat."

"But you still worry . . ."

Neil squeezed his fingers resting on Gwen's thigh. "I do."

"Are you doing everything you can?"

"Yes."

"Then breathe."

As if Gwen had the power to flip his switch, Neil found a deep breath and pushed his head into her shoulder.

Every day he was thankful for this woman . . .

The landline on his desk rang.

He ignored it.

Gwen twisted in his arms. "It's a German number."

Neil's hand shot out, put the receiver to his ear. "Hello."

"A woman matching your description visited today."

Neil leaned in closer to Gwen. Something, anything, in the form of a lead made him smile.

"What was she looking for?"

The line clicked several times.

"Files that very few know exist. And information about a former classmate she may have had a recent encounter with. Perhaps to thank them for giving her something to remember them by."

The line went dead.

Olivia is in Germany.

"What is it?" Gwen asked as she took the phone from his fingertips and set it back on the charger.

"That was Charlie at Richter. We have a break."

"Brilliant."

He reached for the phone. "I need Claire back in the office . . ."

Gwen snatched the phone out of his hands. "Leave those kids alone. Calling Claire back to the office every time you assume they're having sex isn't going to stop them."

"That is not—"

"What did Charlie tell you?"

"Olivia was at Richter. She wanted access to the files we acquired. To find the person who shot her."

"Then she knows who did it."

Neil gently removed the phone from Gwen's hand. "And since the majority of the files are in German . . . and Claire reads German . . ."

Gwen's long fingers wrapped around the phone again, slid it away. "Jax reads German. Sasha reads German."

It was his turn to take the phone.

Gwen held on to it this time.

"But Claire—"

"Is going home after a long day and can help look in the morning."

A ping on his computer told him that Claire and Cooper had arrived in Tarzana. A quick glance showed him that Jax was still at the office.

Neil loved his smart wife but was sometimes annoyed at how well she knew him. "Fine, I'll call Sasha."

Gwen always smiled and sat taller when she got her way. She released the phone. "And Jax . . . I'm sure she won't mind putting in a few extra hours to start the search." Gwen removed herself from his lap and rubbed the nonexistent wrinkles from her pants. "Jax is leaving to visit her family soon, right?"

"Next week."

Gwen leaned down, her lips requesting his. Her kiss was brief, but promising. "Then you might want to start getting used to the idea that Claire and Cooper will have the house all to themselves for a spell."

She turned to walk away, and Neil delivered a playful pat to her butt.

Gwen jumped, looked over her shoulder. "Don't threaten me with a good time."

Twenty years with the woman, and she could still make him hard with just her words.

CHAPTER
TWENTY-FIVE

The after-school programs at the youth centers meant working late. Fitz was driving him back to the office when Neil called.

"Hey," Leo answered. Adrenaline zipped up his back anytime Neil reached out.

"Are you in a position to talk?"

Leo glanced at Fitz. "Not really."

"Call me when you can."

Oh, no, no, no. "Wait. Tell me."

Neil paused. "She's alive. We have a lead."

That adrenaline swelled and washed over him in relief. "Happy hour sounds great. I'll call you when I'm on my way." He ended the call and tried not to smile as brightly as he felt.

"I like happy hour. Where are we going?" Fitz asked.

"Uhm . . ." Leo cleared his throat. "That was Neil. He's having trouble with the wife. I'm not sure he'll want to talk about it if there's a woman around."

"That's unfortunate. I have zero social life lately."

"Next time," Leo offered.

"Yeah, yeah . . . I don't want your pity invites."

"I thought you were having luck on that dating site."

She pulled off the freeway and onto the congestion of Melrose Avenue. "You know what a woman really finds on dating sites?"

"No. But I think I'm about to get a lesson."

She lifted her right hand off the steering wheel to count. "Catfishers, cheating husbands, old men that want to date women half their age, or men my age that want me to have an IQ of twelve and big tits."

That sucked.

"Happy hour next week, then," he offered.

"You're on."

~

Leo pulled through the gates of Neil's home and parked in the circular drive.

He'd never been to the man's home before, and was thoroughly impressed by the grounds alone. Gated estate, long, tree-lined cobblestone drive to a Mediterranean-style home. The sun had already set, but the house was completely illuminated by lighting in the trees and from the eaves.

Leo looked at the camera facing out from the door and rang the bell.

He heard running footsteps before the door opened.

"Hi."

Leo stared at Neil's daughter and realized just how stressed the man must be with his little girl dating. She was as beautiful as her mother, only with dark brown hair. "You must be Emma."

"That's me." She opened the door wider. "You're Leo."

"I am."

"Come in." Emma turned away from the door. "Dad?" she yelled.

Gwen stepped into view. "Really, Emma? Must you?" she asked. Her British accent added an air of elegance to her words. She smiled at Leo as she approached.

"Sorry." Emma found her inner lady and cleared her throat. "Oh, Father . . . your guest has arrived."

Gwen chuckled and reached for Leo's hand. "Lovely to see you again."

"Sorry for the last-minute call."

"At Neil's request. No need to be sorry." She walked him through the foyer and past a massive great room with twenty-foot ceilings.

"Your home is beautiful."

"Thank you." She walked by a pair of forgotten Reeboks and kicked them out of the way. "Kids," she said.

"Those aren't mine," Emma said as she flopped onto the couch.

"Go tell your brother to come down here and clean up his mess."

Leo walked past what looked like forgotten homework spread all over the kitchen table.

Emma started yelling again. "Hey, doofus . . . Mum said—"

"Emma Louise!"

Even Leo snapped his shoulders back when the girl's middle name came out.

Gwen continued through the kitchen and down another hall. "Do you have children, Leo?"

"No."

"They really are a joy." She stopped at a closed door. "Except when they're not."

Leo laughed.

Gwen opened the door to Neil's home office.

Leo was pretty sure the room was supposed to be another living room, or maybe media room. It was at least a thousand square feet. A desk you would expect in the Oval Office sat center stage. Several large chairs sat in various places in the room with coordinating tables. Two oversized sofas faced each other, with a large coffee table separating them.

Neil was on the phone when they walked in. He lifted a hand as if asking them to wait. "We'll make that work. Thank you. I'll do that." He set the phone down and walked over to Leo's side, hand extended.

"Did you run every light on your way here?" Neil asked.

"Only two," Leo said, shaking the man's hand.

"Can I get you something to drink?" Gwen asked.

"I'm fine, thank you."

Neil smiled at his wife. "Blake asked that you call Sam and coordinate dinner next week."

"Lovely."

Gwen excused herself and closed the door behind her.

Leo let out a breath. "You have an exceptional place here, Neil."

He shook his head. "It's all her."

Leo stared at a piece of art on the wall.

It looked expensive.

"Do I have to ask, or are you going to tell me?"

Neil indicated the sofa and Leo made himself comfortable.

"Olivia is in Germany. Or was. She showed up at Richter searching for information about a former student."

"The person who shot her."

"So it appears."

"There's a list of recruits on campus?"

He shook his head. "Potential recruits, though I doubt it's still there."

Leo's hopes dropped. "So . . . ?"

"We procured a copy, of course."

Leo lifted a palm up. "Let's see it."

Neil gave a short shake of the head. "No. There are a lot of innocent names on the list. I have Sasha and Jax going through them now to try and narrow it down."

Sometimes Leo forgot he and Neil weren't exactly on the same team. "We could speed up the search if I plug them into the FBI database." And stop the shooter from getting another chance at Olivia.

"Olivia's name is on there. When Pohl died . . . how many Olivias did what she did and disappeared when the man who hired them was dead? The list is irrelevant to Olivia. She knows the name of the shooter . . . What she is looking for is bigger."

Leo huffed. "Bigger than a list of assassins?" He had a hard time picturing what that could be.

"Secrets. Throughout the years, the board members of the school were responsible for the hiring and firing of the administrative staff. People like Pohl and Lodovica, the headmistress, recruited the board by learning the dirty secrets of parents who placed their children in the school and then blackmailing them."

"So the board members knew what Pohl was doing?"

"Perhaps . . . some. It's unlikely they knew the extent, but they would never ask the hard questions or risk their own exposure. AJ, for example, his mother had an affair . . . AJ was the result. Fast-forward several years and her husband is appointed as America's ambassador to Germany. Things get sticky. Pohl tells the board filled with members like AJ's mom to keep voting Lodovica in so he can farm in . . . literally . . . young orphans such as Olivia, and prime them to become his henchmen."

That was some seriously fucked-up shit. "And the board does nothing."

"Exactly. But for every Olivia there's a Sasha. Orphans placed at the school to educate and protect them . . . teach them to protect themselves. Sasha's father murdered her mother, and would have eliminated her, too, had he known where she was. The secret of who Sasha was when she was placed at the school, and who her benefactor was, is interwoven in those files. None of it dirty, unless given to the wrong person. We of course have no way of knowing what information is damaging, so it remains hidden. Only the board members were scrutinized when the entire thing came down seven years ago."

Leo placed both hands on his knees as if he needed to lean in to digest the information. "And now Olivia is searching for these files."

Neil nodded. "She knows we have copies, but she went to the source instead of asking us."

"To not involve you."

"More proof Olivia has changed from what Pohl had turned her into."

Leo stood and started to pace. "She has a name and wanted any information she could get on this person to find them."

"That would be what I'd do."

"To what . . . kill them?"

Neil shrugged. "Maybe. If the attempt on her was personal."

Leo closed his eyes, hated the nausea that the thought of her going after this person induced.

"Or maybe she wants to find this person's Pohl. Who hired them. I'd be more interested in that name if this wasn't a personal bullet."

"Do we know if she got to these files?"

"No idea. Doubtful."

Leo nodded as direction started to form in his head. "How did you know she was at the school?"

Neil leaned over and picked up a remote from the coffee table and pressed it. The back wall of the office started to move until the panels folded onto each other and revealed a series of monitors that ran the length of the room and added another five feet of depth. "Damn, Neil."

The man actually smiled. "I'm rather fond of that."

Leo crossed his arms over his chest to see what other James Bond shit Neil had up his sleeve.

Another click of a different remote and it all turned on.

The monitors were a patchwork quilt of camera angles from dozens of homes and businesses. It was a larger-than-life version of what Neil had in his headquarters.

Neil moved to his computer, pressed a few keys, and the majority of the monitors turned off, leaving the center one illuminated. He then expanded the image to fill the surrounding monitors and make the picture close to six feet tall and ten feet wide.

"This is Richter."

Leo saw three images.

"Satellite, obviously. The front doors and the service entrance."

"Olivia wouldn't walk in the front door."

"No. And she didn't." Neil scrolled through several different cameras, giving Leo a snapshot of life at Richter. "She is well aware of where these cameras live and knows how to avoid them. Any kid that grew up there would . . . so for people like Olivia, this is all useless information." Neil changed the image of a different time of day. He stopped and zeroed in on a man. "This is Charlie. The kids refer to him as Checkpoint Charlie."

Leo laughed. "Cute."

"Properly named. He was the proverbial guard at the front door of the school. He is a big reason Sasha and Claire are still alive. This is the man who told me Olivia was there."

"Is he on your payroll?"

"No. But he knows what's happening on campus. I've checked in with him several times to make sure a new Pohl wasn't around. He's always helped out. When Olivia left, I messaged him and asked that he inform me of any visitors. He refused."

"Why?"

"Maybe to protect Olivia? I don't know. But she must have said something that convinced him to reach out."

Leo ran his fingers over the five o'clock shadow he'd started to grow for a woman who was running away. "He wants us to find her."

"I think he wants to help save every kid they lost. Including the one who shot her."

Leo could see that angle. "Looks like Checkpoint Charlie needs to be interviewed. We need to know what he told her."

"He's not going to tell you," Neil said.

"That's not going to stop me from asking. Do we know when Olivia was there?"

Neil stared at him . . . silent.

Leo stared back.

Neil looked away, typed on his computer. "Charlie didn't say. The campus is pretty tight. When we infiltrated, we went in late, in numbers, and we hacked the then internal system to go undetected." He stopped the footage from the service entrance to focus on a truck. "If I were solo, I'd blend."

The words on the truck were in German, and Leo couldn't read them, but the image of sheets drying on a clothesline told him what it was.

"When was this taken?"

"Twenty hours ago."

"Just enough time to put Olivia anywhere on the map."

Leo did not know how he was going to get this one past his boss. Not that it mattered. "I need a plane ticket." He pulled out his phone.

"Charlie will never talk to you."

"I can be convincing."

"They won't even let you on campus."

"Then I'll see him when he goes home."

"He lives there."

Leo sat back down and opened a Google search for plane tickets. "If Gwen were missing, would you sit here and do nothing if you knew she was breathing on a different continent?"

"Put your phone away," Neil grumbled. "Your flight leaves tomorrow at ten in the morning. I'm sending Jax with you. Claire and Sasha

Catherine Bybee

were both a part of blowing up the establishment and are scrutinized. Jax walks in unnoticed. Charlie might talk to her."

Claire's singsong voice repeating *warm and fuzzy* sounded in Leo's head. "You're a good man."

"I have a team based just outside of London, they know Jax. If you find information you need to jump on, they are there, and I'll be on the next flight out. Don't be a martyr."

CHAPTER TWENTY-SIX

Olivia had maps of the area surrounding A Róka, the establishment Charlie had told her about. The Fox, aptly named, sat in the center of District Five with the parliament building a short distance north, the Danube to the west, and Liberty Square to the east. The location offered escape routes in all directions, routes she was choreographing now.

This was uncharted territory. There had never been a time she actively sought out one of her own. She was walking an extremely tight rope. Simply walking into A Róka would expose her. Yes, she would wear a disguise . . . but as the saying goes, you can't bullshit a bullshitter. It was easy for her to detect who was camouflaged and who was not. And when you see a familiar face and cannot place them, you tend to look longer and harder, and that would cast attention Olivia didn't want. There was no way around walking into the nightclub. The only information about the place online was that there was a strict dress code, and cell phone use was not allowed inside.

It would take nine hours to drive there. An unavoidable route since there was no way in hell Olivia was going to arrive without a weapon.

She wanted nothing to do with searching out replacements, and getting the weapons past airport security without inside help was too risky.

Olivia's attention started to wane.

Sure enough, it was two in the morning.

She buttoned up her desk, made sure everything for a quick exit, should she need one, was ready to go before taking care of her nighttime ritual and climbing into the hotel bed.

Winding down had become an obsession.

She took her computer and keystroked her way into the path that would show her Leo.

The man had his computer up and online every night. She watched him as he buzzed around his kitchen going back and forth to his computer. Every once in a while, she'd hear him mumbling her name. "C'mon, Olivia . . . would it kill you to say hi?"

She knew he couldn't see her.

But seeing him, hearing him . . . was a comfort.

Only this time, his computer wasn't on. After two attempts, she realized it was useless.

Maybe he was working late?

She closed her laptop and pushed it to the other side of the bed. Leo's side. And if she opened her eyes in the middle of the night, she'd reconnect and look again.

When exhaustion finally took hold and she drifted off to sleep, she reached a hand out, touching the cold edges of her laptop, envisioning Leo.

Her eyes cracked open exactly four hours later and she moaned. Mornings were cruel at the pace she was maintaining.

She checked Leo's feed.

Nothing. It was only nine in the evening in LA.

Strange.

It took her an hour to leave her room and slip down to the café across from the hotel and order a coffee and hot cereal. It was still early, but the place was filling up.

She felt a strange connection and peacefulness listening to most of the customers speaking German. For a moment she remembered a time one year after leaving Richter. She'd gotten past the crushing shock of her employment and had started looking for ways out. At twenty-two she'd sat in a café like this one, in Germany, but she could have been anywhere. She'd look around and find the smiling faces of families and friends, all moving about their lives, and she'd ache. Young people her age would sit in a booth beside her, talking about their night at a pub, a party, or a play. They'd see her and strike up a conversation. And at that time Olivia wasn't worried someone was trying to kill her. So she would talk and even went out with a group on occasion.

Then she'd get a call.

You're going to Prague. I need you in Moscow. There's a situation in Costa Rica. Not every case ended up behind the barrel of a gun. Sometimes she needed to get closer. On the rare occasion, the assignment only involved gaining information. In those times, acts she had to perform didn't kill others, but they did burn away at her soul.

Eventually she'd sit in a café, like the one she was in now, and not engage. She'd put earbuds in and pretend to listen to music so no one would approach her. After an assignment, she'd get as far away from where it took place, find a bar, and use the first man she could to try and drown out the images in her head.

That was until Amelia.

AJ's sister and Olivia's ex-roommate at Richter showed up like a ray of goddamn sunshine in South Africa.

Amelia was there on a work assignment . . . legitimate work . . . and they met in a café. Olivia had no choice but to engage. For hours they talked. Amelia told her about her job, her new condo, her lack of a boyfriend. Olivia told her she'd been around the world, sipped that champagne with gorgeous men and slept with them all . . . even the married ones. A gross exaggeration, but it was what Amelia wanted to hear.

The day rolled into drinks until Amelia started asking hard questions.

By morning Amelia knew the truth. At least the CliffsNotes version of all the ugly. Having a friend was not a risk Olivia wanted to take. Not with Amelia's life on the line.

Olivia had gone to South Africa without Pohl knowing. She sat on a pier daily with the contact phone in her hand, having every desire in the world to throw the thing away.

Amelia was the tipping point.

They stood on the pier together as the cell phone sunk to the bottom of the sea. Next to waking up every day, ripping up Pohl's contract meant putting a bounty on her head.

It was months later that Olivia felt comfortable reaching out to Amelia. They'd put cameras in her condo and Amelia had been the one to teach Olivia how to ghost a computer and use text messages that disappeared almost as fast as they scrolled onto the page. Still, within six months, Amelia was dead. In fact, all three of Olivia's roommates at Richter were dead.

All to flush Olivia out.

Any chance of allowing herself to be open to friendships . . . or love . . . died with Amelia.

Until Leo.

Until Neil and the team.

Now Olivia sat in a café, her head down, her body language closed off.

She really had started to believe that the world thought she was dead.

If only she'd turned to her nightmares and looked closer . . . maybe she would have woken up, come out of the amnesia sooner, so she didn't have to break her heart in order to die again.

~

"Does Neil own this plane?"

Leo was once again in a private jet, which just boggled his brain, for the third time since he met Neil.

Jax sat on the sofa, feet curled under her with a tablet in her hands. "Technically it belongs to his brother-in-law. He's big in shipping."

Leo ran his hands over the leather seat. "Does it ever get old?"

Jax shrugged.

"I take that as a yes."

"My parents have money. They don't own a plane, but they were too good for domestic flights."

He looked down at the clouds that passed by. "It's going to make riding in coach really hard."

"Neil doesn't always pony up for this."

"I can't imagine what it costs."

"You don't want to know," Jax said.

Leo changed the subject. "Why did your parents send you to Richter?"

Jax kept plucking away on the game she was playing. "They didn't want to be parents."

"Ouch."

She put aside the game and looked up. With a perfectly polished British accent, she said, "Of course I have a daughter. Lovely girl. She's at Richter, you know. Fluent in four languages. She'll make a rich man a lovely wife."

"Double ouch." That didn't fit the description of any of the women working with Neil.

She stood, moved to the bar. "Yeah. Pissed them all to hell when I moved to the States and got a *job*. So *dirty* of me." She removed a flute and found a bottle of champagne and a small container of orange juice. "Want one?"

He shook his head. "But when we're done with Richter, you're going home to visit?"

"I'm not due there until next week. You don't dare show up early . . . that throws the whole schedule off."

"Why bother if your parents are such snobs?"

She pulled the cork out of the bottle with a nice pop and filled the glass within an inch of the top. "I don't hate them. They're not bad people, just selfish. And sadly, I really don't know them very well. I was barely in a training bra when they sent me to Richter, and I only went home in the summer and on holidays. And in the summer, my parents would take a month-long something somewhere and leave me and my brother with a nanny."

Poor little rich girl. "Damn."

With her mimosa in hand, Jax sat a little taller and smiled. "I never lose sight of the fact that as crappy as all that sounded, I've been very blessed."

"So what will you do before crashing your parents' house?"

Jax laughed at his description.

Leo envisioned her parents living in some stuffy manor-type home with servants and regal greyhound dogs at the door. The only time something crashed was when the rich drunk uncle dropped his bourbon and everyone blamed the glass.

She pointed up at the plane. "Blake. Gwen's brother. I'm going to his offices in Amsterdam to do a sweep."

"A sweep?"

"A couple of days to check out the office, the docs . . . talk to the employees, see if there are any security concerns."

"So . . . spy on the Dutch?"

"Pretty much. But hey, you have to run a virus check on your computer once in a while to clean out all the clutter."

"Neil has a broad range of what he does."

"The man doesn't sleep. He is always figuring out another way to hire more employees to help out the people he knows. And Neil knows everyone. He's a good man. He really stepped up for Claire. As her best friend, I will always be thankful for that."

Leo turned toward the window again. "Like he did for Olivia."

"Yup. Earning your respect and loyalty without even trying."

"Maybe he'll hire me when I lose my job." He'd told his boss that he got word from Janie and he was going to find her and convince her to turn her husband in.

He wasn't sure Brackett bought the story, and got a truckload of shit and five days to get his ass back to work.

Fitz had looked at him and said, "I hope she's worth it."

"You think you will?" Jax asked.

He really couldn't read that one.

She tipped her glass back. "Like I said, Neil knows everyone."

~

Olivia was leaving for Budapest the next morning. And because she wouldn't hook up to any form of internet when she was in Hungary, she had her laptop open with Leo dialed in. She needed to see him before she left.

With the outcome unclear, there needed to be one more something to hold her over.

One more something.

When her computer pinged, she dropped the pen in her hand and scrambled to get in front of it.

Leo's face came into focus.

The scruff of beard on his face was killing her. She knew, without a shadow of a doubt, that he was growing that for her.

Because of her.

He clicked around on his computer, completely blind to the fact that she was watching him.

She indulged. Something Olivia would never have done preamnesia. It was surprising what a brush with death and finding someone who cared about you did.

She stared at her monitor for what felt like hours. It was only ten minutes . . . but she'd stay there as long as he did . . .

Except . . .

She turned to the window of the hotel room.

When she looked back at the computer, she wasn't observing Leo.

Her chest rose and fell . . . rose and fell.

Pushing off the chair, she moved to the window and opened the blinds wide.

It was the middle of the night in LA. This time of year . . . it was dark everywhere in the United States.

She fell in the chair and pulled the computer closer.

Leo wasn't home.

Olivia looked over her shoulder. The generic art on the wall, the small space.

Leo walked away from his computer and pulled his jacket off his shoulders.

She clicked into his audio.

He disappeared from view, and the sound of a television filled her feed.

Someone was trying to sell cars . . . in German. A tilt of her head and she closed her eyes.

Pulling herself from the chair, she found the unused remote control on the bedside table and turned on the TV.

She shifted through the channels, slowly . . . turned up the volume on her computer.

Then it was stereo.

She squeezed her eyes shut. "Son of an ever-loving *bitch*!"

Leo was not only in Germany . . . he was in Berlin. Or close enough to it to have the local news on his set.

Olivia swiped at the space under her eyes, rubbed her temples, and then pounded both fists on the desk. One deep breath later and she was typing.

You're going to get yourself killed.

Leo scurried into view, relief in his expression. He took a moment, a deep breath.

One keystroke and Olivia unscrambled the signals to find his exact location.

Call me.

He'd been coached.

One fortifying breath later, You've wasted your time.

He smiled as he wrote his reply. Go ahead . . . tell me how much you don't care what happens to me.

You son of a bitch . . . I don't!

He was smiling now. The kind of smile he sent her when she was teasing the hell out of him, his sexy *I have your number* smile.

Then you won't care when I do this.

Leo's image disappeared the second he removed the power from his computer.

"Goddamn it!"

Olivia swung out of her chair and paced. "I don't care."

I don't care!

Back at her computer, she found the hotel where Leo was staying. "A Hilton? Really?"

He had so much to learn if he was ever going to stay alive.

CHAPTER TWENTY-SEVEN

Leo had laid traps many times in his career, most of them on paper, or during questioning.

But this one was so much sweeter.

She was close.

He felt her.

They left the hotel and rented a car.

Apparently, he was destined to be in the passenger seat while a woman drove.

Jax knew the roads, knew what the signs were saying without looking them up on a translation app.

Leo was pleasantly surprised to find that most of the people he'd been in contact with so far spoke English.

"Do you think she's still in Germany?" he asked Jax.

"If she's not, she's likely on her way back. You had the TV on in the room, right?"

"Yeah."

"Then she knows you're in Germany. Which is why she said you were going to get yourself killed."

Leo had concluded the same thing. Disconnecting the computer was one of those *tough love* moments that gutted him.

He knew Olivia cared or she wouldn't have contacted him.

But that had been hours ago.

He was banking on her contacting him again . . . soon.

They drove through the flat countryside of late fall colors while winter's pointy nails put a chill in the air. The terrain, the climate . . . all of it was so incredibly opposite of living in California.

"What are the chances of Charlie talking to us?"

"He won't tell us a thing unless he thinks it will protect Olivia."

"He called Neil. Obviously, he felt she needed something."

Jax nodded. "I wouldn't be here if Neil felt differently." She reached for the volume on the radio and turned it up with a smile. "I haven't heard this song since I graduated."

Leo smiled. It was in German. He didn't understand a word.

The gates of Richter reminded him of old movies where the camera rolled up to a castle.

Jax gave her name to a man at the gate.

"Since when do schools have guards?" Leo asked.

"This is Richter." She leaned out the window, said something else to the man, and waited for the gate to open.

Even though Leo had seen the grounds via Neil's cameras—or more to the point, Neil tapping into Richter's cameras—they didn't do justice to the real thing.

The school loomed ahead like the giant it was. Stone and brick, pillars and glass. Lush trees lined the drive that went on forever. "This is pretty impressive."

"It is all that." Jax looked out the window and up into the trees as she drove. "Cameras are everywhere. Big Brother has nothing on Richter."

"Duly noted."

There were only a couple of cars parked in front of the school. From the maps he'd studied, the staff parking was around the back and only visitors parked at the entrance. "I take it there aren't very many visitors."

Jax put the car in park and cut the engine. "Never really are. More now than when I was here. This is more for dropping off and picking up, and since it's a boarding school, that only happens on weekends and holidays. When there are events, a valet service is hired."

"What is tuition?"

Jax laughed. "Too much. You ready?"

"From the second I got on the plane."

They exited the car and walked the short distance to the front doors.

Jax lost all semblance of the slightly carefree twenty-four-year-old the second she placed one foot on the first step. Her shoulders pushed back, her chin shot up, and she removed her large-rimmed sunglasses as they approached the man standing at the top.

Her first words were in German and met with a smile.

She reached out a hand and shook his.

Both of his hands sandwiched hers.

"Where are my manners?" Jax turned to Leo. "Headmaster Vogt, I'd like to introduce a friend of mine, Leo Kenner." The last thing they wanted was Leo's real name used.

"Mr. Kenner. Welcome to Richter."

"Leo, please." They shook hands. "Headmaster."

The man was slightly shorter than Leo, maybe a decade older. When he spoke English, most of his German accent disappeared. "Only the students call me Headmaster. It's Johan."

Jax placed her hand on Leo's arm and stepped closer. For the next however long they were on campus, Jax and Leo were a couple, and she was showing him where she went to school.

"I told you he was kind."

"What brings you back?" Johan asked.

"Like I told your secretary, I wanted to show Leo where I grew up before he meets my parents."

Johan stepped aside; his eyes found Leo's. "Ahh, the parents. That's always a special time."

"Jax has warned me."

She smiled, patted his arm. "That I have."

They walked into a grand foyer that spread out to the left and right in equal proportions. Straight ahead were massive windowpaned doors leading into a courtyard.

"This is unbelievable," Leo murmured.

"Nothing in America compares," Jax said.

Johan walked them toward the courtyard. "I would certainly hope not."

The courtyard was filled with clusters of students of all ages.

"The scarves are new," Jax pointed out.

"A demand of the students."

"Since when do the students demand anything?" Jax asked.

"You know there have been many changes since you were in attendance. The students having a voice in their lives here is one of them. When scarves for the different dorms were suggested, I honestly thought we'd be asked to hand out wands and teach classes on how to use eye of newt." He paused as they all chuckled. "As it turns out, it's easier to determine if a student is somewhere they shouldn't be."

Jax leaned forward. "They'd just borrow someone else's if they want to sneak around."

Johan laughed. "We are aware. But then it's willful, isn't it?"

Leo felt Jax's fingers grip his arm. "How is willful disobedience handled these days?" Leo asked.

Johan met his gaze. "Not as strongly as it once was. I assure you."

"That's good to know."

The headmaster turned to them, clasped his hands. "I certainly don't need to give you a tour, as Jacqueline is quite capable."

Leo smiled at Jax when her full name was used.

The headmaster continued. "All I ask is that you don't disturb any classes in session. We reserve that for parents considering Richter for their children."

Jax tilted her head. "That's a little far off."

Johan looked between the two of them, his smile wide. "Life sneaks up on you."

"Is there anywhere you'd like us to avoid?" Jax asked.

He shook his head. "We have nothing to hide here at Richter." He started walking away.

"Headmaster?" Jax stopped him. "Is Checkpoint Charlie still here? I'd really like him to meet Leo."

"Yes, Charles spends quite a bit of time in the upperclassmen dorms. You'll likely find him there."

"Thank you."

Johan turned to Leo. "Wonderful to meet you. Do stop by the administration and let them know when you're leaving campus."

Jax let go of Leo's arm as the headmaster walked out of sight. "Anytime someone tells you they have nothing to hide . . ."

"They have something to hide."

Jax sighed. "Let's go find Charlie."

~

Olivia thought she was done spying on Richter.

Until she followed Leo and Jax as they left the Hilton and drove there.

God, it was good to see him.

Goddamn him for following her to Germany.

And damn it to hell . . . what had Charlie told them?

Olivia followed them back to the hotel and then again an hour later when they left to grab dinner. Once she was fairly certain that was the extent of their plans, she liberated a master key from a hotel maid and slipped into Leo's room.

She searched his things but didn't touch his computer. Three women on Neil's team were trained by the same instructors as her.

When it was obvious there wasn't anything in the room that clued her in to something useful, she sat in the lone chair, grabbed a jar of fifteen-euro peanuts, and put her feet up on the bed.

She needed to end this thing and send him back to the States after shattering any fantasy he had about her.

Because that's all she could be.

A fantasy.

Ninety minutes—and half the minibar snacks later—the electronic lock on Leo's door told her it was showtime.

She took a fortifying breath and put on her best resting bitch face.

Leo stopped in his doorway, his eyes aimed right at her.

Ignoring the surge of adrenaline and the increasing beat of her heart, she set the pace. "Close the damn door before someone sees me."

He released the door, let it swing shut, and took a step closer. The relief on his face was so transparent she wanted to cry inside. That was the kind of look that would get him killed.

She lifted a hand. "No, no. This is not a social call."

He stopped. "You look tired."

She stood. "What are you trying to prove?" she asked and didn't wait for him to reply. "That the FBI hires idiots? Because coming here, looking for me . . . you're a dead man walking if anyone connects the dots."

"A chance I'm willing to take." He removed his jacket and tossed it on the edge of the bed.

She dug her nails into her palms. "What did Charlie tell you?"

He smiled. "I find it completely counterproductive for you to tell me you don't care and follow me at the same time."

"I tried shaking you in Vegas." She pointed to her chest. "This Olivia would have used you for a night and kicked you out in the street without your shoes. The woman in Colorado no longer exists. I'm sure Neil warned you about me."

Leo rubbed his chin. "Neil told me a lot . . . but Sasha, she was the one with some insight."

Olivia took one step closer, lowered her voice. "I am not the kind of person you want anything to do with."

Leo sighed, rolled his index finger in the air. "Oh, I know it. The Assassin and the FBI Agent. Believe me, that's been spinning in my head for a month."

Why was he smiling? "I've killed people."

He chuckled. "Killed. Past tense."

"Leo—"

"You're not on any list, by the way. Not one. We've looked. You were truly a ghost in those years you worked for you-know-who." He pulled at the top button of his shirt. "According to my people, you're nothing."

"That doesn't change the facts."

"No. It doesn't. As Neil pointed out . . . you and I know a lot of people who might have ended someone else's life. Half of Neil's team saw combat."

"Not the same."

"Are you telling me you took joy in killing?" He narrowed his gaze.

She blinked a few times. "Like plucking birds from the sky."

He grinned.

She wanted to slap him. "Why are you doing this?"

"I told you my feelings," he said slowly. "When you love someone, you don't sit back while they self-destruct. You try and stop them. In fact . . . that's kinda what you're doing right now."

She swallowed, his words too close to the truth.

He took a step closer.

She held her ground.

"Me loving you will not get me killed," he said. "You loving me—"

"I don't love you." Her words were sharp.

Again with his smile. "That's fine. Not going to change anything."

"Is that right?"

He nodded. "My objective is the same. Find your classmate from Richter before you do."

It was annoying that he was neck and neck with her intelligence. "And do what?"

"Same as you. Find out who hired him or her."

She turned away from him for the first time since he entered the room. What now? Race him to Budapest? *Him or her* . . . Leo didn't have a name. And even if Charlie had given them the same information, she had the advantage.

Olivia moved her head from side to side as she turned. "I've warned you. My conscience is clear." She started to walk by him.

He laughed.

She stopped in front of him, her glare directed to his eyes. "What do you find so amusing?"

"Assassins don't have a conscience."

She needed to leave.

One step and his hand shot out and grabbed hers.

She was out of his grip and had him pinned against the wall, her elbow to his neck, in two breaths. "Don't."

Both of his hands came to her waist. His eyes softened.

Her hold faltered.

Leo grasped her hips and brought them flush with his.

"You're an idiot."

He held her in place and gently removed the arm she had to his throat. "I know."

She stared, breath harsh, and Leo crashed his lips to hers.

She let him . . . for a moment. How she missed him, wanted him even with all the risk. *Push him away. Show him you don't care.*

Olivia followed her inner voice, tried to shove.

He didn't budge.

She closed her lips, denying him.

Leo's hand moved to her neck, her hair, and not so gently pulled it back.

Her eyes opened to find him staring, his thumb stroking her jaw, and when she gasped, he kissed her again.

And she was drowning. The feel of him on her, the taste of his lips . . .

Use him and kick him out.

She could do that. One night.

The second her mind decided, she swept his tongue with hers and pushed against his erection with a fever that matched the stupidity of the moment.

Clothes flew and hands moved. Neither of them said a word. This was raw and physical, the kind of sex Olivia preferred.

His fingers pinched.

Her nails dragged over his skin.

Need. Just need, she chanted in her head.

The second Leo pushed her onto the bed he was inside her and everything stilled.

And just like that, he intertwined their fingers before he started to move. The raw became tender, the physical became more. The *more* that lingered in her chest as he brought her closer to completion.

Only she knew how this man worked. She wrapped her legs around his waist and gave in.

Olivia took what he offered, over and over.

He told her she cared.

She called him a fool.

And with every insult, he made her cry out his name again.

Hours later, they gave in to exhaustion. And somewhere in the middle of the night, she pressed her lips to his chest before sneaking out of his room.

CHAPTER TWENTY-EIGHT

"You have me on a tracker," Leo told Jax as he hoisted his bag up on his shoulder.

"I'm not sure about this."

"You don't have to be. You're going to Amsterdam, I'm following Olivia. I told Neil I'd call for backup if I needed it. I might be a fool for doing this, but I'm not stupid. The fewer faces seen with her the better."

Jax leaned in, placed a kiss to his cheek. "Be careful."

"I will. See you back in the States."

She pointed at him. "You owe me a drink," she said as she backed away.

"I do?" What did he miss?

"Yeah. We get here and we're practically engaged and now you're leaving me for another woman. What will I tell my parents?"

Leo laughed as he turned and walked away.

The second Olivia had walked out of Leo's room, he was up, dressed, and packed. She'd barely gotten back to her hotel and he was waking Jax to give her a heads-up.

As he expected, Olivia was mobilized and running, and he was right on her tail, not even bothering to hide.

He followed in the rental car from the second she left her hotel. They weren't out of the city twenty miles and she pulled over.

He watched as she glared into the rearview mirror and jumped out of her car.

Leo pulled the key and put it under the mat.

"Fuck off, Grant," she said the second he got out.

He popped his trunk and grabbed his bag. "You know, if you don't stop leaving after we make love, I'm going to start believing you really don't care."

She marched over. "I don't."

He met her between the two cars, reached out, and pulled her close. A quick kiss to her ticked-off lips. "Good morning." He left her staring and headed to the passenger side of her car.

"What are you doing?"

He looked over his shoulder as if the answer were obvious. "Taking two cars is a waste of fuel. And since we're going in the same direction . . ." He opened the door to the back seat, threw his bag in.

She marched up, grabbed the bag . . . and tossed it out. "We're not doing this."

He picked it up, tossed it in . . . pressed one finger to her chest to back her up, and closed the door. "Yes. We are."

She glared. "You're really starting to get on my nerves."

"I know."

He opened the door and encouraged her to get in. "I can drive. You don't look like you got any sleep last night."

She walked around him, her middle finger in the air, and climbed into the driver's side.

Leo laughed and took the passenger seat.

As soon as they were on the road, he texted Jax, told her to come and get the car.

"How did you know where I was?"

Claire!

"I can't tell you all my secrets until you stop running away."

Leo noticed her white knuckles as she gripped the steering wheel. "What did Charlie tell you?"

"Who was the shooter?"

She checked her blind spot, grunted.

"I took care of you two to one last night. You owe me."

"I faked it."

He busted out laughing.

Olivia said something in a language he didn't understand.

"The way a woman moans and cries . . . that can be faked. But the way your body pulsates around my—"

"Shut up, okay." She hit the wheel.

"Who is he?" Leo asked.

She stayed silent.

"Claire and Sasha are combing through the files . . . the ones you helped them get way back when. And they already have the recruit names. You can save them some time, and they can start gathering information that might help us when we confront him." Leo kept saying *him*, hoping she would either correct him or go with it. Either way she was confirming and knocking the search down considerably.

"We aren't confronting him. I am."

Score. It's a boy!

He would venture a bet that Olivia before the amnesia would have never let that slip. Or maybe she was starting to trust him just a little.

Leo reclined his seat, crossed his arms over his chest, and closed his eyes. "It's okay. We have a few miles for you to get used to the idea."

"Goddamn it. He told you, didn't he?" Olivia was pissed. "Damn you, Charlie."

Charlie hadn't told them anything. Even denied seeing Olivia in the first place . . . but gee, thanks for stopping by and be sure to do it again after the wedding.

"I'm going to take a little nap. Let me know when you want me to drive. We need to be rested and go over a plan."

"My plan. One that doesn't involve you."

He really was exhausted. He was secretly hoping they were driving for more than a day. "Good luck with that." Leo let his brain settle, and he started nodding off.

~

Only once Leo had fallen asleep did she allow herself to look at him.

Such an annoying piece of beautiful shit.

He wasn't shaking, much as she tried to move him along.

Of course he didn't leave. The night before had been off the charts. All of the memories that they'd shared since they met funneled into those hours and made the night so much more memorable.

What was she going to do?

He would just keep returning. And what would happen if he returned at the wrong moment and was seen? What if . . .

If she told him what she knew and made him promise to stay out of sight. Or devised a plan where he had to stay out of sight to keep her safe . . .

And what of Claire and Sasha? Maybe they could find dirt on Friedrich, the man who had put a hole in her, something she could hold over him so he ponied up the information on who put the hit on her?

Isn't that what she really needed to make the man talk?

Once again, she looked at Leo.

If someone came to her right then, threatening Leo, would she talk? She was so screwed.

Olivia set her hand in the space between their seats and tried to ease the constant tension that lived between her shoulder blades. She wasn't going to stop any of them from getting involved.

Controlling that involvement was her only choice.

Maybe she could get out of this without someone taking a bullet for her.

If she hadn't realized how foolish it was to get involved with someone before, she sure understood it now.

But just like with Amelia, she didn't know what was coming. There was no warning with her. At least with Leo . . . and the others, she knew the imminent risk. They knew to watch over their shoulders. Even more . . . Leo and Neil's team were all seasoned. They could take care of themselves. Maybe not against an assassin's bullet . . .

She sighed, trying to push that image out of her head when Leo silently slid his hand in hers and squeezed.

~

Four hours into the drive and they were just outside of Prague when Olivia allowed him to take the wheel so she could sleep.

When Leo asked if there was a particular route she wanted to use, she told him there wasn't a reason to zigzag until they were leaving.

He opened a map on his phone. "So stay on the 50."

She nodded. "Avoid Vienna." She pointed to his map. "We'll cut through Slovakia to get to Hungary."

Instead of giving any reason for her to believe he had no idea where they were headed, he nodded and took the wheel. "Vienna sounds romantic."

"Just drive, Grant."

It wasn't long before she was sound asleep in the passenger seat, her hands wrapped in his jacket and tucked under her cheek as a pillow.

She was hedging.

He felt it when she let him in the car and confirmed it when he took her hand and she didn't stop him.

When they stopped to get gas, and he used the bathroom and she was still there . . . he breathed.

There he was, driving through countries instead of counties toward complete uncertainty and he couldn't stop smiling.

If for no other reason than he knew exactly where she was, and for now . . . she was safe.

For almost a month that hadn't been the case.

He never wanted that to happen again.

She slept for two solid hours before opening her eyes and doing a cat stretch.

Olivia was beautiful when she was waking up. "Where are we?"

"In the middle of nowhere, but it sure is beautiful." Rain had started to fall, slowing the drive slightly.

A road sign passed, and she looked at her map with a yawn.

"Have you gotten any sleep since you left Colorado?"

She looked at him, blinked several times.

"Don't you think you should go into this rested and ready for anything?"

"It's hard to sleep when someone is trying to kill you," she told him.

"I'm not going to let that happen. Maybe we get a place outside of town and regroup. We go over your plan."

She huffed. "Budapest is more than a town."

So that's where they were headed.

"Still . . ."

"You're not wrong."

"Glad you see it my way. Now, what does one eat in Czechia? I'm starved."

～

Two bites in and Olivia apparently made up her mind.

"His name is Friedrich Schmidt. Better known as Mr. Wet and Sloppy."

They sat across from each other in a small diner in an even smaller town.

"You're kidding."

She shook her head. "And I didn't give him a second chance. Not that it mattered. He moved on within a week, and so did I." She took a bite and chewed in thought. "We had a lot of classes together."

"Was he an orphan, too?"

"I don't remember. I think there was an uncle, but I wouldn't bet money on it. Most people with families didn't talk about them much when they were around those of us who didn't have families."

Leo cut through some kind of beef and filled his fork. "Was there bad blood between you?"

"No. We stayed friends after the ill-begotten kiss. Got in trouble pulling pranks together."

He thought of the kids on the campus. Imagined what Olivia must have looked like in the uniform. "Did he work for Pohl?"

"There was only one person that I knew who worked for Pohl other than me. And the only reason I knew her was because she'd graduated the year before. She was part of the welcoming committee. Unbeknownst to her or me, Pohl used that connection to force my first . . ." She stopped talking, looked around.

Her first kill. "What happened?"

She put her fork down, grabbed her water. "I didn't want to do it. I thought I'd signed up to be a spy. Something close to what you do . . . Sasha and Claire. Hack computers to stop bad people from doing bad things. Sip wine in Vienna and bug a mercenary's room to learn their next victim." She stopped talking, eyes blinking.

Leo reached out and took her hand.

She smiled, removed her hand, and picked up her fork again.

"Pohl put a gun to her head, told me to take the shot or she'd die. She begged me." Olivia snapped out of the memory.

"I'm sorry." Leo couldn't imagine the pain.

"I was twenty-one." She took a bite, spoke around it. "I never saw her again after that night. Couldn't tell you if she was alive or dead. Anyway . . . Did Friedrich work for Pohl? Could have. We competed a lot in school. If I took him down on the mat, he worked hard to pay me back the following week. But that's how the school worked back then. *You're good, but they're better.'* There weren't participation trophies at Richter. You had winners and losers."

"And Friedrich was a winner."

"The guy couldn't kiss, but he knew how to shoot."

Once Leo realized that Olivia had resumed eating, he joined her.

"And you're positive it was him in the car in Vegas?"

"Yes. It's amazing what your brain remembers in times of stress. I saw the long barrel with a silencer, knew it was pointed at me. Our eyes met and I knew I was going to die."

"That didn't happen."

She cleared her throat. "I gave it a good college try." Olivia reached for her water. "Funny, though . . . I'm pretty sure I saw him in the hospital."

That stopped Leo's next bite. "What? When?"

"Early on. After I stopped thinking I was in Atlantic City and before I refused the pain medications."

"Neil's team was there."

"He was in a hall. Looked like any other visitor when they wheeled me to another CT scan. I didn't recognize him, but I remember him looking me in the eye. Of course, that could have been the medication, which makes more sense. If Friedrich was there and he'd botched the job, why didn't he finish it?"

Leo shrugged. "Conscience?"

"You already pointed out we don't have those." Only she was smiling as she said it.

Leo picked up a piece of bread and soaked up the generous amount of gravy on his plate. "What makes you think Friedrich is going to be in Budapest?"

"I doubt he's there, but I might be able to lure him in."

Leo didn't like how that sounded at all. "What stops him from taking a shot the second he sees you?"

"Charlie said it was a sanctuary for us. Or did he skip that detail with you?"

Leo kept silent and smiled. He was happy to see her cleaning her plate. Not only did she look tired, she looked thinner than when she'd left Colorado. "Must have missed that part."

Olivia narrowed her eyes and dropped her hand to the table. "You son of a bitch. He didn't tell you anything, did he?"

Leo wiped his mouth, put his napkin on the table, and shook his head. "Nada. Zip. Wouldn't even tell us what he had for breakfast."

He saw the frustration ripple through her and changed the subject. "So this bar—"

"Nightclub," she corrected.

"Right, nightclub. It's a no-kill zone?"

She moaned. "I can't believe this."

Leo leaned forward on his elbows. "Do you think women are the only ones who can fake it?"

"I'm going to make you eat those words," she warned him. When Leo looked closer, he saw a hint of admiration in her gaze.

"Don't I know it." He removed his cell phone and hesitated. "Is there any reason I shouldn't give this name to Neil?"

"Why ask? You're going to do what you want."

He set the phone down, reached for her hand.

She tried to pull away, and he held tighter until she looked at him. "Full disclosure from this point forward. I needed to get you here so you knew I was serious about doing this with you. I can't sit back and do nothing. If I was that man, you wouldn't want anything to do with me."

She stopped pulling, and her voice lowered. "I don't want you to die."

It wasn't the "I love you back" he was aiming for, but it was a start. "I don't plan on doing that anytime soon."

He waved the phone again with a silent question.

A single nod and he texted the name to Neil.

CHAPTER
TWENTY-NINE

The small town they landed in was a little too close to the center of Budapest for Olivia's comfort, but any smaller and the two of them would stick out as the strangers they were.

The moment she mentioned Friedrich's name, she committed.

All the years she'd been on her own, and now Leo was at her side picking apart her plan, giving suggestions and offering different scenarios. Although she'd executed many plans, very successfully, on her own, there was comfort in having another educated opinion.

And Leo was right.

If he were the type of man who didn't want to jump in feetfirst, she wouldn't have looked at him twice.

All the years Neil encouraged her to join his team, and it was her asking for their help.

Gathering more information on Friedrich was imperative.

She needed leverage. Needed to find the man's weakness.

Just as Leo and, if she were being honest with herself, Neil's entire team were her Achilles' heel, Friedrich had to have one.

They set up in their hotel room and opened a secure connection to talk with Neil.

Olivia was nervous, but there wasn't any turning back now.

Neil came into view, his lips pressed together. "Glad to see you in one piece," he said in greeting.

"I didn't expect to be talking to you like this."

Neil offered a nod. "I know. We're a team. We take care of each other."

Leo reached over and grasped her hand.

She squeezed. "Tell me what you've learned."

Neil started talking. Friedrich Schmidt was nowhere close to being an orphan. But the father on his birth certificate and the man whose DNA he matched were not the same. His parents sent him to Richter, and the uncle, Louis Schmidt, took over as the boy's family. And in the records of secrets, Louis and Friedrich shared the same DNA.

"Are his parents, any of them, still alive?" Olivia asked.

"Mr. and Mrs. Schmidt live in Munich. Uncle Louis is proving harder to locate. We need another twelve to twenty-four hours on this."

"If Friedrich cared for his uncle, he'd make the man disappear," she said. "It might take years to find out where he is."

"We're not working hard, just scouting. Learning where Louis is might result in word getting back to the family that's trying to hide him."

"And if Friedrich knows someone is looking, he would be more inclined to deal," Leo pointed out.

"Or shoot first and skip any deal." Olivia saw the other side of this.

"I have several people asking the same questions in different locations. Schmidt will know that can't all be you. And when someone in your line of work suddenly has backup, the tables shift." Neil looked pleased with himself. "Let's go over A Róka."

For twenty minutes Olivia worked through the neighborhood surrounding the nightclub. There was roof access, street access, and possibly an underground passage. "I'll confirm that before I go in."

"You're not going in. Not at first," Neil told her.

If Neil didn't see the danger in telling her what she was entitled to do or not do, he was going to see it now. "The only way this team will work is if you understand that I do not take orders. From anyone."

"Hear me out." Neil regrouped. "You're dead to this community. Schmidt might be the only one that knows you're alive."

"And whoever hired him."

"Perhaps. But the fewer people that know you're alive the better. We all agree on that, right?" Neil asked.

"Right," Leo answered for them.

"We send Leo in—"

"Out of the question." Olivia pulled her hand out of Leo's, sat back.

"I'm not sitting on the sidelines," he told her.

"I'm not going to watch you die."

Leo turned to her. "I'm walking in and leaving a message in a place that no one knows me."

"People like me know all about people like you, Mr. FBI. People like Mykonos and Navi . . . they love talking to the people mingling in these locations. And the Navis of the world will know you."

"So you turn me into an old man."

She didn't like this. "You don't speak the language."

"Do you speak Hungarian?"

"No, but I have five languages to tap into."

Neil interrupted both of them. "English is the universal language in these establishments, and you know it, Olivia."

Leo took a long breath. "What is it you're really worried about? No one is going to shoot me for asking questions in a place where people ask questions."

"The fewer people that know we're connected the better."

They stared at each other, locked in an argument.

"Olivia," Neil interrupted. "Your argument about the Navis of the world isn't unjustified, but it's weak. And more limited than people who might realize you've returned from the dead. Add thirty years to

Leo's face, send him in not to lure Friedrich around to talk to you, but because Leo has information about a job in Vegas that didn't turn out like it should have. When word comes that Friedrich is in attendance, we send you in . . . with a team."

Olivia turned to the monitor. "Keep your ass in California."

"My London base is already working. The only face you'll recognize is Jax. She'll make sure you don't shoot anyone you shouldn't."

"Jax is in Amsterdam."

"Change of plans," Neil said.

Olivia looked at Leo, then Neil. Neil's plan was solid. Putting others at risk was never a concern in the past. And there were times she didn't really care if she made it out alive.

Leo reached for her hand. "It's a good plan."

"If I find holes, we're changing it," Olivia warned.

"By all means," Neil said, deadpan. "In twenty-four hours, we start rolling. Tell me what you need."

"Communications," Olivia said. "If Leo goes in, we need to be able to hear him."

"Done. What about weapons? Cash?"

She shook her head.

"We'll reconnect in twenty-four hours, sooner if everything is in place." Neil's image disappeared, and Leo closed the laptop.

"You all right?"

"I haven't decided."

He twisted her around and placed both hands on her knees, his eyes level with hers. "If you disappear, I'm searching for you and not watching my back."

He was trying to scare her.

She would never admit his tactics were working. "You'll watch your back."

"Not like I would if I knew you were out there alone."

One hundred percent commitment. That's how this had to be to come out on the other side alive and with the information they needed.

"You're manipulative," she told him.

He smiled. "I'm in good company."

~

Leo sat still while Olivia did her thing.

Not once in his career had he needed to wear makeup, let alone strips of plastic to add weight and disguise his bone structure.

Using paintbrushes and glue, she took her time. Music played in the room, and she worked in silence. The whole time she refused to let him see what she was doing.

Jax had arrived a couple of hours before, bringing with her the communication devices Olivia had requested. Once Olivia told Jax her plan on how to transform Leo, Jax left to return with a suit and padding.

Now, with Leo in one chair and Jax in another, they were both preparing to go in.

A Róka required a serious entrance fee, in cash, and the dress code wasn't negotiable. Leo couldn't help but think there would be more surprises once they were on the inside.

Olivia held out the jacket for him to get into and ran her hands over the lapels before standing back.

"Holy shit," Jax said behind her.

"Looks good?" Leo asked.

Olivia twisted him until he faced the mirror.

Chills ran down his arms. She'd added weight and wrinkles and a nose that appeared to have been broken in the past. The facial hair he'd grown for her had been removed. She'd put a second skin over his head, and now he had the receding gray hairline he hoped to avoid.

He looked like a larger version of his grandfather before he'd passed. "Wow."

She patted his ass, smiled through the reflection in the mirror. "I'd still do ya," she teased.

"Hollywood needs your skills," Jax told Olivia.

Jax stood in a hip-hugging V-neck dress that cut so low it damn near went to her navel. The choice was to add not only a layer of distraction, since it was hard not to stare at her chest, but to display enough side cleavage so that no one could possibly think Olivia and Jax were the same person. Not that many would be looking at her face.

The women gave a red tint to Jax's blonde hair and added some extension by route of a long, loosely curled ponytail. Her makeup gave her a sharper jawline, and the red contacts she chose had literal sparkles around them. Disguises were expected in these places, and eye color was an easy switch. Where Olivia's sun-kissed olive skin was hard to hide when wearing the kind of gown Jax was wearing, Jax's creamy complexion did not look the same. Anyone reporting to Schmidt, or relaying the information about who was asking for an audience, would not mistake a disguised Jax for Olivia.

Jax wore a tracker in her hair, and Leo had one in a cuff link on the chance that the establishment commandeered their cell phones.

A knock on the door sounded their time for departure.

"That's our ride," Jax announced as she reached for a coat.

Leo opened the door, found a man who looked like the perfect chauffeur standing on the other side.

"Leo?" the man asked.

Jax made the introductions as Sven walked in the room. "Sven, this is Leo, Leo, Sven. And that's Olivia."

"A pleasure." Sven's eyes traveled to Jax, his mouth gaping. "Damn, Jax."

Jax smiled, handed her jacket to Leo to help her. "Not to be a girl, but if I move the wrong way, everyone gets a peep show."

"Do you want tape?" Olivia asked as she turned toward her bag of disguises.

"No. Much better if I leave less to the imagination once we're there."

None of them could argue with that. Leo opened the jacket for her to step into.

Olivia clipped her earpiece in with a built-in microphone. They'd already done an equipment check and were ready to roll.

He turned to Olivia, uncertainty written on her face. "We'll be in and out of there in less time than it took for you to do all this." He pointed to his torso.

Sven moved toward the door. "We have a van out front. I'll introduce you to the team."

Olivia's eye twitched.

"Let's do this before I change my mind."

Leo knew none of this was easy for her, any more than it would be for him to be on the outside once she went in.

They exited the room and let the fun begin.

~

Entering A Róka reminded Leo of his history lessons on Prohibition in the States. The first door was not *the* door . . . and the initial fee was not the *only* cost.

Jax hung on Leo's arm like the gold digger she was to portray, and him as the cradle robber.

The foyer of the actual nightclub was a small, dimly lit bar with a dozen patrons sipping cocktails and talking softly.

At the second door, two large men greeted them. "Good evening, Mr. . . . ?"

"Anderson. And my companion, Miss Swan."

His smile was nice enough, but the physical space the man took up told Leo he was capable of enforcing the rules of the establishment.

"I will assume you have been briefed on our . . . guidelines."

"We have," Leo replied.

"Then you won't mind that we secure your weapons."

A contingency they all saw coming.

Leo glanced at Jax and reached for his sidearm. He pulled the magazine and emptied the chamber before handing it to the man speaking.

"I'll feel absolutely naked," Jax said with a pout on her lips.

"Sorry, love." Leo stepped behind her and helped her out of her coat.

The men shifted slightly when Jax revealed the dress and averted their eyes when she lifted it enough to reveal a small holster strapped to her thigh. With her coat and the gun in the doormen's possession, Leo removed an envelope and placed it in one man's hand.

Only then did they stand aside and let Leo and Jax pass. "Enjoy your evening."

The second set of doors emptied into a much grander space with many more people.

"We're in," Leo whispered softly for the team to hear.

A tone in his ear was his only reply. The goal of the team was to listen and intervene only if the proverbial shit hit some kind of fan.

"This looks like it was once a ballroom," Jax said as they walked through the room. Chandeliers lit the thirty-foot ceilings. Long columns flanked the room, with soaring windows looking out over a courtyard. What once might have been a platform for a small orchestra now had a single piano player and a singer entertaining the guests.

There were dozens of tables around the perimeter of the room, dimly lit nooks for people to hide, and enough space between these tables to offer some privacy.

"If this was a ballroom, wouldn't that make this building a private home in the past?"

"Most likely," Jax said.

They kept their conversation around observations to help paint an internal picture for the outside team. They were not going to risk being thrown out for photographing the interior of the space.

The rules of A Róka were relatively simple. No cell phones out. At all. No pictures whatsoever. What people discussed in the club was at their discretion, but no action happened inside their doors. No exchange of money—anywhere—with the exception of the front door. The bars were open, and the hefty entrance fee paid for not only drinks but information, if it was available.

No one believed for a moment that the people seen in the establishment would be kept a secret, nor was it some kind of "what happens in Vegas stays in Vegas" type of vibe. But it was a *no-kill* zone. How the establishment enforced this, Leo didn't know. But he didn't think it was by an escort to the street.

Leo and Jax attracted their share of attention, though Leo saw more eyes on her than he did on himself.

"Bartenders talk with everyone," Leo said.

The two of them found open space at the main bar.

"Good evening." The bartender set two coasters down with a smile. "What may I tempt you with tonight?"

Jax ordered a glass of wine, Leo a whiskey.

"I haven't seen you here before." The bartender was a man somewhere in his thirties and half the size of the bouncers at the door.

"It's our first time," Jax said for them.

The man poured her wine with a smile.

"Meeting someone?" he asked.

Leo accepted his drink. "We're hoping to . . . in the future. Although I'm not sure if my acquaintance frequents this establishment."

"Perhaps I can be of some assistance. I see a lot of people. Some who want to reconnect with old friends, and others that would just as soon be left alone."

Leo leaned one elbow on the bar. "I believe I saw our old friend recently in Las Vegas," he said.

Jax leaned forward so the V of her dress gaped just enough to promise an eyeful if she moved another centimeter. "This gentleman and I share the same alma mater in Germany. Perhaps you've heard of Richter?"

"Of course. A school as old as that has delivered plenty of patrons to A Róka."

"How might we get word to our friend?" Jax asked.

The bartender smiled, his eyes drifting to Jax's chest as he reached for a bar towel. "When was this visit to Las Vegas?" he asked.

Leo gave him the exact date when Olivia was shot.

The man reached for a token behind the bar and scooted it toward Leo. "You'll have to show this to the gentlemen on your way out when you retrieve your coats. It is nonrefundable."

The token looked like a poker chip. "How does this work?"

"In America they call it a tip. We respect the privacy of our clientele should they request it. As we would with you as well. Of course, I speak only on behalf of the staff. We have no control over the patron on the other side of the room."

"Understandable."

"If your classmate is unreachable or prefers to be left alone, you'll be told we were unsuccessful in helping you. If there is a message, we'll be sure and pass it on."

Leo and Jax exchanged glances. Could it be that easy?

"You've been most helpful. Thank you," Jax told him as she brought the wine to her lips.

"Of course." With a smile, the bartender walked away.

"Let's take a look at the architecture, shall we?" Jax suggested.

They moved around the room talking about the walls, the halls, and routes away from the main room. They found the restrooms and separated for less than five minutes.

People looked, but didn't stare.

No one approached.

They exited and retrieved their belongings.

As instructed, Leo handed the doorman the token and received a similar one in a different color along with an envelope. Leo tucked it away in his coat and helped Jax with hers.

Sven was waiting on the street, the door to the back seat open.

Once they were inside and leaving A Róka, Leo relaxed. "That was easy."

"It's never that easy," he heard Olivia in his ear. *"What's in the envelope?"*

Leo removed it and tore the seal. The price tag to the information was revealed. "How deep are Neil's pockets?"

He showed the paper to Jax, who blew out a whistle.

"But look at the fine print . . . your fifth visit to A Róka is half off, and your tenth is free," she said with a small laugh.

Leo read the letter out loud so the team could hear the instructions. He was to return, or whoever he wanted to retrieve the information was to return, and bring the token.

"Now the question is . . . How long do we wait?" Leo asked anyone who had the answer.

"Forty-eight hours," someone said in his earpiece.

"Plenty of time. And if Friedrich doesn't bite, we look elsewhere," Olivia said.

Leo looked behind them to find the surveillance van following, all the while wondering how Olivia handled waiting on the sidelines while someone else was in play.

CHAPTER THIRTY

"Next time, I'm going with you," Olivia said the moment she and Leo were alone in the hotel. Listening in on the conversations in the night-club was not the same as being there.

"I agree."

"I can't sit in a van." Olivia's arms were crossed over her chest.

"I agree."

"No one will recognize me."

"I agree."

She stopped talking and looked up. "You do?"

"There were a lot of people in there, and not one stopped what they were doing to strike up a conversation. Jax and I didn't recognize anyone, but that might be different for you."

Olivia took a deep, fortifying breath. "I'm out of my comfort zone."

Leo pulled his arms out of his jacket and set it aside. "The fact that you admitted that means your comfort zone has shifted."

And that felt like a weakness.

Leo's cell phone rang.

She watched as he looked at his phone and ignored the call.

"Who was that?" she asked.

"Fitz."

Olivia paused. "You're going to lose your job."

"Always a possibility." Leo smiled and set his phone on one of the bedside tables.

"I thought you liked your job."

"Love my job. I hate the bureaucracy. I see how much gets done with Neil's team, and it makes me question what I'm doing with the FBI."

"You don't like playing by the rules?" Considering there were many nights she'd dreamt of working for a legitimate organization, it was strange to know Leo would want it differently.

"Most of the rules are in place to keep the bad guys from having a loophole for a get-out-of-jail-free card. When I saw what Neil's team managed to do for Marie Nickerson, I started to question what I was doing with the feds."

Olivia leaned against the hotel room desk. "I spent months shadowing Marie. Reported to Neil on who visited her. Names, occupations . . . That girl is so broken."

Leo offered a soft smile. "You protected her. All of you did."

"The FBI had a hand in that, too."

"Yes. But with you . . . it's personal. It shows in the outcome. When I had time to think about what Sasha told me about you, all of you, I realized you were a victim—"

"I don't deserve that title."

"You do," he insisted. "And as long as you allow me to be in your life, I'm going to remind you of that. If Neil's team had been around when you were nineteen, this never would have happened. So when you ask me if I'm going to lose my job, I can't help but feel as if it doesn't matter. There is obviously a private sector where I can use my skills. Where we can both use our talents."

Listening to him gave her something she never thought she'd ever feel.

Hope.

Leo started to pull at the skin on his head that gave him the false hairline, and she moved closer to help. "I'm unsure how an FBI agent and a retired assassin are supposed to have a relationship without me getting fired." He sat in a chair, giving her more room to work.

Her fingers shook as she fiddled with the edges of the wig. "A relationship."

"That would be that thing we're doing. The sharing of our time, ideas . . . bodily fluids." His hands rested on her hips.

Olivia trembled as she cleared the makeup from Leo's face. "I've never had a relationship . . . with a man."

He grinned. "Is there something about your sexuality you want to share?" he asked, teasing.

"You know what I mean."

Leo kept her from turning away. "I know you're scared."

"I never said I was scared." Her voice was sharp.

Leo smiled. "You're scared that you give a shit. Probably beat yourself up every time you slow down enough to think about it."

He wasn't wrong.

"I've done horrible things." Her hands stilled, her gaze focused on the back of the room.

"How many of those atrocities have you committed since Pohl's death?" he asked.

"None." She paused. "Well, I might have dabbled in a little information gathering and liberating a couple cars . . ."

She found Leo smiling. "What's a little fraud and grand theft auto among friends?"

"Necessity," she insisted.

"We'll figure out how to move forward once we've gotten through this. And we'll do it together," Leo insisted.

She didn't know if she could do that . . . the moving forward thing. But there was no shaking Leo at this moment. Not with him and Neil's team deeply embedded in the outcome.

"Don't even think about bolting."

"I'm not."

He peered closer, seemed satisfied with what he saw. "Let's get a good night's sleep and regroup tomorrow."

Olivia grinned and proceeded to remove the rest of Leo's disguise.

~

"It's disturbing," Leo said looking through the mirror at Olivia two nights later.

She'd disguised herself as a man.

Her clear complexion was gone. A face riddled with acne scars and a scattering of facial hair was enough to throw many people off.

"Good," Olivia said to Leo.

Leo was back in his Mr. Anderson attire.

Jax donned another revealing dress as Miss Swan.

Neil, despite telling her that he wasn't flying to Europe, was going to sit in the surveillance van dressed to scale a wall if he had to.

"We have coverage from the front of the building and the back," Neil told them.

"We don't even know if Schmidt is in there," Olivia said.

Leo called A Róka and received a message that there was some closure to the answers he sought and he needed to come in to obtain it.

Friedrich's picture circulated between them. "He might look more like Jax and less like this."

Olivia shook her head. "I doubt he'll be in drag. Regardless, if he's there, I will be the one to talk to him. Jax and Leo need to be on the periphery."

No one argued.

"No risks," Neil insisted.

Olivia looked around at the faces of the team. "If he wants privacy, I'm giving it to him."

"He tried to kill you." Leo's voice was hard and steady.

"If he wanted me dead, I'd be dead. If he needs me to cooperate with him for some reason, he'll target one of you." The thought gutted her. "I'm not the one who needs to look out."

Neil was nodding. "Olivia is right. If he isn't there, he's likely casing the place looking for her. I'm more concerned about a lack of an audience than if he is there and wants privacy. Olivia trusted us with the first round, we will trust her with this one."

"Let's get this party started," Jax said with a little bounce in her shoulders.

"Your enthusiasm is killing me," Leo announced.

A few of them snickered.

Leo turned to Olivia. "You ready?"

She nodded, lowered her voice. "I am."

Leo cringed. "I like you better as a woman."

Neil reached for the door. "We arrive in stages. We'll do a mic check en route."

Jax reached her fist out and looked Olivia in the eye.

For a second, she didn't quite know what to do. Then she pressed her knuckles to Jax, who smiled and stood taller. "C'mon, Sugar Daddy . . . I need a drink."

Neil lifted his hand. "Five minutes." He walked out of the hotel room to get a head start.

Five minutes to the second later, Olivia squared her shoulders and left with her driver.

They completed the mic check once Leo and Jax were in motion.

The plan circulated in Olivia's head. Her breathing became a meditation.

A Róka came into view.

"We're here with you," Neil said in her ear.

"Got it." And she pushed out of the car.

Olivia went in first, following the same route that Leo and Jax had a couple of nights before.

Inside was much how Leo had described. Maybe a bit busier since the weekend was in full swing.

With a perch on one corner of the main bar, Olivia ordered a whiskey and avoided eye contact.

Fifteen minutes later, Leo and Jax walked in, her arm tucked in his. Jax created a stir, even if she didn't realize it.

"Welcome back," the bartender said to Leo.

The earpiece gave Olivia the opportunity to eavesdrop.

"Chardonnay and a whiskey, correct?" the man asked.

As the bartender filled their drink order, Olivia searched the room to determine if anyone was watching the two of them.

The room was heavily dominated by men, most gathered in small numbers of two to four. A couple of larger groups congregated in the center of the room. Mixtures of different languages, Dutch, Slovakian, Hungarian, Russian, German, and plenty of English mixed together in a melody that could only happen in Europe.

Leo tapped his token on the bar and patiently waited.

When Olivia looked at others, she noticed half a dozen tokens of different colors weaving between the fingertips of the patrons in the establishment.

Olivia lifted her drink and left her spot to find another angle.

C'mon, Friedrich . . . where are you?

Half an hour passed with Leo and Jax making small talk with each other. The bartender insisted he would be with them to discuss what he'd learned shortly. But time slowly slid by.

Olivia looked around.

The waiting was a test.

The question was . . . Whose test? The establishment's? The bartender's? Or was Friedrich watching and waiting?

Olivia circled the room and realized the vantage point from the floor level wasn't optimal. Above their heads was a balcony space. "I'm going upstairs," she whispered to herself and the team on the other end of the microphone.

A single ping in her ear told her someone had heard her.

She found the staircase and started to climb.

The scent of cigars and cigarettes was strong, the lighting dim.

She looked down and saw Leo and Jax more clearly. She stood in the shadows and searched the room again with her eyes. Other than a couple of men admiring the feat it took for Jax to stay in her dress, the two of them went unnoticed.

Olivia was about to give up when she noticed the flicker of flame as someone lit a cigar several yards away.

The light cast by the flame illuminated a face. A face staring at the floor of the ballroom.

The extra senses on the back of her neck began to tingle as she moved closer to get a better look.

Very few people moved around the balcony space of A Róka, allowing those that were there an extra layer of privacy and quiet.

The man was tall and lanky. Long fingers stretched over the cigar as he sucked the smoke down deep into his lungs.

"Take your shoes off, Olivia. We're gonna get caught." Friedrich held his *shoes up in one spindly hand to show her the way to the stacks.*

Olivia's pulse caught in a rapid fire, brought her to stand just outside of his view.

She waited.

"Hello, Friedrich."

The man froze, took a deep breath, and then pulled the stogie from his lips. "I knew it had to be you."

Olivia cast herself into his light.

It was then he turned to look at her. "You look better than the last time I saw you."

"That's not hard to do. All I have to be is vertical."

Friedrich's face was drawn, the kind of exhaustion Olivia knew all too well.

"I have questions," she told him.

"Nothing I'm obligated to answer," he said.

"I took your bullet. That deserves some kind of payment."

He narrowed his eyes, then looked down at the floor of the nightclub.

Leo and Jax were on the move.

"Get rid of the mic," Friedrich told her.

She hesitated with the sound of a beep in her ear.

She looked at the man and saw the boy within. Nothing about him said he wanted to pounce or escape. Olivia took a chance and pulled the tiny microphone from a button on her jacket.

She dropped the device in her drink and set it aside. "Why?" she asked.

He nodded toward his right and started to walk.

She followed.

~

"Damn it, Olivia." Leo looked at Jax at the same time the team in the van told them Olivia's microphone was dead.

"No one panic," Neil said through their earpieces. *"She hasn't left the building."* He gave them her location, and Leo and Jax split up once they were in the balcony space.

Leo saw her silhouette as she moved deeper into an alcove. "I see her," he announced.

That's when he noticed her hand reach out, palm flat, as if telling Leo to keep his distance.

"Hold up. Give her space," he told the others.

Jax stopped her forward motion from the opposite side of the balcony.

For now, Olivia was flanked.

All Leo could do was wait.

~

"You may not believe this, but it's good to see you."

Olivia sat opposite Friedrich. While he sat with his back against the chair, arms stretched out with his cigar hanging from his long fingers, she kept herself upright, both feet on the ground, ready for anything.

"Considering you tried to kill me . . ."

"I'm told you have people poking around in my life," he said.

Olivia thought of Neil's team asking questions throughout Europe, looking for Louis Schmidt.

"A waste of time so long as you provide the answers I need."

"My parents are already dead to me."

"There is always someone that means something . . . eventually."

Friedrich's cold stare told her there was someone. Maybe more than one.

"You had a chance to finish the job and didn't. Why?"

He shook his head. "You weren't the target."

Olivia did all she could to hide her surprise.

"Everything I learned about you said you'd been tossed in an ocean half a decade ago. No one was more surprised to see you alive than I was."

"Grant," she muttered.

Friedrich tilted his head in confirmation.

The knowledge made her sick to her stomach. "Why is he still breathing?"

"You," he said simply. "He's one of yours. I didn't know. Didn't see you until that night. Made my driver circle twice. I had a choice.

Take him, or take you. Or both, I suppose. I researched the people you associate with. Learned that Budanov was part of that team. Stacking up powerful enemies for a low-paying job wasn't how I wanted to end my summer."

"So you shot me."

Another tilt to the head. "Made it look good."

"A little too good, thank you."

"You're still alive," he countered. "If someone didn't go down, the resource order on Grant would have remained. You took the hit and his bounty dissipated."

"How does that happen?" In her experience, once a hit was out, it didn't go away.

"He was a warning, not an enemy. Pissed off the wrong man."

"Navi?"

Friedrich shrugged.

"Mykonos?"

A tilt to the head. "You don't stand up to these people and survive."

Olivia's head started to put the pieces together. If Leo was the warning, the person they wanted to shut up could only be Marie Nickerson.

"The trial is over. Mykonos is already in prison."

Friedrich pulled a drag off his cigar . . . blew it out slowly. "I owe them a hit."

Olivia held her breath. "Marie."

Friedrich's silence was his confirmation.

"You can't do this. She's just a kid who was forced into this life . . ."

"I don't care. You know how this works. You take a job, you finish the job. I spared you. Kept your man alive to avoid your chase . . . avoid Budanov. The girl means nothing to you. Let it go."

"Don't—"

"Walk away," he told her. "Our world thinks you're dead. Jane Doe in Vegas was nobody. A prostitute, maybe. You open this . . . make it personal . . . and that anonymous face is given a name and you're once again thrust into this life. You don't want that."

"You don't know me."

He shook his head. "Pohl went down, you disappeared. Or was it the other way around? If you wanted to continue the work, you could have. You decided to die."

"So you were Pohl's recruit."

Friedrich remained silent.

"Why didn't you leave? Why still live in this world?" she asked.

"It's all I know."

"Bullshit."

Friedrich laughed. "And how have you earned your money since our benefactor died?"

"Stop buying expensive cigars and Armani suits. You'd be surprised what you can survive on."

Friedrich shook his head. "It's not my lifestyle."

"So sell your soul to the highest bidder," she countered.

"Who are you to judge?"

He was right, but Olivia had to convince him to walk away from Marie. The girl meant something to Neil and his team. She meant something to Olivia. The strength it took for Marie to go against her enemies and call them out . . . the way Olivia never did with Pohl. She had a considerable amount of admiration for the young girl.

"Let this one go, Olivia." He sat forward and stubbed his cigar in an ashtray.

"Your father would be disappointed if he knew."

Friedrich looked directly at her. "I told you my family means nothing to me."

"Let me rephrase. Louis would be—"

"Don't." His voice was tight. "I spared yours. You owe me this one."

She did . . . even though Leo meant next to nothing to her the night she was shot. That had all shifted and now she had a chance to walk away . . . they all had a chance.

He stood and smoothed the wrinkles from his coat with a slight tug. "For what it's worth, it's good to see you alive," he said. "Cross me, and I will kill you."

Friedrich walked out of the shadows, leaving Olivia in the dark.

Leo replaced Friedrich the moment her childhood friend left her sight.

"You okay?" he asked.

No. She had a decision to make and didn't know if she was strong enough to make it.

CHAPTER THIRTY-ONE

Olivia remained silent as they backed out of A Róka and away from the city.

Leo jumped in her car when they left and now regarded her with caution. She'd been told something she wasn't sharing. He could tell by the rapid blinking of her eyes and the way her smile didn't fall on her lips as easily as it had just a few hours before.

Only once they were gathered did Olivia reveal what she'd learned.

"Leo was the target," she told them. "I mentioned both Mykonos and Navi as the ones who bankrolled the hit. Friedrich didn't confirm or deny. When he saw us together, he made the decision to take me down."

"Why would he do that?" Leo asked.

"Combination of things. Shock of seeing me. Realized if he shot you, I'd come after him. When Amelia was killed, I did everything in my power to take out Pohl."

Neil stood by the door, arms crossed over his chest. "Schmidt knew you'd retaliate."

"Yes."

"Why not make sure you were dead?" Jax asked.

"He'd researched your people." Olivia pointed between Neil and Jax. "Sasha had some serious clout at Richter. Her records weren't easily broken, and even if they were, her name was revered. Friedrich knows she's part of your team. He didn't want her as his enemy."

"So there's a price on my head?" Leo felt his stomach reject that idea.

Olivia shook her head. "Friedrich suggested that was lifted once the trial was over. They wanted to make an example of you."

A look around the room confirmed he wasn't alone in his confusion.

"And that's it? You take the bullet so Friedrich doesn't gather enemies. Leo is no longer worth more dead than alive, and everyone goes along like nothing happened?" Jax asked with a shake of her head. "I don't buy it."

"That's what he told me," Olivia reported.

"If Schmidt is Navi and Mykonos's henchman—"

"It didn't sound like Friedrich's loyalties were in any corner."

"A mercenary," Neil suggested.

"That's worse," Sven added.

Olivia shrugged her shoulders. "He didn't kill me. He could have."

"A mercenary with a conscience?" Leo asked. If that was the case, they had something to work with.

"Or at least a past that he was fond enough of to let me go."

Leo sighed. Her memories were Mr. Wet and Sloppy . . . What were his?

"So Navi and Mykonos know nothing of who you really are?" Neil asked.

She shook her head. "I feel like Friedrich would have told me otherwise if they did."

"So that's it? The man shoots you and gets away with it?" Sven asked.

"Considering how many people I've put holes in, I'll count myself lucky." Olivia looked beyond them as if remembering all those faces.

Leo glanced at Neil. They both watched her.

Neil pushed away from the wall he was leaning against. "Let's break this location down and move out."

"Are you having Friedrich followed?" she asked before he had a chance to leave the room.

"Of course."

Leo walked Neil out of the hotel room they were in, leaving Olivia and Jax to strip out of their costumes.

"There's something she's leaving out," Leo accused the moment they were alone.

"Agreed."

"What is the likelihood of a hit man leaving the target standing and still getting paid?"

"Slim to none. But if you were still a target . . . she'd tell us. She wouldn't risk you."

"If not me . . . then who?"

"The one who ultimately put Mykonos in jail."

The two of them stared at each other. "Marie."

"Logical conclusion."

"She's deep in the system because of the hit on her," Leo said.

"But we know who has been hired to kill her."

"Keep an eye on him and we can intervene."

"And if Olivia knows this, she will think the same." Neil sighed.

"What's it going to take for her to trust us?" Leo asked.

Neil shook his head. "I don't know."

~

Spindly fingers held her against the stacks.

His long, wet, forked tongue attempted to enter her mouth. The spiked ends stung as it passed over her lips.

"You really don't know how to do this . . . do you?" Friedrich asked.

She opened her eyes, saw the blackness of his.

Behind him, the faces of those who were gone because of them loomed.

"I never wanted this," she told him.

"Too late to turn back now."

His tongue lapped up one side of her face.

"I can make it right." She struggled against his grip, found her arms forced together in iron chains.

"You're going to lead me to her."

"I'll kill you first."

Friedrich started to laugh, and suddenly the weight of the world dropped from below her feet, and her stomach launched into her throat.

Olivia's eyes sprung open, her hands reaching out to grip the covers on the bed.

It took a moment for the room to come into focus.

She was on a plane.

Neil's.

She looked at her watch. Two hours had passed since she asked to be left alone.

It had been nearly twenty-four hours since her meeting with Friedrich.

Her dream swam in her head. The faces, the heat . . . the misery.

The message, however, had changed.

She wanted to break the binds of the stacks . . . the memories of the past. Keeping one woman alive may not be the redemption that would free her, but perhaps it was a start.

If Olivia had concluded that Friedrich still had unfinished business, then Leo and the others would, too.

Why would Friedrich tell her his target?

Never once in Olivia's time on the other end of a scope had she revealed any names of her victims.

Friedrich had. To serve what purpose?

His words and logic twisted in her head. *The forked tongue of the devil in the stacks can't be trusted.*

"Son of a bitch."

Olivia walked out of the bedroom in the back of the private jet and saw Leo and Neil deep in conversation.

"He's going after Marie," she said in a rush. "He's going to use us to find her."

Neil sat back in his chair, a smile spread over his face.

Leo walked over, placed his lips to hers. "Let's find a way to stop him."

~

"His story fell apart the moment he said Leo was *my man*."

Leo squeezed Olivia's hand. "Well . . . I am."

Olivia smiled at the thought. "But you weren't then. Friedrich had no way of knowing we had zero contact until that night in Vegas."

"He figured out there was a connection . . . eventually," Neil said.

"By following me to the hospital and watching. Noticing how often Leo showed up and that guilty 'you were shot because of me' look on your face."

"He admitted he shot you instead of me. So I'm right about that one."

Olivia rolled her eyes.

Neil waved a hand in the air. "Let's get this back on point. Can we trust that the hit on Leo is gone?"

Olivia released a short laugh, looked directly into Leo's eyes. "He's still here, isn't he?"

"I haven't been hiding since Colorado."

"I'm sure Friedrich had a shot if he wanted to take it. At the hospital . . . the trial . . . on the way to the bathroom after a coffee break." She could think of a hundred ways to eliminate the heartbeat of someone who wasn't avoiding a bullet.

"And now the target is Marie," Leo said.

"We all knew her life was threatened. That's why SWAT surrounded the courthouse. Why Neil had me on point to make sure all those bases were covered."

"Friedrich never had a clean shot," Leo said.

"And when you don't have a shot, you wait until you do. But the protection program does a good job, and even people in my line of work—"

"You're retired," Leo interrupted.

"My *previous* employment," she corrected. "Even we have a hard time finding people in the protection program."

Neil tapped a pen on the notepad in front of him. "Friedrich shoots you but makes sure he's seen so you'll seek him out once you're recovered."

"Must have been a bitch when he learned you'd lost your memory," Leo said with a laugh.

"Eventually I show up . . . he tells me how happy he is to see me alive, paints some kind of solidarity between us. Leads me to think this isn't personal."

"And what is the best way to get someone to do something?" Leo's question was rhetorical.

"Tell them not to," Neil said, deadpan.

"He knows I have people in my corner, and I won't risk you," Olivia said. "He thinks I'll search out Marie myself and go alone to protect her. Two hours ago, that was exactly my plan," she admitted.

"You'd be walking into a trap."

"Or leading him right to her. But like any good sting . . . he needs to believe that is still my plan."

"And if we do nothing? If you don't search for her . . . what then?" Leo asked.

"His strategy will change. He has a resource order with Marie's name on it. She dies, or he dies trying. There isn't a lot of middle ground." Unfortunately, Olivia understood the rules all too well.

"We need to catch him in the act."

"Then that's exactly what we're going to do." Neil removed his phone and dialed a number.

Leo sat beside Olivia and grasped her hand in his. "You made the right choice."

"I've never been a team player," she told him.

He kissed her fingertips. "You are now."

~

"You ready for this?" Leo asked as they sat in his car outside of Neil's headquarters the morning after they'd flown in.

Olivia looked at the nondescript office building with tinted windows and security cameras everywhere. Twice she'd sat across the street watching the space. Or more to the point, the people walking in and out. Once right after they'd all infiltrated Richter and the secret about Amelia's death had been revealed . . . and another time two years before. The first was to assure herself that everyone had gotten out and was well. The second was because she had started to give up on living. She'd reached out to Neil, and eventually he had a job for her she was willing to take. And since she was basically on her own while playing bodyguard to Marie Nickerson, she'd taken the job.

Only now . . . this.

"I have to be," Olivia answered.

He reached out, laced her fingers with his.

She squeezed, took a deep breath, and brought her attention back to him. He was dressed in a suit and returning to his office. The plan was for him to keep his day job for the meantime. His job with the FBI would be imperative to their overall plan on how they would deal with Friedrich.

Leo kissed her fingers. "I know I'll be pulling overtime for the next few days. We can rent you a car if we need—"

"Neil said he had an extra."

Leo sighed. "I'm going to be a nervous new boyfriend . . . text you, follow you home if you're still here when I get off work."

Home.

Was it possible to call any place she stayed home?

The night before, they'd dropped into bed the second they showered the flight away.

The morning had been rushed, and the thought of staying in Leo's home indefinitely hadn't quite sunk in.

Until now.

"If I'm crowding you—"

His open jaw and direct stare stopped the words she was going to say. "Okay . . . I get it."

"Good." He shifted in his seat. "Listen . . . I know this is new for you. I don't expect it to go seamlessly. Just talk to me. I'm a reasonable guy."

She laughed. "You are."

"Then don't cut me out."

"If I was going to do that, I would have done it before now."

He seemed to like her answer.

Leo leaned forward, pressed her lips to his. "I can walk you in," he said once he pulled away.

"I think I'm capable," she said, whispering.

He let go of her hand. "Be safe."

"Watch your back," she countered.

"I always do."

Olivia pushed out of the car and walked to the front door.

One look into the security camera and the door buzzed.

A glance over her shoulder showed Leo waiting until she was inside before he backed out of the parking lot.

She blew out a breath and stepped inside.

"Good morning." Sasha stood as the one-person welcoming committee.

And for reasons Olivia couldn't name, unshed tears stung the back of her eyes. She swallowed the emotion and ignored it. "Good morning."

Sasha let a smile spread over her. "It gets easier."

Olivia blinked to keep the tears back. "I hope so."

"I'm glad you're early. You need to know a few things about the team. First is that Claire is a hugger. No getting around that. Isaac has threatened to tie you up at the first opportunity—"

Olivia laughed, loving the lift in her chest. "He can try."

"I suggested he would be wasting his time. And Lars might actually cry."

Her jaw dropped. "You're kidding."

Sasha shook her head. "We were worried about you. I know you left to protect us. I know walking through that door today might have been the hardest thing you've done to this point."

"It wasn't easy."

"I know. I've been there." Sasha lifted her hands to the building. "The family you choose is often more important than the family you were born to. There's no judgment here. Everyone has a say. If you have a problem, air it. If you have a need, ask for it. It took a long time for me to admit I had a family. This family. We can be that for you."

Okay, the tears were back.

Olivia opened her eyes wide, trying to make them go away. "What the hell . . ."

Sasha laughed. "You'll get used to that, too." She nodded further into the office. "Let me show you around before the place fills up."

Olivia fanned her face with her fingertips as they started walking while shrugging off her coat.

Sasha scanned her frame. "We'll take a couple hours and go shopping."

Olivia glanced at the dark leggings and skintight shirt. All three outfits she had with her looked exactly the same. "You think I need a makeover?"

Sasha shook her head. "I was more concerned about your condom supply."

It felt good to laugh.

Sasha pushed through a door into a room filled with floor-to-ceiling monitors. "Welcome to MacBain Security and Solutions."

Claire was sitting in a chair. She jumped up the second they entered the space and wrapped her arms around her. "I'm so happy you're here."

Olivia looked at Sasha and mouthed . . . *Help!*

CHAPTER
THIRTY-TWO

For the first time in Olivia's adult life, she felt as if the skills Richter had taught her were being used for the greater good.

The first week after returning, Sasha, Claire, and Olivia worked together to build a network of websites and email addresses. Two weeks in, Jax returned from Europe and joined them. Between the four of them, they were able to create legitimate-looking FBI and federal marshal websites that would fool the top hackers in the business.

The plan was to give Friedrich something to follow.

The London team kept Friedrich in sight, and when the opportunity presented itself, Sven, the top hacker on that team, infiltrated Friedrich's room and programed the man's computer to pick up what they were laying out when they were ready.

Isaac tried twice to handcuff Olivia to a chair before he finally conceded. The sparring between them reminded her of her early years at Richter, when fighting was for points and fun . . . and never really meant to hurt someone.

Lars didn't actually cry when he saw her, but he was pretty quiet and went out of his way to ask her if she was okay almost every day. Olivia put him at ease the best she could, and gave him a good ribbing about Pam, who he apparently called on occasion.

At night, Olivia and Leo would either work together on the plan at Neil's headquarters or snuggle on Leo's sofa in front of a fire in his small Glendale home.

And she belonged.

If it wasn't for the fact that Neil's team had eyes on Friedrich, she'd be concerned that they were being watched.

But for now, the only spidey sense crawling up her spine was how quickly she was assimilating into Leo's life. Feeling him lying beside her at night had helped chase away some of the hellish landscape of her nightmares. She knew there was no way to erase the demons of her past, but maybe in time she could achieve some kind of balance.

Once the decoy protection program home that was housing Marie had been secured, and the trail of bread crumbs was in place, it became a twenty-four-hour game of dodge and weave.

Olivia sat in front of one of Neil's computers late in the evening, when it would be morning where Friedrich was in France. Patiently she waited until the man logged in to his computer before accessing the hacks she'd designed and Sven had placed.

"You sure this is going to work?" Claire asked at her side.

Leo was leaning on a table behind her. Sasha and Neil were close by.

"He thinks I'm invested in Marie. The smart thing for me to do would be to find the girl and move her . . . or protect her. And since I'm shacking up with Mr. FBI over here"—she looked over her shoulder and smiled at Leo—"I would eventually infiltrate Leo's system and find a database. But not right away. Friedrich will know this. Even if he doesn't follow my path to fake Marie, we will make sure he stumbles upon the intel." Olivia itched to press buttons when she saw that he'd logged in. But before she put the plan in action, she needed to watch what he was doing.

"There is still a chance he could know we're watching."

Olivia shook her head. "He was good. I was better."

Friedrich's computer powered up completely, and he put in a password.

Claire leaned forward to type. Olivia stopped her.

"We should get his password," she suggested.

"Not needed." Her eyes stayed glued to the monitor. Sasha and Neil walked up behind her. "I changed mine every day."

Friedrich pulled up a Gmail screen.

Hope flared in Olivia's chest.

Leo leaned forward and placed a hand on her shoulder.

Less than a minute later, Friedrich was in Leo's email.

"Holy shit," Leo cursed.

His hand tightened on her shoulder. She reached up to squeeze it. "This is what we want."

"How long has he been in there?"

"I'm going to guess daily," Olivia informed him. "But don't worry, he's waiting for me to hack in to get into the federal database. Harder for him and easier for me because of you." Olivia leaned back in her chair, stretched her arms over her head, then moved to the keyboard.

She sent an email to Leo's address from one of the sites they'd set up. In the subject line she typed "Richter Urgent."

It took five minutes for Friedrich to open the email. It was allegedly sent by Checkpoint Charlie requesting immediate information about a former student that might be on an American most-wanted list. In the email he implied that a mutual friend might be in jeopardy.

"Charlie would never ask this question," Claire said.

"No, but Leo wouldn't know that. So when Leo jumps on his email for the night, he might just log in to his office email and give Friedrich the link he needs . . . or the link that I need." Olivia waited, forcing herself to move slowly to not tip off Friedrich.

A half an hour later she opened the email, as if she were Leo . . . that was when the hack into his computer was up and running.

Friedrich's fingers were typing quickly to catch up.

"I didn't go to hacking school . . . Tell me what's going on," Leo asked.

Olivia typed while Claire explained. "You know how hackers get into your computer and steal personal information through email? A good hack only requires you to open the email. So Olivia sent you a fake message from Charlie, you open it, and now your computer is subject to whatever information she wants to get from you. We open that up for Friedrich to follow along." Claire pointed to the computer screen. "Pretending to be you, she logs into the FBI site, our fake FBI site, and that login and security is now compromised. You would be searching for the name Charlie just dropped, and if Friedrich is paying attention, he will now start working on Marie's whereabouts."

Olivia pretended to search for the name acting as Leo. Twenty minutes in, she logged off.

They all watched as Friedrich moved around the fake website, roadblocks stopping him from getting far. Around midnight, Olivia used the alleged hack as if she were going into the FBI site to search for Marie as well. Unlike Friedrich, she was able to push open a window, a fake one, that sent her to a new site. A trail of bread crumbs and slow delivery of intel had to be paced to keep Friedrich from the truth.

The door to Neil's office opened, and Jax walked in with Cooper. "We're ready for our shift."

Having given Friedrich enough information to keep looking, Olivia and Leo went home, leaving the three younger members of the team watching Friedrich's online movements.

Olivia stretched out beside Leo, exhaustion in her bones.

"How long will this part take?" Leo asked.

"A few days. The last bit of intel will make him think he has a jump on me. He'll want to get there first," she said, yawning. "It will still take him a couple more days once he's on the move."

"Enough time to get to the decoy house?"

It had been an exciting and exhausting day. "Yes. He'll leave Europe with a jump flight, change identities, and get to the US. Once he's here, he'll obtain what he needs for the hit. I don't think he'll waste time casing the location. Only enough to know I'm not there."

"Then we're on to phase two," Leo said, pulling her into his arms.

"So long as nothing goes wrong." She was too tired to think about that now.

Leo kissed the top of her head. "Go to sleep. We have time."

She couldn't keep her eyes open even if she wanted to. "I'm glad I'm not doing this alone," she admitted out loud.

He squeezed her tighter. "Me too."

~

For the next three days, they worked around the clock, dribbling information to Friedrich until everything he needed to know to get to Marie was available to him.

Only then did they leave California to beat Friedrich to the finish line.

The decoy witness protection home sat in an older neighborhood in a suburb of San Antonio, Texas. It had been fortified and surrounded by Neil's team. The occupied home on the south side was a vacant rental, and a logical place for Friedrich to infiltrate to take his shot. The home on the north side was owned by a single man who won a four-night, three-day vacation south of the border, courtesy of Neil's never-ending pockets. The actual home with the address they'd fed to Friedrich as Marie's, Neil had rented from the owners stating a need for a photoshoot. Not only did the owners receive a pretty steep paycheck for the space, they were going to have an entirely secure home with a state-of-the-art security system free of charge.

The European team kept eyes on Friedrich when he left that part of the world. When his flight arrived in Boston, Neil had eyes on him until he left. From there the man flew to Austin and rented a car.

AJ was on point to follow, but the risk was too great when Friedrich veered off of the main highway. That was when nerves started to rumble. Olivia thought of it as the few minutes of silence NASA has to go through when their spacecraft is reentering the atmosphere. You knew it would happen and approximately how long it would take . . . but you never really knew until it was over.

Olivia sat in a huddle with the rest of the team, all of whom were dressed in different costumes and disguises. Or, like her, were armed to the nth degree, wearing combat gear and prepared for the worst.

Cooper sat to Sasha's left, a stick of gum in his mouth, his knee bouncing with energy. Both of them were dressed for war. Claire wore runner's pants and earbuds, giving the illusion that she was out for an evening run. Lars and Isaac were dressed as plumbers, and the surveillance van was a modified work truck parked one block over.

"As soon as Friedrich infiltrates any adjacent homes, we move. Let's do this without one shot fired," Neil instructed. "Sasha and I will take the south home. Leo and Olivia the north. Everyone else, be prepared to move if he chooses a different house altogether."

They'd kept the actual decoy home empty . . . with the exception of the special effects set up to cast shadows as if someone was walking around. The blinds were selectively closed with cloth that would make it difficult for Friedrich to see with an infrared camera or goggles. This would force him to move closer and wait for a shot. Logically, the houses closest would be used.

As Olivia pointed out . . . he would want to get in, kill the girl, and get out without anyone hearing a thing. That's what they wanted, too.

The last thing any of them wanted was a gun battle in a residential neighborhood. Hostages were not an option.

What they needed was for Friedrich to follow the fake intel and get close to the target that was supposed to be Marie, and the team would take him down. Then the third part of their plan could begin.

Olivia placed her hand over Leo's. "This is going to work."

"It has to."

It was midday, and the residential neighborhood was quiet. The homes were spread out enough to offer some protection from people in the neighborhood. The team was accustomed to breaking into homes unnoticed. And in cases like this, Leo and Olivia walked right through the front door like they belonged.

"Team One in position," Sasha reported for her and Neil. Their voices came through the earpiece.

"Team Two in position," Olivia said, looking at Leo as they walked through the vacant house.

"Team Three."

"Team Four."

Time ticked by in slow minutes.

Olivia watched the street from the highest window in the house.

In any other assignment, she'd have her sniper rifle out, her scope dialed in, and her exit ready.

The more time that passed, the more concerned she became.

The time on her synchronized watch said Friedrich should have arrived thirty minutes ago.

"Maybe he was hungry?" Isaac suggested from his position.

"He can't get anywhere close without us seeing him," Neil reminded them.

That didn't stop Olivia's palms from starting to sweat.

Claire's voice sounded in her ear. *"Incoming from the south."*

Olivia blew out a breath, watched the street.

When the Jeep drove by, it was as if the entire team froze.

Lars reported next. *"Exited from the north."*

"Well, shit."

Olivia took a breath. "Hold tight."

Minutes passed.

"He's circling back around."

After two sweeps past the houses, Friedrich parked outside the block and was seen leaving the Jeep on foot.

"Claire?"

"He's taking position from the thicket of trees in the north property," Isaac reported.

Olivia moved her location and found a back window. "Do you see him?" she asked anyone listening.

"He's moving closer. Be alert." Neil's voice was tense.

The movement was brief, then for thirty minutes, Friedrich crouched in the overgrown corner, watching the house they'd set up as Marie's location.

"Drawing him in," Sasha reported.

Without looking, Olivia knew Sasha had turned on the remote setup and activity that would suggest someone was sitting on a sofa watching TV.

"Headed toward you, Team Two."

While Friedrich moved, so did Olivia, ready to intervene the second he infiltrated the house.

"He's cutting the power," Sasha reported.

"Moving in position," Cooper announced.

"Team Four ready on your call, Team Two."

Olivia made eye contact with Leo, who had his back to the wall by the side door.

The light in the hall went dark, the sounds of appliances running went silent.

"Making his entry through the south door. Weapon in his right hand."

Time moved slowly and Olivia counted every heartbeat she felt inside her chest. She heard the lock moving and crept closer to flank the door with Leo.

Leo stood prepared to pounce, his weapon an extension of his arm. His opposite hand stood ready to make the move at the same time.

The door opened.

A silencer poked through first.

Leo signaled and they both rushed.

Olivia reached for the weapon, and Leo pulled the man inside.

The distinct sound of the gun firing shot through the ceiling as Friedrich managed two rapid rounds before Olivia relieved him of his weapon.

Neil was yelling commands through their communication system, and Leo was wrestling Friedrich to the ground.

The element of surprise had worked long enough to take the gun, but not to stop the fight for dominance.

Leo tossed his gun the moment they both hit the floor.

Olivia secured the weapon and pointed it at the two of them.

Friedrich managed an elbow to Leo's kidney and lifted a fist to strike another blow.

"Freeze," Olivia yelled, her aim ready to make him stop.

Friedrich hesitated and looked her way.

Only then did she realize the team had filled the house. Half a dozen guns were leveled . . . red dots covered Friedrich's face and chest. One wrong move and he'd resemble swiss cheese.

Friedrich slowly opened his long fingers and lifted his hands in the air.

Leo was on him, forcing Friedrich's hands behind his back and into a pair of handcuffs.

"I want to see my attorney."

Leo lifted him up to his knees.

"That's not how this is going to work," Olivia announced.

Cooper walked in the back door and tossed Friedrich's bag onto a table and started to rifle through it.

"What are you doing?" Friedrich asked.

"Leo was never a target," Olivia said to him. "Navi isn't as stupid as his 'cousin.' You popping me was not a split-second decision."

He stayed silent.

"You had one target all along. It wasn't until after Budapest that I remembered a lone SWAT member on the opposite side of the courthouse whose position was optimal for a kill shot. Only your intel was off. Marie wasn't exiting the door you expected. Your exit wasn't secure."

Friedrich remained silent as Olivia spoke.

"You were unable to touch her. So you slap me. Make damn sure I saw you before I went down to guarantee I'd come looking for you. You tell me to walk away. I'm a ghost and no one needs to know I'm alive. All I have to do is look the other way."

Olivia glanced around the room. "Only you'd done your research. Knew enough about this team to understand that we don't walk away from a job half done. So you waited for Leo and me to track down Marie so we can protect her. And in turn lead you right to her."

Friedrich's next words were muttered in German.

"Stealthy bitch indeed," Olivia repeated.

"She's not in Texas, is she?" he asked.

"Couldn't say."

"What do you want from me?" Friedrich asked.

Olivia turned to Cooper and exchanged the silenced handgun for the burner phone he had in his hand. She waved it in the air. On the other end, Mykonos Sobol, not his "cousin Navi," would be taking the call. Funny how phones like these ended up in prisoners' hands.

"You're going to make the call."

He shook his head. "I can't do that."

"You can. And you will." The phone dangled in her fingertips. "Mykonos only has to believe Marie is dead to achieve what he desires. To make an example of the girl and brag to those he wants to control that he made sure she was dead. Since Marie has no intention of a resurrection, no one will ever know."

Friedrich narrowed his eyes. "Even if I did this, what do you do with me?"

"You disappear. Find an island somewhere. I understand Bali is a great place to retire."

Friedrich's expression shifted. His lips pressed together in a thin line. "Leave him alone."

"I'm not threatening your father," Olivia told him. Her eyes looked at Neil, who offered a nod. Their tracking had found Louis Schmidt in Bali, where he was enjoying the life of a king . . . all bankrolled by his thankful son who loved him unconditionally. "This is your exit, Friedrich. Take it."

"If Mykonos learns that Marie is alive, the bounty is put on me."

Olivia looked around the room. "The bounty is on you now."

Friedrich attempted to look smug. "You want me to believe that everyone in this room is willing to shoot an unarmed man?"

Leo leaned close to Friedrich's head and spoke for all of them. "It's Texas, and you're breaking and entering with a gun that has your prints all over it. There doesn't need to be a bigger reason than that in this part of the country."

For the first time since Leo had put Friedrich in handcuffs, the man looked less than confident.

Olivia approached, the phone in her hand.

Neil turned away from the scene and walked out the back door.

"Time to call this in."

"And if Mykonos wants proof?"

"We're professionals. We don't take trophies." Did he think she was new?

Olivia held the phone up, her finger over the call button. Burner phones were one-time use with one number on the other end and were destroyed once the message was relayed.

Friedrich gave a single nod, and Olivia pressed the button.

It rang twice before it was picked up.

Mykonos Sobol's voice answered. "Tell me," he said in Russian.

"It is done," Friedrich answered in the same language.

Leo looked at Olivia.

She kept her expression neutral.

Olivia rolled her finger, telling Friedrich to continue.

"I expect our agreement to be fulfilled within the hour. You'll never hear from me again. I expect the same from you."

"A pleasure" were Mykonos's final words before Olivia disconnected the call.

The color in Friedrich's face had turned ashen. "What now?"

"We return to your hotel, wait for the funds to hit your bank, and then get you on a flight."

CHAPTER THIRTY-THREE

Leo kept one hand on Friedrich and one hand on his weapon as the team divided in two.

Half traced back to the hotel with Friedrich, and the others stayed to clean the scene.

With the Jeep left behind, Sasha drove with Neil, Olivia, and Leo in the back of the van keeping watch.

"You're just going to let me go?" Friedrich asked for the third time.

Olivia nodded.

Leo watched the man's movements and the growing uncertainty displayed by his constant questions.

"How much was Marie worth?" Leo asked, dragging every bit of information from the man that he could while he was still in their presence.

"Half a million euros. Double if she was taken before the trial."

Leo glanced at Neil. Everyone in the van knew that Mykonos was hammering the final nail into his jailhouse coffin at that very moment. The second that half a million landed in Friedrich's account would seal Mykonos's fate to spend a lifetime in prison.

"That money would go a long way in Bali," Leo told him.

They arrived at the motel as the Texas sun was setting.

Neil and Leo flanked Friedrich as they escorted him to his room to retrieve his belongings. Just as Olivia had predicted, Friedrich had stashed passports and cash in the vent space of the room. A tablet served as his computer, and an extra weapon was quickly given to Neil once it was retrieved.

With the hotel key left behind, they returned to the van and headed toward the airport.

"Log in to your bank," Leo instructed.

"Why?"

"We need to make sure Mykonos believed you. If the money is there, you get on the plane."

Friedrich opened his tablet and logged in to his bank. He swiped back and forth until he found what he wanted before showing the screen to Leo.

Leo saw the transfer and gave the tablet to Neil.

With a flip to the communication link in his ear, Neil gave the report. "The transaction is complete." He rattled off the account information to whoever was listening on the other end.

"I'm never going to see that money, am I?" Friedrich asked.

Leo shook his head. "It's in the hands of the feds. Abandoned by an assassin who hunted down a twenty-year-old girl. Maybe you felt the heat."

Olivia smiled. "Maybe you developed a conscience."

"Either way, Mykonos goes down with the evidence. No testimony from you is needed."

"What stops the Sobol family from coming after me?"

"Nothing," Olivia announced. "We will circulate that you're dead. Leave notice at A Róka for anyone asking. Inform Checkpoint Charlie. Maybe they accept that fact and move on . . . maybe they have an ongoing resource order for your demise."

The Texas sun had set, and Sasha pulled onto a dark stretch of road that emptied onto a private airstrip.

Leo looked out the window, his eyes in constant motion. Getting Friedrich on the plane was the final piece of the puzzle. Neil had eyes in Indonesia waiting to confirm the man made it and had an escort the entire way.

"Go buy a rice field in Indonesia and take up yoga. I'm guessing you have a small fortune stashed away. Enough to live comfortably for the rest of your life," Olivia encouraged.

As soon as the small plane came into view, Neil called ahead to the pilot.

Olivia reached out, placed a hand on Friedrich's shoulder. "We're even. Disappear or don't. But I never want to see you again. Don't give any of us a reason to come after you."

Neil opened the sliding door of the van and stepped outside, hand on his AR, eyes alert. "You have an escort and a free ticket to your destination. If you break the chain, you will be brought in one way or another. If Mykonos can take your call in prison, he can make sure you don't survive if you're still taking jobs."

Olivia, Sasha, and Leo moved into position.

"You wouldn't want to dirty your hands with my murder?" Friedrich asked Neil.

Sasha stepped in front of Friedrich, her face up against his. She spoke in Russian, tension rippling through her body, her eyes laser focused on his.

Beside Leo, Olivia chuckled at what was being said.

When Sasha was done with her lecture, Friedrich attempted to act unaffected, but he offered a single nod in response.

"Do I want to know what she said?" Leo asked.

"Probably best you don't, love," Olivia told him.

The door to the airplane opened.

"Stay alert," Neil instructed as he, Olivia, and Leo walked Friedrich to his private ride.

They made it halfway to the waiting plane when all hell broke loose.

The night sky lit up as gunfire came at them from two directions.

Leo's breath caught in his throat, his weapon became an extension of his arm, and he started firing in the direction of one gunman. "Get down," he yelled as if he needed to.

Olivia and Neil were crouched low and running toward the plane.

Out of the corner of his eye, Leo saw Sasha pulling the van around for cover.

Dirt blew as gravel kicked up from both the engine of the aircraft and wheels from the van.

"Fuck," Olivia managed to squeeze out within feet of the plane.

Friedrich reached the plane first and dove in.

Sasha skidded to a halt, the door to the van open.

Then everything happened in slow motion.

Leo saw Neil follow Friedrich into the plane.

Olivia turned toward Leo, and a spray of bullets dusted around them.

Her eyes met his and she twisted to the ground.

"No!" he screamed as he crumpled on top of her to stop any more projectiles from hitting her.

He heard Neil yelling through the chaos.

"Get out of here." Sasha's command rose above the noise of the engines. "I've got this."

Leo held Olivia to the ground as the plane started to move. "Hold tight, hon."

The van Isaac and Lars had used sped onto the runway and gave them the coverage they needed.

Leo lifted off of Olivia enough to see her looking at him.

Sasha shouldered her rifle and moved to their side.

Together she and Leo brought their arms under Olivia's and ran toward the van.

Without stopping, Sasha jumped in the driver's seat and peeled away.

Above them, the single-engine plane with Friedrich and Neil lifted into the sky.

They sped off the airstrip with Isaac and Lars right behind them. Olivia's body started to shake.

"We're clear," Sasha announced from the front of the van.

Leo sat back as the last of his adrenaline dumped from his system.

Olivia rolled onto her back and started to laugh.

"Holy shit, it worked," Leo said as he dropped his tired arms at his side.

Sasha slowed the van to a stop and turned up her comm link.

They heard Friedrich's panicked voice mixed with Neil's.

"Who else knew you were here?" Neil yelled.

"No one. I work alone."

"Someone was following you."

"I was careful."

"Not careful enough."

"It has to be Mykonos. He's the only one who knew I was searching for Marie," Friedrich pleaded. "I swear to God."

Leo reached for Olivia, pulled her into his lap. Even though he knew the whole thing was a setup, watching her go down a second time felt as real as it had been the first time. "He's crapping his pants," Leo said.

"The only reason I'm not snapping your neck myself is because Olivia said you both deserved a chance at a new life. If she's dead . . ."

"I had no way of knowing this was going down."

Friedrich continued to plead, and Neil opened up a new asshole for the man.

The communication link faded as the airplane moved out of range.

The door to the van opened, and Claire and Cooper stood in full combat gear covered in weeds and dirt. The assailants climbed into the van with handshakes and pats on the back.

Claire started to laugh. "Now *that* was fun!"

Olivia rested her head on Leo's chest.

He squeezed her tight. "Let's go home."

EPILOGUE

Jax walked along the uneven crowded streets of Ubud. Her long hair was braided in a way that kept it out of her face. Her skin had been kissed enough to suggest she'd been in Indonesia for several weeks.

With mala beads around her neck, and flowing skirts swishing at her ankles . . . she blended.

This was the kind of assignment she liked.

Every day, she passed the entrance to Friedrich and Louis's home.

From the outside, the colorful doors looked just like everyone else's.

On the inside, a lush courtyard sat center to a private home with a personal chef and housekeeper that lived on-site.

Friedrich Schmidt was now known as Ted Miller, an ex-pat who had sold his small chain of fast food restaurants to retire at an early age.

If the man was itching for a different life, Jax couldn't tell.

When it was her turn to pass the baton, she walked by Friedrich's mail slot and left him a token and a note. Jax used a mixture of Russian and German, a code she and Claire had come up with at Richter and some of the other students had adopted.

The note simply said . . .

If information circulates among our joint enemies and your location has been compromised, another token will find its way into your home without explanation. If you are informed of a threat to "the team," we expect the same in return.

Jax watched from a distance as Friedrich sat and read the note.

Afterward he burned the paper with the end of his cigar.

He looked around as if knowing he was being watched and smiled.

At that moment a Balinese monkey jumped up on the table beside him and grabbed a date from a bowl.

Friedrich reached to pet the animal before standing up and walking out of view.

Sven nudged Jax's shoulder. "So this is what you've been doing all winter?"

"I'm working hard here."

They both laughed and enjoyed their one day together before Jax headed back to the States.

~

Olivia stretched her cold feet toward the roaring fire that heated the Lake Tahoe cabin.

Neil had found a remote location for her and Leo to spend the remainder of the season.

The sting to shut Mykonos down and remove the possibility of parole had worked.

Even if the cost was Leo resigning from the FBI.

Working outside the department's radar, regardless of the outcome, wasn't tolerated.

For three weeks Olivia and Leo picked up where they'd left off before her memory returned.

They had snowball fights and ate a lot of mashed potatoes while they contemplated what they were going to do next.

"I think we should take it," Leo announced.

The written description of Neil's job offer solved all of their problems.

Olivia took the proposed contract from him to read it again.

"It looks more like we'd be working for his brother-in-law." With her head resting in the crook of Leo's shoulder, she read a few details.

The European arm of Harrison Shipping, specifically the Amsterdam offices, was in need of an investigative group. There had recently been a consistent loss of cargo, small at first, but increasing at an incremental pace. Harrison would need both Leo's investigative skills and Olivia's hacking and language abilities to get to the bottom of the missing cargo and money. It would, however, require relocation for the both of them for an undisclosed amount of time. The job came with a housing budget, travel, a company car, phones, computers . . . everything one could possibly need. And a six-figure salary and benefits.

"The only thing this offer is missing is bicycles," Olivia announced.

"Excuse me?"

"No one drives a car in Amsterdam."

Leo laughed and pressed his lips to her temple. "I think we should take it."

"You're ready to become an ex-pat?" she asked.

"I'm ready to take on all the new titles. Ex-pat. Ex-FBI. Ex-bachelor . . ."

"Ex-boyfriend," she teased.

"No. I don't like that one." He kicked his foot next to hers as if dismissing her idea.

She sighed. "I still can't believe what you've given up for me."

Leo placed a finger to her chin and made her look at him. "I didn't give up anything for you. Ask Neil. My cold house in Glendale provided temporary shelter for a workaholic that took on unending undercover assignments because I had nothing better going on. And in the end, it was Neil and his team that brought closure to that. I completely understand how Neil recruits so many quality employees. The hands of the FBI are tied up in so much bureaucracy that nothing gets done. Or if it does, it takes years." He reached for the job offer, waved it in the air. "Not only does the private sector pay better, something tells me it's going to prove a lot more fulfilling. Especially with my wife at my side."

Olivia shifted into a sitting position, her eyes wide. "Who said anything about a wife?"

Leo smiled. "You didn't read that part in the contract?"

She reached for the paper, but he pulled it away and scrambled off the sofa. He then pretended to read what she knew wasn't there.

"Since Harrison Shipping is investing such a large sum of money for your services, we would like the guarantee that Leo and Olivia form a more permanent bond in the form of marriage to ensure no one gets cold feet and runs off."

Olivia was smiling, and even though Leo's words were a joke, the insecurity she'd created by running from him twice was in his voice. "I love you, Leo. I'm not going to leave."

Every time she'd confessed her feelings in the past weeks, Leo rewarded her with a kiss and a devotion of his own.

He leaned over the sofa and pressed his lips to hers. "Prove it."

"Olivia Naught is dead. She can't get married."

"We have a quiet ceremony, and I remind Mrs. Grant how much I love her every day for the rest of my life."

Mrs. Grant.

A real name.

One Olivia could keep.

"The FBI agent marries the assassin. What could possibly go right?" she asked.

"The ex-FBI agent and ex-assassin . . . Our life will never be dull."

She reached her lips toward his. And when he kissed her, she grabbed the contract from his fingertips and scrambled off the sofa. "It says here I don't have to wear a ring."

Leo was smiling. "Why not?"

A small ache in her chest was still there. "A ring tells the world there is someone's life that is more important than my own and uses that knowledge against me."

"Shhh," he coaxed as tears threatened in the back of her eyes. "All anyone has to do is look at me looking at you to know what you mean to me. Rings are not necessary."

Olivia closed her eyes and wished she could erase her past.

All she could do was move forward and live a life to be proud of from this moment on. "I love you," she said to his chest as his arms circled around her.

"I love you . . . Mrs. Grant."

She leaned back and smiled. "I'm wearing red at our wedding."

Leo's smile illuminated the room. "Never going to be boring."

They sealed their agreement with a kiss.

ACKNOWLEDGMENTS

That time has come again when I thank the people and chosen family in my life for all their help in making each book possible. This book was written in the challenging year of 2020, which may evolve into the "year we will never mention again" once it is over. But alas . . . here I am, typing and thanking my tribe.

Thank you, Montlake and Amazon Publishing, for giving me the freedom to write the books I want to write. Holly Ingraham for helping me shape this story and the others before it. Maria Gomez for your continual support book after book.

My dazzling agent, Jane Dystel, who I love and adore. Thank you for all you do.

My sisters from different misters, Kari and Brandy, who were with me as I was putting the finishing touches on this book. I could not have pulled it off without you. You are both always there when I need you the most. Kari, my guide to all things federal agency and now private investigator. Thank you for all the tips along the way. I still can't believe you carry a gun for a living, and I ended up sitting at a computer typing.

Fiona . . . who is the reason I have more people to dedicate my books to. I cherish every moment of our friendship, and I'm deeply grateful for the technology that gives us the opportunity to keep in touch. Your daily support and whip cracking all the way from Western Australia is spectacular. Thank you.

Now, on to Ethan and Eloise . . . By the time this book is in print you will already be married, and the ceremony and time leading up to it nothing but memories and photographs. It saddens me so profoundly that COVID has robbed me of traveling to Australia and being there to celebrate your special day. However, marriage is more than one moment and one celebration. I remember holding you, Ethan, the day you were born. Perhaps I can be there again when and if the time comes for me to hold one of yours. I say this next part with a thickness in my throat and tears in my eyes. Your father would be so proud of you and your choice in a wife. He lives in you and is never far away . . . I hope you know that.

May you both hold on to your happily ever after and find joy in every day you have together.

Congratulations!

Catherine

ABOUT THE AUTHOR

Photo © 2015 Julianne Gentry

New York Times, Wall Street Journal, and *USA Today* bestselling author Catherine Bybee has written thirty-five books that have collectively sold more than eight million copies and have been translated into more than twenty languages. Raised in Washington State, Bybee moved to Southern California in the hope of becoming a movie star. After growing bored with waiting tables, she returned to school and became a registered nurse, spending most of her career in urban emergency rooms. She now writes full time and has penned the Not Quite series, the Weekday Brides series, the Most Likely To series, and the First Wives series.